What a woman wants

ALSO BY BRENDA JACKSON

No More Playas

Unfinished Business

The Playa's Handbook

A Family Reunion

Ties That Bind

The Midnight Hour

The Savvy Sistahs

ANTHOLOGIES

The Best Man

Welcome to Leo's

Let's Get It On

An All Night Man

Mr. Satisfaction

AND COMING SOON

Slow Burn (A Madaris Family Novel)

What a woman wants

Brenda Jackson

St. Martin's Griffin ⚑ New York

WHAT A WOMAN WANTS. Copyright © 2007 by Brenda Streater Jackson. All rights reserved. Printed in the United States of America. No part of this book may be used or reproduced in any manner whatsoever without written permission except in the case of brief quotations embodied in critical articles or reviews. For information, address St. Martin's Press, 175 Fifth Avenue, New York, N.Y. 10010.

www.stmartins.com

Library of Congress Cataloging-in-Publication Data

Jackson, Brenda (Brenda Streater)
    What a woman wants / Brenda Jackson.—1st ed.
        p. cm.
    ISBN-13: 978-0-312-35934-8
    ISBN-10: 0-312-35934-9
    1. African American women—Fiction. 2. Female friendship—Fiction. I. Title.

PS3560.A21165W47 2007
813'.54—dc21

                                                    2006048683

D   10   9   8   7   6   5   4   3

Acknowledgments

To Gerald Jackson Sr., the man who continues to show me what true love is all about.

To all my readers who continue to enjoy my love stories.

To the 1971 Class of William M. Raines High School, Jacksonville, Florida, for our 35th class reunion. Ichiband!

To my Heavenly Father who gave me the gift to write.

Listen to advice and accept
instruction, and in the
end you will be wise.
—PROVERBS 19:20

Part one

Hope deferred makes the heart sick,
but a longing fulfilled is a tree of life.
—PROVERBS 13:12

Prologue

Adrianna Ross-Fuller walked out of the Hilton Head trauma center's ER and toward the waiting room. She paused a moment in the corridor and took a deep breath. Although their patient hadn't survived, she'd thanked her trauma team for doing an outstanding job. It wasn't their fault the woman stopped fighting for life long before she'd been wheeled through the doors to ER. A shudder ran through Adrianna. Why would that poor woman have wanted to die? Why would anyone?

"Dr. Ross-Fuller?"

She recognized the police officer immediately. They had met a few months ago when he rushed into ER on the tails of the EMT crew, who brought in a two-year-old child. The toddler had nearly drowned in his neighbor's pool and was in shock. That day, hours later, Adrianna walked out into the waiting room smiling, ready to deliver good news: the little boy would recover. Today the news wouldn't be so positive.

She shook her head sadly at the inquiry in his voice. "She didn't make it, and it was apparent she didn't want to live."

Lt. Neil Upshaw nodded. "That doesn't surprise me, considering this was an attempted suicide." The fifty-something-year-old man then shook his bald head and hunched his shoulders in absolute desolation.

"No longer an attempt, Lieutenant. She succeeded. Do you have any idea why?" The words came out in a sigh.

"I'm sure the letters she left behind will explain all."

Adrianna lifted a brow. "Letters?"

"Yes, four of them. One addressed to no one in particular and three others to women she knew. Those three were sealed. The first one wasn't, and all it said was, 'I don't want to live any longer.'"

She shivered again. How could a person get so hopeless that they imagined death was far better than living? She couldn't imagine what would make an attractive thirty-four-year-old woman want to end her life by overdosing on a prescribed medication. Adrianna thought of all the trials she had endured in her thirty-five years as an Amerasian. Even when she'd felt her lowest, she had never thought of taking her own life.

"Has her family been notified?" she asked. If he was anything like her, the officer probably disliked that part of his job most.

"Yes, and they're on their way from Charleston. She has an older sister, a brother, and an elderly mother."

Adrianna nodded as she checked her watch. It was almost two in the afternoon. In a few hours she would be catching a plane for Virginia. Tomorrow night her grandparents were throwing a party in her honor to mark the first anniversary of the day she had entered their lives. How unfair that even while the people she most cared about had every reason to celebrate, there was a family on its way to Hilton Head Island with reason to mourn.

Her heart surged with compassion, and then a cold feeling of loss filled her chest. Times like these, she questioned her decision to become an emergency room trauma doctor. But that reservation was short-lived. As she bade good-bye to the lieutenant and made her way toward the elevator, she knew if she had it to do all over again, she would choose the same profession.

She shook her head, still thinking of the woman whose life had ended prematurely that day. What a terrible waste.

1

"Ashes to ashes. Dust to dust."

Faith Gilmore watched as the coffin was lowered into the dark earth. A part of her still could not believe what she was seeing. She glanced over at the two other women standing beside her. Monique Hardings and Shannon Carmichael were in the same daze of disbelief as she was. It was like they were all stuck in some sort of weird dream.

Tomorrow they would wake up from it, and Cely would take them all to task when they told her about their strange nightmare. *Me commit suicide? No way. There isn't that much depression in the world. I am the most levelheaded, laid-back, not-a-care-in-the-world person you know. There's no way I would* ever *get in a funk so blue that it would trigger me to take my own life.*

Yet she had done exactly that, and this was no dream.

"This ends the memorial service for Cecilia Graham," the minister was saying. "You may all return to your cars."

Faith blinked. Return to their cars and do what? Mourn some more? Leave? Ask themselves for the thousandth time how could this have happened? *Why* this happened? Especially to Cely, who had always been the strongest of the four of them.

She felt someone touch her hand, glanced up to see Monique and Shannon standing right in front of her. Faith looked at them mutely, noting that their eyes were as red as hers, their cheeks just as tear-streaked.

"It's time to go," Monique said softly, and Faith could hear her fighting to hold back more tears.

"Yes," Shannon chimed in, her voice just as tight. "I need to get away from this place. Quick. I need a thick slice of pizza, a strong drink, and to get laid. Hell, I need something, anything, to make me forget everything I've gone through today. This week."

Faith almost rolled her eyes. Shannon had always been the one they all thought had the weakest disposition. Cely had always worried about how Shannon went about dealing with stress. "How about if we go back to my hotel room, drink some wine, and chill. I'm really not in the mood to go to the repast," Faith suggested.

Monique understood. "Neither am I. I'm sure Cely's family will understand if we wait and visit tomorrow before we leave."

"Yes, I'm sure they will," Shannon agreed. "They know Cely was more than a friend to us. She was like our sister."

Faith nodded. That was true—ever since the four of them had met so many summers ago as teens on Hilton Head Island, they *were* sisters. Cely's grandparents had operated a hot dog stand on the beach, and she had been their little helper. Like Faith's parents, Monique's and Shannon's families had owned time-share condos and made the trip each summer to the island, where the four girls had become the best of friends for life.

But now one of their lives had ended. The circle they had formed more than twenty years ago was broken, and somehow they had to repair it and move on. "All right, let's go. But first let's say good-bye to Mrs. Graham. I don't want her to think we're deserting her."

A couple of hours later, Faith, Monique, and Shannon had replaced their dark mourning dress suits with slacks and blouses, and they were sprawled on the bed in Faith's hotel room. They were remembering the good times they'd shared all those summers long ago, from the time they were thirteen.

"Do you remember the summer when we began noticing boys for the first time?" Shannon asked, laughing between sips of her wine. "Cely was acting so shy that day when that hunk from FAMU tried to come on to her. That was the first time any of us had been noticed by a college guy."

Faith chuckled. "Yes, I remember! We were sixteen, and the guy thought we were naive enough to fall for his game."

Monique nodded, grinning. "Yeah, he wasn't very smart."

"But he sure was a looker," Shannon couldn't help but add, her eyes twinkling in mischief. "I think he really did like Cely, though."

"Yes," Faith said, "and I think she really liked him, too, which is why she did sneak off to see him that night."

The room got quiet for a moment. Then Faith finally asked the question she'd been dreading: "Have either of you read the letter Cely left for you?"

Monique shook her head. "I couldn't make myself do it. I can't imagine how depressed she must have been to do what she did. And to know even then she had been thinking about us, our friendship."

Shannon placed her wineglass aside, inhaling sharply. "I haven't read mine either, although a part of me is very curious. Maybe it will explain why she did it."

Faith nodded. "I think we should read them now. Here. Together. There must be something she wanted to tell us—otherwise she wouldn't have written them."

Monique took a sip of her drink. "I'm not sure I want to know what she was thinking that day. Cely was the most fun-loving of all of us. I remember how things were for me after Paul's death. When things seemed to fall apart, she was there to help me keep things together. I can't imagine anything getting her so down, she thought she couldn't share it with us or wouldn't know we were there for her, no matter what. Nothing could have been that hopeless when she had everything going on. The last time I talked with her—a few weeks ago—she was doing great. She had met this neat guy, she had finally made the decision to have her mother move in with her instead of go to a nursing home, and she was up for a promotion on her job. I can't imagine what would make her do what she did."

"Then let's read our letters and find out," Faith repeated, not really wanting to do so but feeling that they must.

The other two women nodded. As always, they would share everything. They each left the bed and walked to where they'd set their purses. They had been given Cely's letters that morning from a kind police officer who had arrived before the start of the funeral. Fifty-something and bald, he had introduced himself as Lt. Upshaw.

Shannon pulled the letter out of her purse and glanced at it thoughtfully before turning to the others. Tears clouded her eyes. "It doesn't seem fair. Cely was the one we called when we needed to be told to get our shit together."

Faith walked over to a chair and flopped down with the copy of her letter in her hand. "Yeah, she was the first person I contacted when I found out Virgil was one of those down-low brothers. She talked me out of getting a gun and blowing his balls off. Now she's gone and we have to move on, keep going, the way she would have wanted. Come on, let's read our letters."

They each took a turn and read their letters aloud. Moments later they glanced up at each other with more tears in their eyes. Monique took a deep breath. "Even in what she thought was her darkest hour, she was thinking of us."

"Yeah," Shannon said, wiping her eyes. "But the letter doesn't explain why she did what she did."

"In a way it does," Faith said in a quiet tone. "There was something going on her in life that made her think she didn't have an out. And she doesn't want that from us. She's pleading for us to live each day to the fullest and do whatever we want to do to enjoy life and not live up to others' expectations and standards."

Monique nodded. "Cely was always trying to please everyone. Maybe she got tired of trying."

"But to the point where she would commit suicide?" Shannon snapped, clearly frustrated and hurt. "I can't imagine her ever getting that low. I bet it has something to do with a man."

Faith rolled her eyes. "Why are you so quick to blame the opposite sex?"

"Because they're usually the ones who deserved to be blamed. And you said she had met this great guy, Monique. She never mentioned him to me. Who is he? I wonder if the police checked her cell phone to see if he called her right before it happened. I wouldn't put it past him, whoever he is, to be the one who pushed her over the edge. Maybe we need to do a little investigating of our own."

Faith and Monique exchanged glances. Nothing had changed over the years. Shannon still harbored ill feelings for most men because of what her father was doing to her mom, but then Shannon's mom's behavior wasn't too much better.

"Well, I personally think it wasn't just a man but probably a mixture of things," Faith decided to say. "But we'll never really know, because she didn't tell us in her letters. And forget about doing our own investigating. There was a suicide note—four of them—so as far as the police is concerned, the case is closed. Even if Mr. X isn't blameless, the police won't arrest a man for 'pushing someone over the edge,' if that's what he did."

"Faith is right," Monique said softly. "In her letters Cely is asking us not to dwell on the reason she did what she did. She wants us to make changes in our own lives. So what are we going to do?"

The room got quiet, and then moments later Faith spoke up. "I have an idea. Remember we all said that one of these summers we would get together and spend it on the island like we used to do? I say let's do it. Let's have one more summer in Cely's memory. Let's get together on Hilton Head Island and do just what she's suggested, like we used to do all those summers when we didn't have a care in the world. Let's plan to take time off our jobs—a month to six weeks—and take on new adventures and broaden our horizons. In Cely's honor let's do as she's asked. Live each day to the fullest and do whatever we want and not worry about anyone's expectations."

"I don't worry about anyone's expectations now," Shannon said curtly, taking another sip of her wine.

"Don't you?"

Shannon cut a quick glance at Monique. "I know when and how to put my parents in their place."

Monique rolled her eyes. "If you say so."

Shannon opened her mouth to say something but then closed it. She turned to Faith. "I'm all for what you're suggesting. I just won't sign up to teach any classes at the university over the summer months. What about you two? Can you take that much time away from your jobs?"

Faith shrugged. As an advertising consultant, she was constantly in demand, but . . . "I think I will. I have money saved that I haven't touched since my divorce. It will be worth it. Besides, I can use a break."

"So can I," Monique replied rather quickly, smiling now. "I hadn't planned to say anything until later, but Cannon Insurance is downsizing, and guess whose department will be the first to go?"

Faith leaned forward, giving Monique her full attention. "Yours?"

Monique said, "That's right."

Shannon looked disgusted. "But you've been working there for almost fifteen years, right out of college. Don't corporations believe in loyalty anymore?"

"I guess they feel they have to do what they need to do to survive. It's all about profits, not losses," Monique said, shrugging.

After sipping her drink, she added, "So count me in for the summer. At least I'm getting a nice severance package that will tide me over. I don't plan on looking for another job for a while. I need to chill before entering the job market again. Hell, it's been so long, I don't know what's even out there. Companies aren't hiring their own insurance adjusters anymore. They're using independents. I might decide to go into business for myself or change careers altogether."

"So it's decided," Faith said. "We'll spend this summer somewhere on Hilton Head Island." She smiled. "And I know the perfect place. My parents finally got rid of their time-share and bought a house on the beach. They won't be using it this summer since they plan to vacation in Europe instead. It's big and roomy and will fit our needs perfectly."

Monique smiled back. "Wonderful. Then it's final. This summer will be ours to do as we please."

"Yes, and we'll have a wonderful time in Cely's memory, just like she asked." Shannon grinned like a woman who was looking forward to doing whatever rocked her boat.

The three women raised their glasses in a grateful toast. They would make this a summer they wouldn't forget.

2

*Four months later,
summertime*

"Will this complete your order, sir?"

Shane Masters looked over at the young woman behind the register. It was hard to ignore her *I'm interested if you are* smile. The kid had to be no more than nineteen, and although it was good for his ego to catch the eye of someone so young, at forty he was old enough to be her father.

"Yes, that will be all," he said, handing her enough cash to pay for his groceries.

Moments later he walked out of the supermarket feeling like a man on top of the world. Retirement was everything people said it would be, and he was glad that because of smart investment moves, he was able to do it now rather than later. The first thing he'd done was purchase a home on the beach in Hilton Head. His ultimate dream home.

He unloaded his groceries in the truck of the rented SUV and was about to get into the vehicle when his cell phone rang. He smiled—it was his sister. He came from a rather large family and had six siblings, all of them born and raised not far away in Savannah, although now they were spread far and wide all over the country. Quinece was his youngest sister and twin to his brother Quinn. And she was the one determined to keep up with everyone.

"What's up, Que-Two?" That was the nickname they had given her when she was born. Quinn they called Que-One.

"I'm calling to remind you about the party Grey is giving Brandy in a few weeks. I don't want you to get so absorbed in your tennis games that you forget."

Shane chuckled as he opened the door and climbed up. "Don't worry. I can still manage to keep a calendar pretty good. How's the kids?"

"They're fine, and by the way I'm pregnant again."

He shook his head, grinning. "Congratulations. You were always the one who wanted a houseful, and it looks like you're getting what you want."

"Yeah, and I'm thrilled that Kendall is more than happy to oblige. I talked to Quinn earlier today, and he and Alexia are trying."

Shane wasn't surprised. "More power to them." Inwardly he was happy for his brother Quinn, a highly successful entertainment attorney, and his gorgeous wife, Alexia Bennett Masters, a nationally known recording artist whose current record was number one on the R & B charts.

"I'm sure Mom will be happy with all these additions to the Masters clan," he added. His attention was drawn to his rearview mirror when he saw a woman getting out of her car. She had the most gorgeous pair of legs he'd ever seen.

His gaze moved upward, and he thought she was definitely a looker, with medium brown skin, a nice set of eyes, and luscious lips. Her hair was fixed in twists, and she had a headful that came to her shoulders.

Hell, forget about the rearview mirror. He turned his body to look out the back window. It was all he could do not to hang up on his sister and give the delectable female his total attention. She made one hell of a moving object as she crossed the parking lot wearing a denim skirt that was short and tight—but it fit her body perfectly. And he couldn't overlook the small waist that—

"Shane, are you listening?"

Quinece reclaimed his attention, but not all of it. "Sorry, I was noticing something else at the moment."

"Probably some woman," she guessed.

"You're too young to play the role of mama with me. Look, I won't miss Brandy's party. I'm driving up that Friday morning."

"Good. We're depending on you."

He raised a brow, not liking the sound of that. "Why?"

"Why what?"

"Why are you depending on me?"

"Umm, I'd rather not say. You aren't going to like it."

His attention was split between what his sister was saying and the woman he was still watching. She had some walk, and with every step she took, he could feel blood thicken in his veins as well as a number of other places. She was more his speed, since she looked to be in her late twenties or early thirties and wasn't daughter material, like cute little Suzy at the checkout counter.

He frowned, trying to remember the last time he'd shared a bed with a woman, and it suddenly hit him that it had been months ago, way before his retirement. Damn, he'd been so busy lately, he'd forgone any kind of a social life. He'd always been careful to keep his relationships restricted to women who only wanted a good time. Those with high hopes and expectations he left alone.

He then realized what his sister had said. "What is it that I'm not going to like, Quinece?"

She hesitated a minute, then said, "Grey mentioned Brandy's mom is bringing someone, a cousin who's visiting from Seattle."

"What does that have to do with me?"

"She's looking for a husband."

Shane snapped his seat belt in place, wishing it were around his brother Grey's neck. "Fine, she can keep looking, since a wife is no longer on my interest list. I almost had one, remember? It was unfortunate for her that a week before the wedding I found out she had gotten pregnant—but not from me."

"I remember that, and I do understand. But you know how

pushy Brandy's mom can be. We're not asking you to marry the cousin, just be nice to her. Is that too much to ask?"

"Yes, it is. Now good-bye." He then clicked off the line. The conversation with Quinece was all but forgotten; however, the woman who'd distracted him earlier was still on his mind, even after she had disappeared into the grocery store.

He was tempted to get out of his car and go back inside the store. There had to be some item he had failed to get. He would be the first to admit he'd been guilty of neglecting his libido for way too long, which was probably the main reason he was even considering sniffing behind a woman.

Going without a female in his bed had never gotten to him before, and he couldn't help but wonder what was there about Miss Short Skirt and Long Legs that had him hot all over, with an exhilarating rush pricking every inch of his skin.

Although the men in the Masters family were well aware of their keen sensuality, not to mention the strength of their passion, he wasn't a randy sixteen-year-old anymore but a man of forty. There were some things you just had to know how to control, and the power of lust was one of them. Sheesh. There wasn't a male born to Annabel Masters who didn't possess a certain degree of civilized behavior.

He pulled out of the parking space. Still, it wouldn't bother him one bit if he were to run into the woman again, and he hoped he did so before leaving the island the day after Labor Day.

Faith bit the inside of her cheek as she studied the watermelons carefully. They were all huge, plump, and definitely looked ripe. She had been given the task of bringing back the sweetest one she could buy, and she intended to do just that.

She smiled. The first week at the beach house had gone great. She, Monique, and Shannon decided to just chill out for a while— rest, relax, take in days lounging on the beach—before getting down to discuss what they wanted to do this summer, a topic they'd been putting off for too long. Tonight at dinner they would finally talk about it and make their decisions. All day she had been toying with the question of just what a woman wanted, or more specifically, what she herself wanted.

Surprisingly, the notion of being loved and truly wanted by a man was no longer at the top of her list. She had grown a lot since her divorce four years ago. She had refused to let what Virgil had done—and who he'd done it with—shatter her whole world. As far as she'd been concerned, he was the one with the issues, not her. And contrary to what her parents thought, she didn't need a man in her life to make it complete. She liked the way things were going and wasn't in need of a makeover. She dated whenever she wanted and didn't have any hang-ups with the opposite sex. She was smart enough to know all men weren't like her ex, who thought there was nothing wrong with having both a wife and a significant other. She enjoyed her independence, she had a job with a good income, and she had a nice savings account. The condo she'd purchased a year ago in downtown Minneapolis was perfect, just what she needed, and was an acceptable distance from her parents' home in Green Bay. Yes, life was good, and she was looking forward to spending the summer with two of her closest friends.

Her mind then drifted to Cely, and she dismissed the hurt she still felt in knowing her friend had chosen to bear her troubles alone—whatever they had been—and not share them.

"I think that's the best one."

Faith glanced up and looked at the man standing beside her. She inwardly smiled. He couldn't be any older than twenty-one or twenty-two, a college student perhaps. She had to admit he was kind of cute if you went for young. "This one?" she asked, pointing to the watermelon she had been eyeing for the past ten minutes.

"Yes, that's the one," he said, giving her another brilliant smile. If she'd been interested, that smile—not to mention his fine physique in the jogging suit he was wearing—would have made her a goner.

"So, what are you?" she asked, returning his smile. "A melon expert?"

He gave her his killer smile again before saying, "Not really. I just can recognize top quality when I see it."

It didn't take a rocket scientist to know he was trying to hit on her. A part of her felt somewhat flattered when his gaze moved to her boobs. "Is that so?" she asked, meeting his gaze when it finally returned to her face.

She started to cross her arms over her chest but decided, *Hey, what the heck, let the pup look.* It wasn't as if she were indecently exposed. She was thirty-four and proud that she had a nice set of breasts. She worked out periodically and tried to stay in shape—not for anyone in particular, but mainly for herself.

"I think I'll take your advice," she said when his gaze moved from her face back to her breasts before moving downward past her short denim skirt to her legs.

"On what?" he asked, meeting her gaze again.

"The watermelon."

"Oh, yeah. Do you need help getting it to your car?"

She couldn't help but chuckle. He had a lot to learn. He was a total stranger, and she had no intentions of letting *Junior* help her take anything to her car. Did she look like she was born yesterday? Hadn't he ever heard of Ted Bundy, the serial killer who snagged his victims by being helpful to them. "No thanks, I can manage."

And to prove her point, she effortlessly picked up the melon, placed it in her buggy, and shot him a smile before moving on. She resisted for a moment and then glanced over her shoulder. He was still standing there, beside the produce, staring at her. She couldn't help wondering if he made it a habit to hit on older women. He would certainly fit the criteria of a boy toy, if she were interested in one.

Unfortunately for him, she wasn't. Oh well, regardless, she had to admit that his lustful interest had certainly made her day.

Monique's lips twitched as she took a sip of her tea and glanced at Faith over the rim. "And this guy actually came on to you?" she asked.

Faith chuckled before placing a slice of melon in her mouth. At least he'd been right. The watermelon she brought home was delicious. "Yes. Can you believe it?" she asked, feigning shock.

"Of course she can believe it," Shannon said, coming to join them at the table. "We're still fairly young, we look good, and I bet in bed we could hold our own. If he had come on to me, I would have taken him somewhere and made his day."

Faith didn't doubt it. Shannon had walked in a few minutes ago after spending most of her day on the beach, and the bikini she'd been wearing bordered on being downright scandalous. "I see you're still taking casual sex to a whole new level."

A smile touched Shannon's lips. "Don't knock it until you tried it. Besides, I screw smart."

Monique took another sip of her tea and laughed. "Screw smart?"

"Yes, I'm cautious, selective, and discreet. I take safe sex seriously. I'm particular about what man I take to my bed, and I don't believe in letting the entire world know about it."

"I'm glad to hear that," Faith said, shaking her head affectionately. Of the four of them, Shannon had been the first to lose her virginity and had come back and told them all the gory details. Faith had been sixteen then, and it was another five years before she had decided to try it for herself, when she'd met Virgil, "the perfect man." Boy, had she been wrong.

"So, I see you're still not into serious affairs," she decided to say, knowing that would be what Cely would have done had she been there. Cely had always been the one to give them food for thought, regardless of whether they were hungry for it or not.

"Of course not," Shannon replied quickly. "Remember I'm Lorenzo and Alma's child. I know all about adultery and emotional abuse to last a lifetime. I lived them firsthand, with my parents. After witnessing their joke of a marriage, there was no way I was going to try it for myself. I would never be that stupid."

"All marriages aren't bad," Monique said quietly. She still felt that little flutter in her stomach whenever she thought of Paul, the man she had married right out of college—and whom she had lost much too soon in a car accident four years ago.

Shannon reached out and touched Monique's hand gently. "You were one of the lucky ones," she whispered. "They don't make men like Paul anymore."

Monique nodded. She had quickly found that out once she'd started dating again. "That's the main reason why I plan to spend the rest of my life single. Don't get me wrong, I'll still date and all, but it wouldn't bother me any if I never married again. Right now all I'm interested in is companionship, someone to go out to dinner with occasionally, take in a movie, talk to—"

"Sleep with," Shannon said, hoping it was somewhere on the list. She couldn't imagine it not.

Monique shook her head. "Yes, that, too, on occasion, but not with the same frequency as you, Shannon. Lack of sex doesn't bother me. I could go years without even thinking about it."

Shannon laughed. "I could, too, if I had my toys handy."

"Can we change the subject, please?" Faith asked. Being around Shannon was always an education, and it was the kind she'd rather do without tonight. "We're supposed to decide on what we really want to accomplish this summer."

"I'll go first," Monique said eagerly. "I can't wait to tell you guys what I've decided."

"Then please do," Shannon said, sitting straighter in her chair and all ears.

Monique smiled like a schoolgirl with a secret. "It's something I thought of doing lately."

"What?" both Faith and Shannon asked.

"You know that I began doing some recreational running for about six months now, as a way to stay healthy and in shape. Well, what I would really like to do is take my running seriously and compete, and I understand there will be a triathlon here on the island in August. That will give me a about a month to get in shape."

Shannon waited on her to say something else. When Monique

didn't add anything, she just stared at her for a moment then asked, "That's it?"

"Yes," Monique said, grinning. "Don't you think that's enough?"

"No," Shannon was quick to say. "You want to spend the rest of your summer here getting all hot and sweaty?"

Monique laughed. "Basically, yes."

Shannon shook her head when she saw that Monique was serious. "But I don't get it," Shannon said. "Isn't there something else you'd rather do this summer? Something that you really want to do?"

"That's what I really want to do, Shannon. I want to be ready to compete in that Beach Bum Triathlon. I know there's no way I will win, but I think it will be worthwhile to get my body ready to compete."

"I agree, and I think it's a wonderful idea," Faith jumped in with her opinion before Shannon could deliver a thoughtless comeback. "And now it's my turn to tell what I've decided to do."

"What?" Monique asked.

Faith smiled brightly. "I want to learn how to play tennis."

Shannon stared blankly at her. "Tennis? But you took lessons a couple of years ago."

"No, I was supposed to take lessons but never got around to it. This summer I will."

Shannon leaned back in her chair, looking from Faith to Monique and back. "Correct me if I'm wrong, but I thought we were supposed to do use this summer to take on new adventures and broaden our horizons. We're to live each day to the fullest and do whatever we want and not worry about anyone's expectations."

Monique and Faith nodded. "Yes, and that's what we'll be doing," Monique said, smiling.

Interesting, Shannon thought. "I find it strange that neither of your plans for the summer includes a man."

Faith seemed amused. "What's so strange about it? I didn't have to come to Hilton Head to get a man. There are plenty in Minneapolis. Besides, I don't consider a summer fling as a way of broadening my horizons—and I certainly wouldn't think of it as an adventure."

"Umm, you could make it one," Shannon said, throwing her a teasing smile.

"Yes, but that's not what I want," Faith said in all earnest. "You may find this hard to believe, Shannon, but a man is not at the top of every woman's 'to do' list."

"And I agree," Monique piped in.

A smile appeared at the corners of Shannon's lips. "Well, he's at the top of mine, and with that said, I've decided what I want this summer is an affair to remember. I want to show some unsuspecting male that that he's not the only one capable of being a panther whose ready to pounce."

Faith blinked. "You're serious, aren't you?"

"Yes," Shannon said, without batting an eye.

"God, I feel sorry for your victim," Monique said, shuddering at the thought.

"Whatever," Shannon said, remembering all the good-looking hunks she had seen on the beach that day. Some had bodies that could make a woman drool. "So you see, ladies, I plan on spending my summer doing something I've always wanted to do. While you're getting all hot and sweaty, Monique, and you're making out with your tennis racquet, Faith, I plan to go on a manhunt."

3

The next morning Monique glanced around the beach, glad she had turned down Faith and Shannon's invitation to eat breakfast at that café on the strip. She had wanted to begin her early morning jog—she intended a run down the beach every morning to become a ritual for her.

With the triathlon only a month away, she wanted to get in the best shape possible. The three-mile beach run wouldn't be a joke, and she intended to take it seriously. Although she knew she didn't have a snowball's chance in hell of winning, as she'd told Faith and Shannon, just to compete would be a major accomplishment.

After doing a few warm-ups, she was about to take off down the beach when she heard her name. She turned. Recognizing the man jogging toward her coaxed a smile from deep inside. "Lyle? Lyle Montgomery?"

Her smile deepened when he got closer and she saw that it really *was* him. Gosh, how long had it been? Eights years since her brother Arnie's wedding. She remembered the first time they had met. He had been Arnie's roommate in medical school, and she'd been no more than sixteen or seventeen when Lyle had come to spend the summer with them. Arnie had thought a guy from Indiana would appreciate the sweltering Louisiana heat, and she recalled how her parents had practically adopted Lyle into the Olivier family that summer. Everyone had liked him. She had liked him.

"Monique Olivier. I can't believe it," he said, coming to stand directly in front of her. "I thought it was you."

Her smile deepened and she automatically gave him a hug. "What are you doing here in Hilton Head?" she asked. The last time she had talked to her brother and Lyle's name had come up, Arnie had said he was living somewhere in Texas and making a name for himself in the medical field.

"I'm here for the summer running a medical symposium at the hospital." He then quirked a brow. "And what about you? You're a long way from Lacassine, Louisiana."

"I know," she said, enjoying the ease of their conversation. "I'm here with a couple of girlfriends for the summer. We worked hard all year and decided to come here and have some fun." She didn't want to go into details of what really had driven them to the island that summer. That would mean explaining everything, including Cely's death, and she didn't want to do that. It was still so hard to accept it herself.

"And you're a jogger, I see."

She grinned. "A jogger wannabe. I got into the habit of running at least two or three times a week back home, but I've decided to get into some serious running to compete in the triathlon next month."

"Me, too," he said as they moved farther off the boardwalk so another couple could jog past. "I've been running now for a couple of years but never took the time to compete in anything. Since I'm here, I decided why not."

"Good for you."

"And how's your dad? I heard about your mom passing, and I'm sorry that I couldn't make it to the funeral. I was out of the country when I got the news."

Sadness came into Monique's eyes. "Dad's fine. Losing Mom was hard on all of us, but in the end the cancer took such a toll on her, we didn't want to see her suffer any longer."

Lyle nodded. "And I was sorry to hear about your husband as well."

Monique inhaled deeply. Paul had died within a year of her mother, and it had taken everything she had to hold herself together after suffering the impact of losing the two people who had meant the most to her. "Thanks. You never met Paul, but I think you would have liked him."

Lyle nodded again as a small smile formed on his lips. "I'm sure I would have. Arnie said he was a nice guy."

"He was. The best."

"Then I'm glad you got to share whatever time that you had with him."

"Thanks."

"Well, let me let you get started since I just finished up. I'm going to head to that café over there for a cup of coffee. Are you staying somewhere close by?"

"Yes, in one of those homes in the newest development of Sea Pines. What about you?"

He said, "Then I'm practically in your backyard. I'm leasing a condo in the Sand Dunes. Will you be back out again in the morning?"

"Yes."

"How about if we jog together and then go somewhere for coffee? I'd like to talk to you, and see what's been going on with you over the years."

"That would be nice." Monique shook her head, and her shoulder-length hair swayed around her face.

Smiling, Lyle reached out and pushed a few wayward strands back from her face and then said, "Okay, Nicky, then this same place tomorrow but an hour earlier. It's best to get out on the beach before the crowds come."

"Okay. I'll see you in the morning with my running shoes on."

His laughter was one of the best sounds she'd heard in a long time, and she watched him turn and jog off toward the cluster of shops. It then occurred to her that during their conversation he had called her Nicky, the nickname he had given her that summer. No one else had ever called her Nicky but him.

Nothing about Lyle had changed. He was older, true, but still good-looking. That first summer he had come home with Arnie, Lyle had been quiet and reserved, but in no time Emily Olivier had stepped in as the mother figure he'd never had in his life, and he had become just like another member of the family.

She remembered the last time she had seen him, at Arnie's wedding. She had been talking to the bride-to-be and glanced up to see him walk into the church for rehearsal as one of the groomsmen. And she had been all giddy that he had been paired with her, which made all the other single girls downright envious. She figured he would be around thirty-eight now, the same age as Arnie. Lyle had certainly aged well. Tall, dark, and handsome, he would capture the attention of any female the moment he walked into a room. She'd heard from Arnie that he never married; instead Lyle had dedicated his life to his occupation, that of a renowned heart specialist.

As Monique took off jogging down the beach, she looked forward to seeing him again the next day.

An hour or so later, Lyle was giving his body a brutal workout in the gym at his condo complex. Seeing Nicky had had one hell of an effect on him.

Deciding he had had enough, he left the gym to go back to his place for a shower. It had been a long time since he'd given his body so much physical abuse, but thoughts of a woman could do that to you.

Moments later, while standing beneath a spray of hot water, he thought maybe he should be taking a cold shower instead. Desire was drumming through him, taking him back in time and making him recall the exact moment he'd fallen for Nicky, all those years ago—a secret he was determined to take to his grave.

He had noticed her that first summer, and since she had been merely sixteen when he was twenty-two, he had felt guilty about lusting after his best friend's kid sister. Even then she'd been a beauty, and when he had seen her again years later at Arnie's wedding, he was in awe of just how much that beauty had blossomed.

He had always intended to revisit the Olivier family after that summer with the full intention of making his interest known when Monique got older. But he never got the chance. It wasn't long after that summer that the private investigator he and his brothers had hired to find their sister had done so, and for the following years after that, he and his brothers, Logan and Lance, had made bonding with their long-lost sister their top priority. More than anything, they wanted to make sure Carrie knew that she was wanted and loved. The next time he'd talked to Arnie and asked about Monique, he'd been given the heartbreaking news that she'd married a guy she met in college.

That's when Lyle decided that since he'd lost his first love, he would dedicate his life to his second love—the medical field. Remarkably, in a very short time he had advanced in his career and was proud of his status as one of the youngest but most noted members in his profession.

As he stepped out of the shower and dried off, he remembered the hurt and pain he'd endured knowing another man had married the woman he'd always considered to be "his Nicky."

The only persons who'd known of his broken heart had been his brothers. He spilled his guts one night when the three had been sitting around Lance's condo in Chicago, after overindulging in too much drink while celebrating the arrival of the New Year. Logan had sympathized with him, but Lance, who'd at the time had considered himself the ultimate playa, had been too jaded to care and had even gone so far as to tell him that women were a dime a dozen and to get over Nicky and move on to another. That was easier said than done, and although he'd dated over the years, a piece of his heart would always belong to Monique.

What was the likelihood of their paths crossing after all these years? With his busy schedule, he hadn't kept in contact with Arnie the way he should have. He knew Arnie headed the neurosurgical department at Massachusetts General and that he and his wife, Cheryl, had three kids, a son and two daughters.

Pulling on a pair of shorts and T-shirt, he headed for the kitchen and smiled. It seemed that fate was giving him another chance to make Monique a part of his life, and the big question was just what he was going to do about it. He could tell from the way she'd mentioned her deceased husband that she had loved the man and probably still did. Unfortunately, Lyle wanted to claim her and her heart.

He grabbed a beer out of the refrigerator and went out on the patio and sat down, stretching his legs out in front of him to think. He didn't know the first thing about being one of those aggressive males who went after what he wanted. Lance was the one who'd eventually gotten his shit together to claim the heart of the woman he loved.

Lyle was a heart specialist. Of the three Montgomery brothers, he was considered the least outgoing. However, when it came to repairing hearts . . .

His smile widened as a number of possibilities formed in his head. He would not lose the woman he loved a second time. He would do what he did best—repair a person's heart, and he fully intended to work on fixing up hers, starting tomorrow morning.

4

Shannon pulled her car into the auto repair shop, determined to find out what was causing that consistent knocking sound she'd started hearing yesterday. She believed in keeping her car in top condition and fully intended to find out what was wrong with it. Since she made her home in Durham, North Carolina, she had driven to Hilton Head instead of flying in as Faith and Monique had done. She never liked airplanes, and although she had flown on quite a few, she avoided doing so whenever possible.

Besides, the drive had been rewarding, and once she got off the interstate to take U.S. Highway 278, the scenic four lanes that took you right over to the island, she had made the trip in six hours.

The cook at the diner where she'd eaten breakfast that morning had recommended this shop, saying it was the best on the island to repair sports cars. She glanced around but didn't see anyone. And then she glanced at her watch. It was noon. Evidently the owner and workers were out to lunch.

She decided to sit and wait. She turned off the ignition and leaned back in her seat, lowered the volume on her radio and began thinking of her conversation with Faith and Monique a few nights ago.

She knew she hadn't really shocked them by saying she would spend her summer going on a manhunt. From as far back as she could remember, she had been the most aggressive of the four when it came to showing interest in the opposite sex. She blamed it on her overly strict parents. They had raised her to be what they considered a "good girl," and she had pleased them by always acting the role of obedient, humble, and easily controlled. But when she was out of their sight, it was a different story. She'd had a tendency to get buck wild.

And although over the years she could admit to having a fair amount of lovers, she didn't consider herself promiscuous or easy. In fact, she was downright nitpicky when it came to letting a man in her bed. She had standards that she refused to lower and was not one to be swept away by sweet talk, a savvy walk, or a well-built body.

She had decided years ago after opening her eyes and acknowledging her parents' mockery of a marriage that she would live the rest of her life as a single woman. Her father engaged in affairs like it was his God-given right to do so, and her mother was just as bad, taking on a series of lovers who were usually half her age. Yet, while out in public, they presented themselves as a loving couple: the highly educated, highly sophisticated, overly dignified, and wealthy Drs. Carmichael. Both were college professors at Yale who had made names for themselves in the academic world.

While growing up, she couldn't wait until she was old enough to leave home and swore that she would return to her Connecticut hometown only for visits. She liked her teaching position at Duke University and was glad miles separated her from her parents. It was enough to see her father occasionally on CNN whenever he was called to flaunt his expertise on foreign policies or to watch her mother on various talk shows like *Oprah,* where she would give her expert opinion about the workings of the human mind.

A sound grabbed Shannon's attention and made her look around. The sight she came upon had blood immediately rushing through her veins. A man dressed in a T-shirt and jeans was coming down the stairs from what looked like an apartment that was built over the garage. To say he looked sexy would be an understatement. He practically dripped sex appeal.

She closed her eyes and reined herself in. Hell, what was the matter with her? The man worked in a garage, for heaven's sake, and he was not the type of person she should be attracted to. How many times had her parents drilled into her the importance of dating someone her equal, someone within her intellectual and academic class? A Carmichael dated only the best and, as far as her parents were concerned, that did not include blue-collar workers or someone who had not achieved a certain status in life—definitely not a person who got grease under his fingernails for a living. She dated doctors, lawyers, politicians, accountants, and so forth and so on. So her instant attraction to this guy was totally unacceptable, unexpected, but undeniably hot.

As if he heard her breathing hard, he turned and glanced over at her car. She wished he hadn't done that. It was bad enough that he had a good-looking body, now his face actually had her licking her lips. Medium brown skin, dark eyes, clean-shaven head, nice set of ears, and a jaw in need of a shave . . . and when he started walking over toward her car, it took all she had to hold her desire in check.

"May I help you?" he asked when he reached her car.

She swallowed. He had a nice voice, too. It practically caressed her skin. Oh yeah, this guy could help her in a number of ways, and all of them were too scandalous to think about right now. "My car."

He raised a brow. A few moments later, he smiled and asked, "What about your car?"

Although he was smiling, a part of her could actually detect his restrained laughter. He was probably aware of what he did to women and even found it amusing. She didn't like the thought of that one bit. That arrogance set her nerves on edge and gave her a measure of control she hadn't had earlier. "It's making a sound, and I want you to fix it. You are the owner of this place, right?"

"Excuse me."

She glared at him. "You're the owner?"

"No, I'm not the owner."

"Then you must be one of the workers, so you'll have to do."

He was smart enough to move out of the way when she pushed her car door open. "My car is making a clicking sound, and I want you to find out what it is and fix it. And I would like to have it ready by this afternoon," she said, handing him the keys as well as her business card. "Is that understood?"

"Yes, ma'am, it is," he said, and again she thought she heard laughter in his voice. "I'm sure you want us to inform you what's wrong with it as well as the cost before any repair work is done, right?"

"Of course. And you can reach me at that mobile number on my business card. I've already called for someone to come pick me up. Is there a place where I can wait for them to get here?"

He nodded toward a bench. "Yeah, over there."

She saw the wooden bench was in an area where the sun was beaming straight down over it. "You don't have an air-conditioned area where I can wait inside?"

"Yes, but I don't have the keys to open it up. The owner is out to lunch."

She huffed a breath, not liking his answer. "Fine, I'll wait over there, then."

Lucky for Shannon, at that moment Faith pulled up. Without saying anything else to the mechanic, Shannon quickly walked over to her friend's car and got in.

"What took you so long?" she asked Faith, refusing to give in to temptation and glance back over at the mechanic as they pulled away.

"I stopped for gas. Remember I told you that I would."

"Oh, yes, I forgot." Although Shannon didn't want to think about the mechanic, she had to admit he was a looker—a well-built looker. Her pulse raced, and she hated the thought of dealing with him again when she came later to pick up her car.

Adam Corbain couldn't help but grin as he watched the woman drive off in the car. She had to have been the snootiest yet most beautiful woman he'd ever seen. Dark brown shredded hair fell to her shoulders, and her eyes had been the color of gingerbread.

When she'd walked off, he had tried not to stare, but he hadn't missed the generous curves showcased in the pair of shorts she was wearing.

She had tried looking down on him like he was a cockroach, but that was only after he detected that hot look of interest in her eyes. Sexual chemistry was hard to resist, and he had felt it the same moment she had, when their gazes first connected. And when she had given him her car keys and business card and their fingers had touched, he had actually felt her tremble, which sparked a need he'd ignored for the past six months. His desire for her had been just that spontaneous. In all his thirty-seven years, he had never experienced such a thing before. He glanced down at the business card in his hand.

Dr. Shannon Carmichael
Professor of English and American Literature
Duke University

"Hey, man, whose car is this?"

Adam turned around at the sound of his old friend's voice. For as long as Adam could remember, Kent Scott was a person who loved tinkering with automobiles, so no one was really surprised after they'd graduated from high school that Kent went to college to obtain a degree in mechanical engineering. After working a few years designing cars for General Motors, he began his NASCAR career and earned the reputation of being both a high-performance mechanic and a fearless race car driver. However, the latter came to a screeching halt when he met and later married Lori. Now he was a family man and the owner of several profitable high-performance repair shops around the country. His clientele included sport figures and celebrities looking for classic cars to add to their collection.

"A woman brought it in," Adam finally answered. "She heard a knocking sound and wants you to check it out."

Kent raised a curious brow. "And she just left it here?" he asked, eyeing the sports car, a sleek and stylish Porsche.

Adam smiled as he handed him the keys and the business card. "Yes. She thought I was one of your mechanics."

A grin flickered across Kent's lips. "You, a mechanic? Not Mr. Ivy League graduate. Mr. Suave Attorney. How on earth could she assume such a thing?"

"Probably from the way I'm dressed, which wasn't to impress," Adam said, glancing down at himself. His jeans and his T-shirt had seen better days.

Shaking his head, Adam walked over to the car he had been about to work on before he'd noticed Ms. Carmichael sitting in the parked car. In a way, it was kind of comical that for the next month or so he would be just what Shannon Carmichael thought he was. A mechanic.

Kent had contacted him a few months ago, letting him know he'd located a 1969 Pontiac GTO, and that all it needed was a little work. "A little work" to Kent meant a lot of work to anyone else. So Adam took a month's leave from the family law office in Memphis to come to Hilton Head. And because he intended to spend the majority of his days and, in some cases, late into the night working on the vehicle, Kent suggested he occupy the empty apartment over the garage. Perfect.

So for one month he would shed the role of Adam Corbain, the cool, sophisticated, and suave Memphis attorney and become a man on a mission to restore what he considered as the beauty of all muscle cars. He intended to make the vehicle into nothing less than one hell of a commemorative collectors' item that would be an added bonus to his five-car garage.

"So was she good-looking?"

Adam glanced over his shoulder. "Who?"

"The woman driving this set of wheels."

Adam smiled. "You're married, remember."

"I wasn't asking for myself but for you."

Adam lifted the hood, not wanting to meet Kent's eyes when he said, "She looked all right."

"She drove this kind of car and just looked all right?"

Adam shrugged. "Couldn't see just how good she looked for her uppity attitude." Adam wished he could claim that her snobbish manner had been a turnoff, but in essence everything about Dr. Shannon Carmichael had been a total turn-on.

"Well, I'll check out her car and see what's wrong with it," Kent said.

"She wants you to call her before any repairs are done."

"Hey, that's the way we do business around here. By the way, Lori wants you to come to dinner tonight. She's grilling steaks."

"Then count me in," Adam said, smiling.

He couldn't help listening when Kent started the engine on Shannon Carmichael's car. A few minutes later, he called out to Kent and said, "Sounds like it could use a tune-up for starters."

"Yes," Kent joked, "maybe the same thing holds true for the woman who drives it."

Adam rolled his eyes. "I didn't come here to get involved with a woman. Don't have the time. This baby here is the only thing that will be getting my attention over the next four weeks."

"If you say so."

"And I do," Adam said before grabbing a wrench and beginning to work.

"Are you sure you don't want me to wait on you?" Monique asked Shannon as she got out of the car.

"Yes, I'm sure," Shannon told her. "The person who called said my car was ready, so all I have to do is pay for the repairs and leave. No big deal."

Monique glanced around, and the first thing she noticed was that there weren't any junky-looking cars all over the place. At least the place looked neat and clean. "All right, if you're sure." She then quickly asked, "You got your cell phone, right?"

Shannon grinned. "Yes, Mother, I have my cell phone."

Monique aimed a *don't play with me like that* smile at her friend.

"Of all the people in the world, please don't tell me I'm sounding like your mother."

"But you are."

"Okay, I get the message. I'll see you back at the house." She waved and drove off.

Shannon took a moment to thank her lucky stars that Monique had been the one to bring her to the auto shop and not Faith. No matter how she might have insisted, Faith would not have left her here alone. Shannon then glanced around. Well, she wasn't alone exactly. It seemed the man from earlier was still there. His back was to her, and she couldn't see his face since his head was stuck under the hood of an old beat-up-looking car. But she would recognize the lower part of him anywhere.

With every step toward him, she felt tension reaching its full height within her. What was there about this man, this mechanic who probably had no aspirations to be anything else, that was making her nervous? No, *nervous* wasn't the right word. *Hot* was better.

The man who'd called to tell her how much the repair would cost and then again to let her know it was ready to pick up wasn't this guy. They had exchanged few words, but she knew it wasn't the same voice on the telephone.

He must have heard her footsteps because at that moment he pulled his head from underneath the hood of the car and turned. What she suddenly felt then was totally unexpected in one way, and not such a surprise in another. She stopped walking when his gaze slowly made its way down her body, and she all but suppressed a gasp. Her lower body started to sizzle in the intensity of his stare.

Yes, she'd seen him earlier that day, but now she was *really* seeing him. He looked more handsome, manlier, sexier—and dirtier. His T-shirt was smeared with grease and oil, and there was a tear on the knee of his jeans that hadn't been there hours ago. There was even a smudge of grease on his chin, but she barely registered any of that, mesmerized by his stance as he leaned against the vehicle he was working on.

There was something utterly raw and savage about him, an attitude that almost bordered on uncivilized. In the past, a man with a clean-shaven head had never set any sparks flying with her. But not only were they flying, they were landing on some pretty interesting spots.

He was looking at her with a concentration that intensified the attraction she felt toward him, making it that much wilder. Her pulse rushed, her skin felt hotter, and she had to concede that although he was probably the most unrefined man she'd ever willingly encountered, he was also the most intriguing. The words *bad boy* were written all over him.

She gathered the composure to speak. "I got a call that my car is ready."

For a moment he didn't say anything. He just looked at her with intense dark eyes before he finally said, "Kent's inside."

The sound of his voice was like the feel of fingertips grazing across her skin. She swallowed. "Kent?"

"Yeah, the owner."

"Oh. And who're you?"

He lifted a brow. "Who am I?"

"Yes, don't you have a name?"

"Yes, I have one."

When moments ticked and it appeared he wouldn't give it to her without her asking, she did. "Well, what is it?"

"Adam. Adam Corbain." Then as if he didn't have anything else to say to her, he turned his back, leaned forward to resume what he'd been doing under the hood of the car. The urge to take a few steps and snuggle up against his back, wrap her arms around him, settle her body right smack up against his well-defined butt, was a temptation Shannon had to fight hard not to give in to. Instead she quickly walked over to the door of a small office.

When she walked back out of the office less than ten minutes later, he was still there with his head underneath the hood of the car. She glanced his way for only a second before walking to her car and getting into it. He turned around when he heard the sound of her engine.

Their gazes locked, held, and she could actually feel heat leap across the span of distance separating them. Nothing like this had ever happened to her before, and she couldn't understand it. Why, of all the men she could be attracted to on this island, did it have to be him? A man who looked the part of a Neanderthal with a capital N. A man named after the first man on this earth. Adam. The same man whose rib started womanhood. Go figure.

She pulled out of the garage, determined not to glance back in her rearview mirror, but she couldn't help herself and did anyway. He was leaning against that car and staring, and for a brief moment it looked as if he would actually smile. But he didn't. She'd dare any woman to actually make his lips tilt at the corners. Just try it. The thought of doing so captivated her, made every cell within her body vibrate, made her already scorching body even hotter.

She breathed in slowly. At that moment, as crazy as it was, she knew her manhunt had ended before it had a chance to begin, in forbidden territory. Although she didn't know anything about the man, she had to accept the obvious.

She had found her prey.

5

Adrianna Ross-Fuller scooped up a handful of laundry from the dryer and went into her bedroom to fold and put it away. She smiled, remembering the call on her answering machine from that morning: Zach had let her know he was coming to Hilton Head for a visit.

Technically Zachary Wainwright was her god-brother, but it was hard to think of him that way, since the two of them had met only a little over a year ago. The day he had tracked her down in her emergency room in San Diego was unforgettable. In a span of a couple of hours, he had convinced her that the family she thought had renounced her more than thirty years ago had actually been looking for her. They had not disowned her because her late father had married a Vietnamese girl during the war.

That day changed her life. He had convinced her to return with him to D.C. and meet her father's family as well as the godfather she hadn't known existed. It was an incredible night filled with amazing people. Since then, she'd forged a close relationship with her paternal grandparents, uncle, and his family, as well as her godparents and the cousins she'd been introduced to. But nothing came close to the impact that Zach Wainwright had made on her life. She'd felt initially overwhelmed by the magnitude of love pouring forth from virtual strangers, but he had been right there for her, just a glance away, reassuring her that he was a friend she could count on. She had believed him. She'd trusted him, and eventually she fell in love with him.

She began folding up her underthings, utterly contented. Zach was not a hard person to love. One of the brightest and most sought-after attorneys in D.C., he was the subject of speculation: Zachary Wainwright. Would he eventually follow in the footsteps of his father, the senator from Florida, and choose a political career? Adrianna couldn't help noticing that whenever anyone brought up the possibility, he was quick to deflect the rumor.

It was also her opinion that Zach was extremely handsome, always the perfect gentleman, soft-spoken, caring, and private in certain ways. According to his sister Noelle, whom Adrianna had also gotten close to over the year, Zach had developed an extremely disciplined social life since his wife's death five years ago, on September 11. She had been a flight attendant on the Washington-to-Los Angeles American Airlines Flight 77 that ill-fated day.

Adrianna sighed deeply. No one knew about her inner feelings for Zach, and she planned to keep it that way. There was no telling what her newfound family would think if they were to discover her secret. And there was certainly no telling what Zach would think. He saw her as a close friend and nothing more. And she refused to do anything that would ruin that friendship, despite the voices she sometimes heard in her head: *Go ahead, take the first step. Let him know how you feel.*

But she couldn't take that step. She had been rejected once by the family of a man she had intended to marry, and she couldn't risk another loss like that, especially not with this family, a family she could finally claim as her own. So when it came to Zach, she had to keep a good head on her shoulders and never act reckless.

Adrianna continued to fold up her clothes, taking slow, deep breaths, trying to rein her overjoyed heart. Zach would be coming to see her in a few weeks, and that alone made her extremely happy.

Washington, D.C.

Zach Wainwright turned away from the window when he heard his parents enter the room. He met their curious gazes. It was late afternoon, and he knew they were wondering why he had called that morning with such urgency in his voice, asking to speak with the both of them.

He studied them before speaking. Noah and Leigh Wainwright were always such a striking couple, even after thirty-seven years of marriage. His tall, handsome, and dashing father, Florida's senator Noah Wainwright, and his beautiful wife, Leigh Murdock Wainwright—lovely, vivacious, and the most gracious hostess in all of the District of Columbia and surrounding areas. Zach knew how very much in love they were. Over the years they had given him and Noelle strong role models for healthy relationships. He had always wanted to bring what his parents had in their marriage to his own, but he hadn't been given the chance. He had lost Shaun after only a couple of years of marriage, and for the longest while, all his hope and dreams had died with her on board that plane. Only strong family support and love had gotten him through that time intact.

"Zach? Are you all right?" The concern in his mother's voice matched the worried look on her face.

His father, on the other hand, just continued to stare at him with those intense, dark eyes of his, and not for the first time did Zach wonder if Noah Wainwright could read his mind. It wouldn't surprise him if he could, since they had always been so close. The retired senator was one of those men who'd always made time for his family, no matter what political aspirations he had. Family had always come first, and Zach knew it always would.

Zach crossed the room and gently took his mother's hand in his. "I'm fine, Mom. I just wanted to talk to you and Dad about something that's important to me."

Leigh nodded before glancing over her shoulder at her husband, and Zach could tell from her expression that she was wondering if he were already privy to what this was about. Guessing exactly that, Noah chuckled and said, "No, sweetheart, I don't know why our son called this meeting, but I'm sure he won't be keeping us in the dark for long. Let's go ahead and sit down."

Zach's parents perched on the sofa in the Wainwrights' study. It occurred to him that on that same sofa, over a year ago, he had ended his father and Randolph Fuller's search for Adrianna Fuller. She had sat there beside Zach while he held her hand, giving her the courage and confidence she needed to confront the family she assumed had turned their backs on her for thirty-four years. That night lies had been exposed, understandings forged, miscommunications cleared up, and, in the end, all the love Noah Wainwright had felt for his deceased best friend—and all the love and admiration Randolph Fuller had felt for his deceased brother, Ross Donovan Fuller—was alive, cultivated anew in Ross's daughter, Adrianna, whom everyone called Anna.

"Zach?"

The sound of his mother's voice brought his thoughts back to the present. Again he heard that apprehension. She was anxious to hear what he had to say. "I'm sure you saw the article in the papers this morning," he started off.

His father nodded automatically. "The one that claimed you'll be making an announcement soon as to whether or not you plan to ever run for public office?"

"Yes, that's the one." For the past couple of years the media had speculated on the possibility. As far as they were concerned, he was following in his father's footstep and a stint in the political arena was inevitable. But Zach hadn't made any commitments, and at first he had laughed off the media's inquiries as ludicrous. But now . . .

"And what about it, Zach?" his mother asked, bringing his attention back to her. She had to be the strongest and the most genuine woman he knew, even in a town where most people constantly performed, as if they were on a stage.

"I've made a decision."

His father lifted a brow. "And?"

"And I've decided to throw my hat into the ring next year and run for senator, but only on one very important condition."

His father offered him a smile while his mother's expression gave nothing away. He knew it had been their shared dream that he would one day go into public office, but they had never tried to coerce him in any way, preferring to let it be his decision. "And what condition is that?" his father asked, meeting his gaze.

Zach took a deep breath. He didn't think his statement would come as a surprise to his parents, since they knew him so well, but . . .

"Yes, what is this condition, Zach?" his mother chimed in, repeating his father's question.

He was watching his parents' reactions when he said, "Anna. My decision to run for office will depend on how Anna feels about it."

His parents contemplated what he'd just said. But he knew them. They would want him to be more specific, and he would be. "Why are Anna's feelings about your decision important, Zach?" his father finally asked.

Zach wasn't surprised by the question. He had expected it. They were forcing him to admit something that he'd been harboring in his heart long enough, but seeing her a few months ago had really brought it home. At the little party her grandmother, Julia Fuller, had given for her, he'd made a decision to act on his feelings. It was a party to celebrate the first year of Anna's being a part of their lives.

"The reason it's important is that I'm in love with Anna. She doesn't know it, and in fact I'm certain she doesn't have a clue, but I intend to make my feelings known to her."

He watched his mother's brow rise. "Just like that?"

He shook his head, grinning. "No, Mom, not just like that. I have more charm and sophistication than that. After all, I am your son. But to answer your question, I plan to take things slow when I visit her in Hilton Head."

"You're going to Hilton Head?" his father asked.

"I intend to spend some time with her. I'm sure she assumes, like a few others, that I'm not over losing Shaun. I admit Shaun will always hold a special place in my heart, but I truly do love Anna. I didn't realize how much until I noticed her grandmother introducing her to so many eligible bachelors at that party four months ago."

Leigh's eyes lit up. "Oh, so you noticed that, did you?"

"I couldn't help but notice," he said with an edge in his tone. "I decided then it was time for me to make my move, and what I do in the future and how she feels about it are important. She may not want to live a life that will constantly throw her in the limelight."

His parents understood completely. It was no big secret that the reason Anna had sought refuge on Hilton Head Island was to maintain her privacy. She'd also inherited a huge tract of land on the island from her great-grandmother, Mattie Murphy. Her family had once owned most of the property on the island before they had given in and sold it to developers. Mattie's share had been split between her grandsons, Ross and Randolph. Upon Ross's death, Anna had inherited her father's portion as well as his share of a private island across the Intracostal Waterway called Glendale Shores.

Upon her family urgings, Anna resigned from her job at the hospital in San Diego and moved to D.C. But there she was constantly hounded by the media, who'd found her story fascinating: HEIRESS FOUND AFTER 34-YEAR SEARCH.

While living in the nation's capital those three months, she hadn't known a moment of peace and eventually transferred to the trauma center on Hilton Head. She had a beautiful beach house built on the property she had inherited there. For Zach to make his feelings known would also mean asking her to be a part of his life and his future. He had to be sure she would feel comfortable being a politician's wife.

"And if she wants no part of that type of life?" his mother asked softly.

"Then I won't have a part of it either. She is more important to me than anything."

His father said, "Then I wish you all the best, son. I think you know how we feel about Anna."

"Yes, Dad, I know, and I want to do the right thing. I will do the right thing, and I wanted you and Mom to know it. I also plan to visit Uncle Randolph as well." Randolph Fuller had always been such a part of his life growing up that Zach considered him an adopted uncle.

"When are you going to Virginia to see Randolph?"

"First thing in the morning. And then later this month I'm going to Hilton Head, where I plan to spend the next month or so."

"Month?" his parents said simultaneously.

"I'll take even more time if I have to. I'm putting in a leave at work—a much-deserved one, I might add—and that's where I'll be for a while if anyone needs me for anything."

"Will you and Anna will be attending the Fourth of July celebration on Glendale Shores?"

Zach smiled. She was asking about the huge gathering the Fuller and Wainwright families held every July Fourth. "We do plan to be there. And I prefer that you not mention what I've discussed today with Noelle. She has a tendency of trying to play matchmaker, and I prefer doing things my way."

"Okay, we won't, but you know your sister. I think she has an idea already about how you might feel."

Zach laughed before conceding, "Yes, she might, but I still want to do things my way." He checked his watch. "Well, I'd better get going if I'm to leave for Virginia in the morning."

His parents stood and his mother crossed the room and gave him a hug. "I wish you the best of luck where Anna is concerned. I knew from the first time I saw the two of you together that one day this would happen, and I'm happy for you."

"Same here, son," his father said, also giving him a big, strong hug. "Anna is a very special young woman."

"I know. And that's the reason I fell in love with her."

6

"*If he was* that hot, I'm surprised you didn't jump his bones when you had the chance," Faith said, grinning after Shannon told her about the guy she'd met at the auto repair shop.

Shannon, sitting on the sofa, crossed her legs, at the very thought. She smiled. "The idea did cross my mind, but I decided to make this an adventure, work up my level of expertise before I go in for the kill. Besides that, I have to make sure the guy clearly understands this will be a summer fling and nothing more than that. I don't want him to get any ideas."

"Oh, and what kind of ideas are you talking about, Shannon?" Monique asked, coming to sit in one of the chairs in the room to join them. They had eaten dinner, each doing their own thing. Now Monique wished she'd had a salad like the one Faith had prepared instead of the hot dogs and fries she'd grabbed on the way back from town. She needed to purchase a few new jogging suits. She and Lyle had been meeting each morning, going jogging for almost a week, and if she was going to continue to do so, the least she could do was look good while getting all hot and sweaty.

"*Several ideas,*" Shannon answered.

"And of course the main one being that there's no way Dr. Shannon Carmichael can even think about getting serious with a blue-collar worker. She only involves herself in relationships of intellectual compatibility," Monique recited.

Shannon frowned, not liking the way Monique had talked to her but then having to admit that what she'd said was true. "So what's wrong with that?"

"For you, nothing."

Her eyebrows rose in obvious displeasure. "And what's that supposed to mean?"

Monique glanced over at Faith, who gave her an eye that said, *Please, let's not go there tonight,* but Monique ignored that look because she *wanted* to go there. Maybe it would be hopeless to try to make Shannon see just what a snob she could be when it came to dating, but still, it wasn't a topic they hadn't tangled with before. No one had been more passionate about it than Cely, but no matter what they'd said to Shannon, she refused even to consider that when it came to men, their annual income didn't matter. Shannon's defense had always been that her parents raised her in such a way as to eventually marry well, and falling for a guy—no matter how decent, honest, and attractive he might be—who didn't make at least twice as much as what she made was not a good match, definitely a step down.

"It means, Shannon, that you still have a lot of growing up to do."

"Why, because I'm selective when it comes to men?"

"No, I think we're all selective. You just take the selection process to a whole other level. You have this stubborn assumption that a woman has to become seriously involved only with someone she considers her professional equal—or better yet, her superior. Knowing your parents, I'm sure from the time you could talk they drilled it into your mind to marry a doctor, a lawyer, or definitely someone who could keep you in all those name brands you like. I'd bet the money I have in my bank account that qualities like honesty, loyalty, integrity, and sensitivity in a man were never discussed. All I'm saying is that you should consider all options. Blue-collar working men should be given equal respect and not looked down upon."

Monique could tell Shannon just didn't get it, and she wondered if her friend ever would.

"I hear what you're saying, Monique, but I have my own taste in men and you have yours—and I doubt my taste will change."

"So what about this mechanic?" Faith butted in to ask, the look in her eyes expressing that she was more into making a point rather than indulging in idle curiosity.

"Like I said, he'll be just a summer fling. When I leave here, it will be out of sight and out of mind."

"And do you think it's fair to him to be used that way?"

Shannon shook her head, smiling with audacious confidence. The hot mechanic would be a perfect summer lover. "Trust me, he'll get his time's worth as well. Don't get me wrong, I believe this guy has some level of social skills and he can communicate well enough but his social and communication skills aren't what I'm interested in."

Neither Faith nor Monique had to ask just what she *was* interested in. Faith then turned to Monique. "I saw you jogging when I went to that shop on the beach to get my nails done early this morning. And the guy you were with looked good. Who is he?"

Shannon turned and stared at Monique, and before Monique could answer Faith's question, Shannon asked, almost shocked, "*You were with a man?*"

Monique shook her head, smiling with the knowledge that *with a man* to Shannon meant an entirely different thing. "No, I wasn't 'with' a man. I was merely jogging with him. He's someone I've known for awhile who I ran into a week ago, and we decided to jog together every morning."

Faith couldn't help but wonder why Monique hadn't mentioned it if it was so innocent. "Who is he?"

"Lyle Montgomery." Monique then watched both Shannon and Faith as they tried to recall where they'd heard that name before.

Of course it was Shannon who remembered. "Isn't he the guy who was your brother's roommate while in medical school?"

"Yes."

A glitter of a smile touched Shannon lips. "I remember him coming to stay with your family one summer. When we saw you those two weeks, he was all you could talk about. You kept going on and on about how good-looking he was and stuff."

Monique laughed. It was both warm and spontaneous. "Yes, I remember, and he's still good-looking."

"What's he doing here?" Faith asked curiously. "Does he live on Hilton Head?"

"No, he's a doctor and is here teaching a medical symposium. He's into jogging and plans to compete in the triathlon as well. Since we're both competing, we've decided to work out every day together."

"Umm, that sounds *interesting*," Shannon said.

"Please get your mind out of the gutter, Shannon. Unlike you, I don't lust after every man I see."

Shannon grinned. "And neither do I. I'm a very selective bitch, remember?"

Monique couldn't help but smile. "There's no way we can forget."

Shannon had decided to call it an early night, which left Faith and Monique up chatting. Faith could tell Monique was excited about seeing Lyle Montgomery again.

"Why didn't you tell us you'd run into him and that the two of you were jogging together every morning, Monique?" Faith asked, studying her friend.

Monique shrugged. "Because I didn't want a big deal made out of it."

Faith nodded and then said, "I recall you had a crush on him."

Monique drew in a full breath. "Yes, but just for that summer. The next summer I had a crush on Charles Moore."

"Yeah, and let's not forget Morris Potter." Faith grinned.

Monique covered her face with her hands, wishing there was a way she *could* forget. "You have a long memory, Faith, and speaking of Morris, I ran into him a few years ago at an insurance convention—and he's gay."

"Umm, maybe I should try and get him and Virgil together."

Monique glanced over at Faith and couldn't help but laugh.

Faith soon began laughing with her. "I'm glad you've put that ugly ordeal behind you and can finally laugh about it."

"Well, yeah—what else can I do?" Faith said, smoothing her silk bathrobe across her knees. "I cried myself out when it happened," she said. "I'm just so glad I had you, Cely, and Shannon to unload on. The three of you helped me to see it wasn't about me but was about him."

"Yes, it was and still is. I'm amazed that the two of you can still be friends."

Faith could believe that. "Well, you're not the only one," she said. "My parents are amazed as well. If Dad had anything to do with it, Virgil would be a dead man. He fooled everyone, including me. Especially me."

"Yeah, and the sad thing is that he's not the only man doing it," Monique interjected. "When I first heard about it I thought this *down-low brothers* thing was a guy's vivid imagination whose aim was to sell books on *Oprah*. Now every way you turn you hear more and more about men having affairs on their wives with other men. The next man I become involved with I'm going to come right out and ask him."

Faith couldn't stop from rolling her eyes. "And you really expect him to tell you the truth?"

"No, but I bet I could learn a lot from his shocked expression," Monique said, leaning back against the couch.

"Umm, speaking of learning a lot, I finally got around to meeting my parents' neighbor today. I had promised Mom that I would go over and introduce myself while I was here. It seems the woman made a lasting impression on my parents when they came to sign the papers to buy this house."

Monique raised a curious brow. "Who is she?"

"She's an Amerasian who's about our age and is a doctor at the trauma center at the hospital. Her name is Adrianna Ross-Fuller. I forgot to mention that I invited her to dinner tomorrow night."

Monique couldn't suppress her surprise. "Someone's fixing dinner? I thought we all agreed it was a free-for-all while we're here."

"I know, but I like cooking every now and then and decided to spend some time in the kitchen tomorrow."

"Hey, it's plenty big enough, so knock yourself out. I plan to get up early for my jog with Lyle, and then later just hang out at the beach and do nothing."

"Just be back by five."

"Oh, I will. And you better let Shannon know about dinner tomorrow. I have a feeling she's going to go after her mechanic then."

Faith wasn't sure she liked hearing that. "You think so?"

"Yeah. I think she's been planning her strategy and is about ready to go in for the kill."

Part

two

What has been will be again, what has been done will be done again; there is nothing new under the sun.

—ECCLESIASTES 1:9

7

"*It's going to* be another beautiful day."

Monique whirled around at the sound of the deep, masculine voice. She'd been doing her stretch exercises and hadn't heard Lyle come up. He was leaning against a wooden post on the boardwalk and wearing a pair of running shorts. Usually he wore a T-shirt, but this particular morning his chest was bare.

She recalled the first time she'd seen his chest, back when he and Arnie had left to go swimming at the park. At sixteen she'd been dazzled by that bare chest; now at thirty-three she felt it razzling her mind. She appreciated a man who kept himself in shape, and Lyle was one who definitely did. She'd noticed that much from the first morning they had jogged together, although she kept trying not to stare. But there had always been something about his dark and hairy chest that had totally fascinated her. It was muscular, definitely well defined, and whereas before it had only been dusted with dark hair, now there was quite an abundance of it. His stomach was flat and lean, and the drawstring to his shorts clearly emphasized the path of hair that led to the waistband.

"Yes, I'm going to agree, Dr. Montgomery," she said, moving her gaze from his chest to his face, forcing her mind to concentrate on their conversation and not on his body. "The weatherman said it's going to be a great day on the beach, and I intend to spend my time on it."

She forced herself to look out toward the Atlantic Ocean. "I love the ocean. It's beautiful, isn't it?"

He followed her gaze. "Sure is." He looked back at her face. "Have you had your coffee yet?"

She shook her head. "No, I don't like dealing with caffeine in the morning. I'm an herbal tea person. It's better for you."

He chuckled. "Hey, you're not going to get an argument out of me. It's definitely better for your heart." He then added, "Natural fruit juices aren't so bad either."

She grinned. "Yes, doctor."

He glanced down at her feet. "Your shoelace is untied. Put your hand on my shoulder, lean in, and lift your foot up to me."

"I can tie it."

"It's no problem for me to do it, Nicky." Deciding they would be wasting time arguing about it, she placed her hand on his shoulder and lifted her foot up to him like he'd asked. "Umm, nice leg."

She barely heard what he'd said. Her concentration was focusing on the feel of his skin underneath her fingertips. It felt warm as well as solid. And then there was the spicy male scent that clung to him. Lyle Montgomery was one enticing male.

"Okay, you're good to go now." His words snapped her back to attention. It made her realize where her thoughts had been. For crying out loud, this wasn't just any other man. This was Lyle, the guy who used to be Arnie's best friend, his ace-boon-koon, in college. What in the heck was wrong with her today? What had been wrong with her ever since they started jogging together?

"Thanks, Lyle," she somehow managed to say, putting her foot back down.

"Don't mention it." He then looped his arm through hers. "The beach awaits us," he said, pulling her down the steps to where their feet hit the sand.

By sheer effort, Monique made her body move as they jogged side by side, in perfect sync. Something was different this morning. Maybe it had been Faith's reminding her last night of the crush she'd had on Lyle. Maybe it was the fact that he wasn't wearing a shirt, which made him much too sexy.

As they continued running, she knew that in the end, about an hour from now, she would be all hot and bothered as well as hot and sweaty, but she couldn't think of any other way she'd rather spend her mornings than with such a good-looking running partner.

Shannon yawned as she pulled another outfit off the rack. If anyone had told her she would be shopping at the crack of dawn, she would have called them a liar. But here she was doing just that. She couldn't believe she had actually walked out the door before Faith got up just to be at this shop when it opened at nine o'clock.

Monique had whipped by her on the way out to jog and had taken only the time to tell her that Faith was cooking dinner and had invited a guest—some woman who lived next door. That was fine with Shannon. Faith was a whiz in the kitchen, and if cooking rocked her boat and she wanted to impress her parents' neighbor, then let her go for it.

Now back to the business at hand. She looked down at the outfits already slung over her arms, items meant to entice, arouse, and stimulate even the most resistant mind. For the past couple of days she had spent her time wondering what was there about Mr. Mechanic that pushed all her buttons. Just thinking about what she had planned sent a subtle shiver through her body. This would be the first fling that she herself had initiated. In the past, the men did all the work, and if they met with her extreme satisfaction then so be it. After a brief period, they would part ways. She was never left with a reason to ever look one of them up again and vice versa. A fling was just was it was meant to be, a fling.

"Do you want me to hold those for you, miss?"

Shannon's thoughts were interrupted by the saleswoman's question. "Yes, please. I intend to get a couple of more items."

"Oh, take your time."

Shannon smiled. And she intended to, even tonight when she showed up at the mechanic's apartment over the garage she planned on taking her time. Boy, would he be surprised. But she had yet to know a man to turn down a thrilling and sensual rendezvous if it was presented to him in the right way—and as she pulled another outfit off the rack, she considered herself the mistress of innovations.

"*I'm glad to* see you weren't a figment of my imagination that day."

Faith turned to see if the statement had been directed to her, and when she saw that it was, she blinked. She'd never considered the produce section of any store as a place men would try to pick up women, but evidently she had underestimated the opposite sex—this was the second time in weeks that it had happened to her.

She sighed. All things considered, she was glad the person staring at her with intense dark eyes was not the young kid from that other day. No, this was a man in every sense of the word. He'd made the statement as if he'd seen her before, but she knew for a fact she had never seen him. He was not a man any woman would forget easily—or at all. To say he exhibited an overwhelming presence would be an understatement.

It had been a long time since her adrenaline was acting up to the point where she could actually feel the pulse beat in her neck. And when was the last time just looking at a man made heat pool in the area between her legs? He had to be over six feet tall and then some. His skin tone was the color of rich chocolate. He had a straight nose, lips you probably could die from kissing, and to top things off, there was a dimple in his chin. *Of all the nerve.* That in itself caught her attention when he smiled, and he was smiling . . . at her.

Okay, she had a choice. She could ignore him or she could choose . . . not to ignore him. The decision was quick and easy. She would not ignore him. She would go along with this game men liked to play whenever they thought they had an easy mark within their scope. In the end she would show him that although she was in awe of the package, she had a level head on her shoulders and wasn't a woman easily swayed by a handsome face.

"Am I supposed to know you?" she asked, placing the bag of lemons for the lemonade she intended to serve with dinner in her buggy.

He leaned against the display of cabbage. "No, we haven't officially met yet, but I saw you one day, a week or so ago. You were at this same store in the parking lot and were coming when I was leaving. I watched you get out of your car."

"Oh."

"Now, I'd like to introduce myself," he said, straightening his form and coming to stand in front of her. At five-eight she wasn't considered short by any means, and he did a job of towering over her. He held out his hand. "I'm Shane Masters."

Shane Masters. For some reason she liked that name. It sounded . . . sexy. "And I'm Faith Gilmore," she said, placing her hand in his and immediately feeling the warmth, the texture, the strength of his grip.

She thought about easing her hand back, but that was before she began drowning in the darkness of his gaze. Oh, he was good. If his smooth words didn't get you, then those eyes of his definitely would. After Virgil she should be immune to the antics of a handsome man. Evidently she wasn't. She swallowed hard. It wasn't her fault she was a traditional girl and still wanted to hold on to those values.

Once upon a time she'd longed to be sexually liberated like Shannon, but that lifestyle wasn't really for her. In her book, the ideal situation was when you met someone, got real close to him, then after a while had sex . . . and maybe if the timing was right, fell in love and eventually got married.

Even though things hadn't worked out with Virgil, she still wanted to believe in happily ever after. If she didn't, she *would* turn into another Shannon, and the very thought of that was downright scary. That was probably the reason the men she went out with since she'd emerged back on the dating scene a few years ago were stable, serious-minded, with relationship potential. She tried staying away from those who were only looking for flings or had commitment issues. She had a feeling the man standing in front of her was only interested in a fling.

"So are you an islander?" she asked, deciding it was time to reclaim her hand, and so that it wouldn't look so obvious she was doing so, she slid it out of his as she turned to study the squash—not that she was really interested in the yellow beastly things. They were her least-liked vegetable.

"For the time being. I recently purchased a vacation home here but still have a place in Michigan. What about you?"

"A couple of girlfriends and I decided this is the place we wanted to be this summer, since it's where we met years ago in our early teens. Our families would come here for two weeks every year."

He smiled. "Boy, weren't you the lucky ones. But then I wasn't too far away. My family is from Savannah."

"That's a beautiful city."

"Thanks, and I would have to agree." He leaned over and picked up a squash and Faith couldn't help noticing how he held it in his hand: tight but not overly so. She then watched how his thumb rubbed against the hard rind surface, and she found herself staring, imagining. . . .

"You enjoy cooking, I see."

His statement made her glance back into his face, where she was once again snagged by his eyes. She swallowed. "What makes you think that?"

He smiled again. "The amount of food in your buggy."

He had her there. "I like cooking when the mood hits," she explained.

"And the mood has hit?"

"Yes." She wondered if he was hinting at an invite for dinner. If that was the case, then he could forget it. It was going to be an all-girls night with her parents' neighbor. No males allowed, and definitely not one who was a total stranger.

Faith could feel his gaze on her when she bent over to check out the heads of iceberg lettuce. She wished to God she could ignore the man, but there was something about him that stirred all kinds of reactions in her. She was even feeling breathless, and no man, not even Virgil, had made her feel breathless before.

Deciding it was time to end their little chat, she glanced over at him and said, "Well, I don't want to hold you up from doing your own shopping."

"You're not. I just came in to grab a six-pack."

"What about dinner?" she regretted asking the moment the words tumbled from her mouth.

"I have a freezer full of those microwave dinners. That's all I need." When she didn't say anything to that, he then asked, "So how long will you be on the island?" He fixed her with that deep, dark stare again.

After placing a head of lettuce in her buggy, she moved on to the tomatoes before saying, "Another three to four weeks."

"Now isn't that a coincidence, same here before I head back to Detroit for a while," he said. "Since we're both going to be here for almost another month, how about if we—?"

At that moment her cell phone rang and she quickly reached into her purse and pulled it out thinking, *Saved by the bell*. He'd been about to suggest that they hang out or something, and she wasn't in the mood to do that. This was her summer to do what she wanted, and what she wanted didn't include a man, at least not in the sense she knew he was interested. Men always thought below the belt.

"Hello," she said in the phone.

"Where are you?" she could hear Shannon ask on the other end. "I need your opinion about something."

"About what?"

"An outfit I plan to wear later this evening."

Faith sighed. "Don't tell me you're still out shopping."

"Yes, but I'm headed back to the beach house now."

"All right, hang tight. I'll be there in a minute." Faith then clicked off the phone and looked over at Shane. "Well, grocery shopping must come to an end for now. It was nice meeting you, Shane."

"Trust me when I say the pleasure was mine, Faith. Take care, and I hope you enjoy the remainder of your stay on the island."

She smiled. "And I hope you enjoy the rest of yours as well."

Gripping the handle of the buggy firmly in her hand, she pushed it past him and toward the checkout counter. And unlike the last time she had left a male in the produce section staring at her, she knew Shane Masters was one she wouldn't be forgetting any time soon.

8

Faith's instincts had been right. Adrianna Ross-Fuller was the type of person who was able to blend in well and get along with just about anybody, even someone who could be as standoffish as Shannon. Adrianna had even suggested they call her Anna like her family and friends did.

Not that Faith wanted to brag, but dinner had been great, and now they were sitting outside on the screened porch watching the waves from the ocean while sipping wine.

A shiver ran through her. She couldn't keep her mind off Shane Masters. He had certainly been dominating her thoughts—even while she'd been cooking, which was another first. In the kitchen, the ingredients she would be using had always been foremost as she went about preparing what she wanted to be a mouthwatering meal. But for the two hours she'd spent in the kitchen, the only mouthwatering thing she could think about was Shane Masters.

"So, Anna, your grandmother's side of the family actually owned land on this island? Back in the day?" Monique asked, reclaiming Faith's attention to the conversation going on.

Anna smiled. "Yes, that's how I got the beach house. Part of this new subdivision was built on land my family owned and later sold to the developers." Anna was proud of her family's history. It was history that had been shared with her since becoming an acknowledged member of the family.

"Hilton Head is home to Mitchellville, organized in 1862 as one

of the first settlements of free blacks in this country," Anna continued. "In fact, before the developers came, most of the sea islands,
since the eighteen hundreds, were the home of free black men who
formed a number of communities. These communities consisted of
farmers, basket weavers, and fishnet makers. During that time the
Gullah culture was still preserved," she added.

Monique lifted a brow. "What's Gullah?"

Anna smiled. "The Gullah was a strong group of African Americans, many of whom were born on the sea islands like Hilton Head,
who spoke the Gullah dialect. My family did manage to retain possession of one island, Glendale Shores. It's where my paternal grandfather was born and is across the water a ways from here. All of us
have agreed not to sell out, although developers have tried twisting
our arms to do so. But that's before they came up against my uncle,
Randolph Fuller. Once they do, then they—"

"Whoa, wait a minute," Shannon interrupted. "Are you saying
the Randolph Fuller is a relative of yours?"

Anna smiled proudly. "Yes, he's my uncle, my father's brother.
Do you know him?"

Shannon shook her head, grinning. "No, but I've heard of him.
Who hasn't? He is and always has been an attorney extraordinaire. I
used to hear my parents sing his praises all the time. He's made history several times by winning a number of high-profile cases."

Anna looked pleased. "Yes, he has."

"You're part Vietnamese, right?" Faith asked. She thought Anna
was simply beautiful with her medium brown skin, almond eyes,
and mane of long, gorgeous black hair.

Anna took a sip of her wine before answering. "Yes, my father
fought in the Vietnam War and eventually lost his life over there. Before he died, he married my mother." She decided now wasn't the
time to share too much of her family history, especially not the part
about where she had been separated from them for thirty-
something years, thinking they wanted nothing to do with her. That
was a part of her past she was trying to put behind her. The person
who'd been responsible, a woman by the name of Angela who'd once

been married to her uncle Randolph, hadn't been operating with a full deck. Angela eventually really went off the deep end when her and Randolph's son, Trey, married the daughter of a woman Angela despised.

"So are the three of you enjoying your vacations so far?" Anna asked, to keep the conversation flowing. It had been a long time since she'd allowed herself time to just sit back and chill and had been grateful for Faith's invitation to dinner. She had met Faith's parents last year, and all they'd talked about was the daughter they were proud of. Besides, engaging in conversation kept her mind away from the fact that Zach would be arriving in a week or so. She had taken some time off work. The Fourth of July was coming up, and they would be joining the others at Glendale Shores.

"Well, I've enjoyed our get-together," Shannon said, standing and glancing at her watch. "But I have somewhere to go."

She turned to Anna and smiled. "It was nice meeting you, Anna, and I can't wait to tell my parents that I met Randolph Fuller's niece."

Anna leaned back in her chair and returned Shannon's smile. "It was nice meeting you as well."

Shannon made a quick escape into the house, and Anna couldn't help noticing the worried expression Faith and Monique shared.

A half hour later, Shannon saw that the auto repair shop was closed. Evidently they ended their workday early on Wednesdays. She weighed her options. She could either go back home and try this seduction thing tomorrow or she could get out of her car and check to see if perhaps the person she was looking for was still there— namely the mechanic who had more than stirred her interest. Since he lived over the garage, there was that possibility he was home. But what if he had a girlfriend in residence? Things could get ugly if that were the case. But then he didn't have a ring on his finger, so in her book he was still fair game.

Making a quick decision, she got out of the car and walked over to the thick glass-paned window and peeped in. She dragged in a deep breath when she saw that although the garage was closed, the mechanic was still there and working on that same car. She glanced down at herself. She would be the first to admit that on any other woman the dress she was wearing would probably look somewhat sleazy with so much skin showing. But she thought that on her it looked right . . . considering what she needed it for.

Drawing in a deep breath, she tapped on the window. In fact, she did it several times before he finally pulled his head from underneath the hood of the car and glanced her way with an agitated frown. He stared, leaning against the car for a moment as if trying to figure out who she was and what she wanted. She knew the exact moment he recognized her as the woman from last week. He tossed the wrench he'd been holding in his hand aside and began walking toward the huge garage door that was connected to the bay he was working in.

Her breath caught when the door rolled up and he was there, standing in front of her. The scent of a sweaty man filled her nostrils, and she raked her gaze over him, taking in the grease-smeared T-shirt and the well-worn jeans. Another thing she noticed was that he had a beer can in his hand. She returned her look to his face and noticed the beautiful dark eyes that were boring into hers. The heat that suddenly flushed between her legs was like a blast from a furnace.

"The shop's closed."

She cleared her throat. "I know." Her body was beginning to ache. Now in addition to the heat between her legs, her breasts felt tender against the material of her dress. And talking about the dress . . . he was noticing it. He glanced up and down at her in a way that was winding her up real tight, and then he took a huge gulp from the beer can before tossing it into a nearby trash bin.

"If you know the shop's closed, then why you're here?" he asked in a raw whisper that not only assaulted her senses, but zapped every feminine thing about her.

She knew he was waiting on an answer. He wanted her to spell it out for him, did he? Well, she had no problem doing that . . . if she really had to.

Taking a step forward, she deliberately brushed her body against his. "Do I really need to answer that?"

He angled his head back and continued to stare at her . . . and her dress. Finally he answered by saying, "No, I guess not." He then stepped aside. "Come on in."

The first thought that came to Shannon's mind was that what she was about to do was crazy. She knew nothing about this man other than what he did for a living as well as what he did to her each time she saw him. What if he was a mechanic by day and a rapist by night? What if he was a serial killer? What if—?

She shook her head, ridding her mind of any visions of being held hostage or him doing her bodily harm. For some reason, even with his rough and raw nature she felt safe with him, so she dismissed all those crazy ideas going through her head as her mind started going crazy on her. She was the one in charge of things here.

Besides, she had questioned a couple of people about him, and although none knew him personally, the cook at the café, the one who'd referred her to this place yesterday, said that all the mechanics who worked for Kent Scott were fairly decent guys and didn't get into trouble. He'd further gone on to say that although he didn't know the mechanic who had moved above the garage, he must have been a close friend of Kent's to live there, and the few times he'd come into the café to buy coffee, he'd seemed like a nice fellow.

Shannon also figured she had her back covered, since Faith and Monique knew where she was, and she would make sure he knew it in case he took it upon himself to try any sort of funny business. So, despite any misgivings she might have harbored, she stepped over the threshold, and when he pushed the button to lower the huge garage door back down, leaving her completely alone with him inside the warehouselike building, she boldly met his gaze. And the only thing she could think about was the possibility that for the first in her life she had gone a little too far.

Adam stood at the sink to wash any grease and grime from his hands as he watched Shannon slowly move around his work area like she found everything she saw fascinating, including the pile of grease rags stacked in the corner. He definitely remembered her from last week and if the truth be told, she had entered his thoughts several times since then.

He could tell that she was nervous, which was a good sign that she hadn't done anything like this before. A woman showing up alone to pick up a man wasn't a real smart move, considering all the sickos in the world. He might be a lot of things, but a weirdo he was not.

Back in Memphis, most women thought of him as the lone wolf, skillfully predatory, yet painstakingly detached when he wanted to be. And he was a cautious man by nature. It came with his profession, since he'd heard and seen it all. One thing he was definitely leery of were women bearing gifts, especially the *let's get naked* kind. And that dress she was wearing could mean only one thing. She had sex on her mind, and he was the male she had targeted. Sheesh, lucky him.

Oh, he knew her kind. Being the oldest son of Judge Warren Corbain, he was the object of numerous women's pretended affections because of his family's name and status. They were ladies who were well refined and dignified and who in the end would show their true colors only after a wedding ring had been placed on their finger. Those were the Exhibit As. Shannon Carmichael was one of those he tagged Exhibit B—high-class society women, the kind who dated one type of man during the day and slept with another type at night. She got her kicks walking on the wild side whenever the mood struck—preferably after dark—and indulging in fantasies that would never cross a "good" girl's mind.

He was glad Sydney, his one and only sister, who was eight years younger than him, never got into the casual dating scene before she married Tyrone. Her long-term affair with Rafe, everyone thought, would surely end in marriage. He had been shocked as hell when

Sydney announced to the family one day that she and Rafe were through. A little more than a year later, she was making another announcement that she had fallen in love with and was marrying a guy by the name of Tyrone Hardcastle. She had left the family firm to move to D.C. with her husband, and almost two years later they were expecting their first child.

Times were too dangerous to have too many sleeping partners for both physical as well as emotional reasons. Some men didn't know the meaning of being a gentleman, but then he had a feeling a true gentleman was the last thing Dr. Shannon Carmichael was interested in tonight. But still, if she thought he would immediately fall victim to her wiles, she had another thought coming. Oh, he intended to eventually give her just what she came for, especially since seeing her dress this way painfully reminded him how long he'd been without a woman. But he would sleep with her on his time and his terms.

But first, there was something he needed to get out of the way. Now that he was seeing her again, a degree of passion he'd felt the moment he set eyes on her escalated to an alarming rate. But then he knew her full breasts, tiny waistline, spectacular, long sexy legs and attractive face had a lot to do with it.

He slowly walked over to her, saw the uncertain look in her eye before it was replaced by a glint of red-hot lust. Oh, yeah, she came here for only one thing, but he was going to show her he wasn't easy.

When he came to a stop in front of her, he heard the thickness of her breathing at the same time he inhaled her scent, a seductive fragrance that he knew had been deliberate. He hadn't been born yesterday and was well aware of how some women operated with seduction on their mind, and this one was working it.

"So," he said slowly, reaching out and letting his fingertips stroke up and down her arms, feeling the goose bumps appear on every area he touched. "Since you're here, I think there's a few things we need to get out of the way, don't you?"

He watched her swallow, and the movement of her throat gave

him an adrenaline rush that made his body harden even more. He was taken back by the force of his reaction to her. He didn't know a woman alive who could shoot his libido up sky-high.

"Things like what?"

The sexy tone of her voice, filled with feminine curiosity, sent more adrenaline shooting through his body. If he didn't get in control of things—and fast—he would be putty in her hands in no time.

"This, for starters," he said, and before she could react, he grabbed her elbow and brought her closer to the fit of him before lowering his head and capturing her mouth.

Whenever he worked on a car, his body seemed to be filled with excessive energy, which he suspected was the reason he was plunging into this kiss, lapping her up like there was no tomorrow. And he was beginning to feel weak in the knees when he realized she was lapping him back.

Kissing, when you really thought about it, required no degree of experience or skill. All you needed were willing mouths and greedy tongues, and the two of them had both. It seemed they had this segment of lovemaking down to a science. There was no way this could have been a simple kiss, not by the way he was tangling with her tongue like it rightly belonged to him. Mating his mouth with hers was as intense as it could get, and the more he thought about it, the greedier he became and the more he wanted to devour her in a way he had never done with another woman. He bet she would make one hell of a sex partner and knew that in time he would find out just how good she was in bed. He had a feeling they were as sexually compatible as any two people could get.

When he felt himself losing control, he broke off the kiss and pulled back, but thought, "Oh, hell," and leaned in for another sweep of his tongue across her lips before diving that same tongue right back into her mouth.

Moments later he pulled back and stared down at her. The intensity of his gaze had to be setting her on edge, but he didn't care. The woman was a witch. She had to be one to have trapped him, the elusive Adam Corbain, this quick and easy.

"So, what's next?" she asked when he leaned forward and zoomed in for her mouth again.

He blinked, knew he needed to get a grip. "What's next?"

"Yes. You said there were a couple of things that we needed to get out of the way. So, what's next?"

Adam breathed in easily. He was tempted to whip her luscious body around, flip her naughty-looking dress up, unzip his jeans, and take her against his car by plunging into her, giving her just what she came for. But he ripped that tempting notion from his mind. No woman had the upper hand when it came to him, especially not this one, who thought she could just breeze into his world—the one she assumed was his—and call the shots. This good ole Tennessee attorney was about to teach the good doctor a lesson about judging a book by its cover. And he would enjoy every minute while doing so.

His lips tilted into a smile when he reached out and handed her a clean rag. When he saw the look of total bemusement on her face, he held back a chuckle when he said, "Next, you can make yourself useful by helping me work on this car."

9

"*I must have* misunderstood you," Shannon said, after finally recovering her voice to speak.

"No, you didn't misunderstand me," Adam replied, leaning against a fender of the car and crossing his arms over his chest.

She glared at him. "Don't be ridiculous. Do I look like I'm dressed to work on a car?"

Adam glanced at her up and down, and the power of his gaze actually made her panties—the skimpy lacey ones she was wearing— wet. He seemed to linger on the strappy sandals on her feet, and she couldn't help wondering why. She knew some men had a fetish for women's feet and wondered if perhaps he were one of those kind.

"I'm very well aware of how you're dressed, Shannon," he said, breaking into her thoughts by using her given name for the first time. "I also know why," he added. "But it has come to my attention that you and I need to get a few things straight, right off the bat."

Shannon's thoughts whirred. What the hell was he doing, or trying to do? She was the one calling the shots, not him. She tossed down the rag he'd given her and tilted her head slightly to establish perspective. "Look, I think I'm the one who needs to get a few things straight with you," she said, as if he was one of her students at the university. "When it comes to affairs, I go about handling them a lot different from most women. The only thing I'm looking for is a good time. I've never been married nor do I ever plan to marry. And I'm not looking at life through any rose-colored glasses. I know the real deal when it comes to relationships, even the supposedly committed kind. When it comes to bed partners, I'm very selective, so consider yourself one of the fortunate ones. You're not exactly the type of man I'm usually attracted to, but there's nothing I can do about that since I am attracted to you. But to get the record straight, to get you straight, all I want from you is a summer fling for a couple of weeks. Nothing more, nothing less. When it's over, I'll go my way and you can continue to tinker with cars."

She took a deep breath and with a graceful toss of her head then said, "Now, is there anything you would like to say?"

Adam had to fight to keep from laughing out loud at Shannon's saucy, I'm-the-one-in-charge, my-way-or-the-highway spiel. With her hands braced on her hips, she looked absolutely luscious, and a part of him longed to give in to her terms and bestow upon her every single thing she wanted, while taking joy in every pleasant thrust. But he had no intentions of doing that, and before he sent her on her merry way, he would teach her one thing. That sassy mouth of hers was better used for kissing.

Pushing away from the car, he slowly closed the distance between them until he was standing directly in front of her. Later tonight he would probably call himself all kinds of fool for sending her away, but she had a lesson to learn that there was more to life than just great sex. Respecting those she had a tendency to look down her snooty nose at would also be nice.

"Yes, there's something I'd like to say."

"What?" she all but snapped.

"You talk too damn much." And before she could utter what he knew would be a blistering response, he leaned in and took claim of that sassy mouth.

Shannon gave up trying to deny she wanted this kiss and simply . . . gave in to it, participated in hopeless desperation. The will to pull away was lost within all the sensations she was feeling. When he released her mouth for a brief moment, she closed her eyes

and breathed in the scent surrounding them. Oil, gas, fumes . . .
man. Adam.

And when he took her mouth with finesse, she couldn't help but
moan in irresistible pleasure. She felt herself being lifted into strong
arms and placed on the fender of the car. She felt her pulse race uncontrollably when he stepped between her open thighs but he didn't
make a move to get her out of her clothing. Instead he slid a hand
between her legs and with a guttural moan he ripped the flimsy material of her panties apart and off her. And then his hand was there,
at her wet entrance, the very heat of her. She shivered at the touch,
moaned out loud at his strokes, and then groaned at the invasion of
his fingers that filled her body with a sexual intensity she didn't
know was possible. Those fingers that he used to work on cars were
definitely working on her, flickering to life a fire that she did not
know could burn so hot.

Her fingers dug into his shoulders, and when an orgasm struck,
she let out one sultry cry followed by one high-pitched scream as
sensations hit her like a shot from cannon. They pulled everything
from her while at the same time giving everything to her. The world
around her seemed to be spinning on its axis; she was afraid if she
opened her eyes, she would see that the moon had actually fallen
from the sky. Never had she experienced anything so starkly sexual
and so mind-blowingly good. Moments later, like a rag doll she fell
forward onto his chest, moaning and breathing in the scent of
grease, oil, and sex from a miraculous finger job. And then he tilted
her chin and was kissing her again while moving his hand slowly
over her hips and belly.

Without any warning, he broke off the kiss and stepped back.
Pulling her dress down, he closed her legs and placing his hands beneath her butt, he lifted her off the car. Her body wanted to scream
that although what he'd done had been spectacular, wonderful, out-
of-this-world brilliant, she wanted everything else that came with it.
She wanted an invasion of the most profound kind. She wanted him
inside her.

The sound of keys made her eyes open, and she looked at him.

He was handing her purse and her car keys to her. "Good night, Dr. Carmichael. If you decide to stop by again, please come dressed to work."

A few minutes later Shannon was driving away, fuming. *How dare he!* No man had ever denied her what she'd wanted before. Who in the hell did that two-bit mechanic think he was, anyway?

Her body began humming a tune that said, "Umm, for starters, he's an expert kisser, and those fingers weren't so bad either. He made you scream, break loose your impeccable sophistication, and give in to an uninhibited nature where if he'd just said the word, you would have placed yourself on a platter just for his taking. No man has ever made you go that far. No man . . ."

And although she didn't like the thought of being mere putty in any man's hands, especially the one who had given her an orgasm on the fender of some damn car, she refused to give up on him just yet. Just before walking out the garage door, she had glanced back at him and the look in his eyes had turned just as cold as the metal her butt had rested up against while on that fender.

But still, the man had a lot to learn when it came to the handling of a refined woman. Oh, she would be back, and she, not he, would decide how she would be dressed.

10

"*So, how did* your date go tonight?"

Shannon wasn't surprised to find Faith and Monique still up, waiting on her. She knew they hadn't approved of her going to the repair garage to see Adam. They thought it was a bad and thoughtless move on her part, but they'd also known once she made her mind up about something, there was no talking her out of it.

She threw her purse down on the coffee table and joined them on the sofa. They were her closest friends, and she loved them to death, but a night like tonight was one you just didn't share. Not in full details, anyway. So she decided to give them the watered-down version. "It went fine and he was a perfect gentleman."

Monique gave her a smug smile. "And I bet that surprised you since you think men who use their hands for a living lack a level of fine grooming and social skills."

Shannon frowned. "I never said that."

"No, but your actions speak louder than words, Shannon. I hate to say this, but one day you're going to meet your match."

I might already have, she thought to herself, remembering just how her night had gone, down to each finest detail. Her missing panties, the ones he'd ripped off her, were a definite reminder. "Keep your predictions to yourself, Monique," she said, standing and yawning. The magnitude of that orgasm had taken a lot out of her. "I'm turning in, so I'll see you ladies in the morning."

"Not me, remember?" Monique said. "I go jogging with Lyle every morning."

"What's with you and this Lyle guy?" Faith asked before biting into another large pretzel.

Monique smiled. "He's nothing but an old family friend. I told you guys that. No big deal."

"And if it is a big deal, no sweat. You don't owe us any explanations," Shannon said, and took the pretzel bag from Faith to start munching on a few. "You're a woman. He's a man."

Monique lifted a brow. "Meaning?"

"Sex. You're going to eventually do it sometime."

"Why do you think that everything dealing with a man and woman always equates to sex, Shannon?" Monique asked, clearly frustrated.

"Because it does. You'll see." Then without saying anything else, she left the room with Faith and Monique staring after her.

Almost a week later and Monique was still trying to forget what Shannon had said, but she couldn't. Why did everything have to boil down to sex with her?

Monique shook her head; she knew the answer. They hadn't just met Shannon yesterday. They were her closest friends, her confidantes. They'd recognized as teens how her mind had begun to work after finding out about her parents' sham of a marriage. As far as Shannon was concerned, she didn't believe in love and wanted no part of it. The love-forever-after bit was meant for only a select few, and she wasn't one of them. Cely had been the one to make it her goal in life to try and rid Shannon of such foolish notions, and with Cely gone, she guessed the task now fell on her and Faith. Lord knows they would try but . . .

"Been waiting long?"

Monique glanced up and met Lyle's heart-stopping smile. He was leaning against a light pole, dressed in a T-shirt and jogging shorts, and he looked a lot more relaxed than she felt. She tried not to notice all those things about him today that she had every day; his fine body, his muscular physique, and his all-too-handsome face. Those were all sexual things, and she refused to give in to Shannon's theory that when it came to a man and woman, it was all about sex. But then, inwardly she would be the first to admit that she *had* been thinking more about it lately since running into Lyle and jogging with him every morning.

"No, I haven't been waiting long. You're right on time."

"Good." He began walking toward her, and once again she tried not to notice how good he looked. Even his walk had a certain suaveness to it. When he came to stand in front of her, his lips hinted at another smile. "Hey, you're okay?"

She nodded. "Sure. Why do you ask?"

He studied her for a moment. "You seem nervous about something this morning. Are you sure you're all right?"

No, I'm not all right, her mind wanted to scream. *I'm beginning to see you as a man—a very desirable man—and I don't want to.* "Yes, Lyle, I'm fine. Really," she said, as a way to convince him.

No one, except for Cely, knew that she hadn't slept with a man since losing Paul three years ago. She'd had the time but not the inclination. Cely had known and understood and had taken Monique's secret to the grave with her. She knew if she were to confide in Faith that she, too, would understand. But Shannon wouldn't get it. She would snatch her off to a shrink and then they would leave there and go to the nearest "toy" store.

Monique inwardly smiled. They all knew about Shannon's "toy" collection, but Monique hadn't needed or wanted any toys. The memories of what she and Paul had shared had sustained her.

Until now.

Seeing Lyle as a man in the flesh starkly reminded her of what she'd not been sharing with a male, which only confirmed Shannon's sordid theory on relationships. Her and Lyle's relationship was based on friendship and nothing more, but that didn't mean she was wrong to notice him as a good-looking man, was it?

"I don't have to report to class until later today. Would you like to have breakfast with me?"

Lyle's statement interrupted her musings. She glanced up at him. "Breakfast?"

"At my place after we finish our jog. If you recall, I can cook."

Yes, she did recall that. Their parents were convinced that if it hadn't been for Lyle's expertise in the kitchen, Arnie would have starved to death in med school. To say her brother would have tried to survive on chips and sodas would have been an understatement.

"And you're willing to go out of your way and do something like that for me?" she asked, sending him a smile. She knew his time had to be tight while teaching those classes at the hospital each day. They had been around Shannon enough to know that preparing to teach a class was time consuming.

"Sure I am. Besides, although we've been jogging together for a couple of weeks, we've talked about a lot of things but not anything personal, and I want to bring you up to date on what's been going on in the Montgomery family. There have been two weddings that I haven't had the time to tell Arnie about."

She knew he was right. While jogging they barely had time to talk, and afterwards he usually had to rush off for the class he was teaching. But she was enjoying the time they did share together. "In that case, yes, I don't have anything planned for the rest of the morning, so having breakfast with you would be nice. But first I want to go home and shower and change. Usually I'm all hot and sweaty after running."

His smile widened. "That's fine. Now let's get our jog out of the way so I can feed you."

Faith glanced around the prestigious-looking clubhouse. Sea Pines was the site of the island's best-known landmark, a maroon-and-white-striped lighthouse at the Harbour Town Yacht Basin. That was where the New England–style village was located that contained shops, restaurants, and places for all sorts of water sports. She and Shannon were making one of the cafés there their favorite place for breakfast.

Her mind was pulled back to the clubhouse. From where she was standing in the lobby, she saw that one side of the building was the site of an eighteen-hole golf course and the other side were the eight tennis courts. She also took note of the Olympic-size pool, a smaller kiddie pool, and a playground for children.

Children.

For a brief moment she allowed the thought, the question of whether or not she would ever have any children to form in her mind. That had always been her dream; to grow up, get married, and have babies. Unfortunately, the latter part of that dream never came to pass because of Virgil. For a long while she had thought about adopting, but then had decided to just wait. If she could, she wanted to experience bringing a child into the world. She wouldn't take such drastic actions like Shannon had once suggested before denying herself the full experience of motherhood.

"We meet again, I see."

Faith whirled around, recognizing that deep, masculine voice. It was the man from the grocery store a week or so ago. She really should not have been surprised at seeing him again. After all, the island was small. Besides that, when she'd left the store she had an inkling their paths would cross again. Somehow she had known it.

The first thing she noticed was that he was as handsome as her eyesight had led her to believe. The second was that he was holding a racket and was dressed for a game of tennis.

"Yes, and I see you're about to play tennis."

He smiled. "That's right, I am. This island has the best tennis courts."

"Sounds like you're an expert player."

"I do okay. In fact, I teach tennis to the kids in my community when I have the time. If it was left up to me, every child in this country would own a pair of jogging shoes and a tennis racket before they turn twelve. What about you? Do you play?"

She shook her head sadly. "No, I didn't get to participate in a lot of sports as a child. I suffered from a severe case of asthma, and to say my parents were overprotective would be an understatement. Now that I've grown out of the condition, I'm trying to make up for lost time. I learned how to swim a couple of years ago, and now I want to learn how to play tennis. I'm here to sign up for a class. I hear they offer several."

Shane nodded. "They do, but actually they are tennis clinics and not classes. Beginners need one-on-one instruction. You can inquire, but I think you'll have to visit another clubhouse for the individual teachings, and I understand they're rather expensive. However, I'd like to make a suggestion, if I may."

"And what suggestion is that?"

"That you let me teach you."

Faith quickly shook her head. "Thanks for the offer, but I don't think that's a good idea. I'm sure you have better things to do with your time than to spend it teaching me to play tennis."

He smiled. "I can't think of a better way to spend my time other than with you." He'd lowered his voice a little, and the provocative and sexy sound sent shivers all through her. Although he was only offering tennis lessons, somehow it seemed her body didn't understand that.

"I'm not sure I'll be able to catch on as fast as you'd want me to," she said, fishing for any excuse. This man did things to her. Things she wasn't sure she was ready for. Shannon was the one dead set on having a summer affair. She wasn't.

Faith watched as Shane took a slow step to stand directly in front of her. "May I ask you something?" he inquired, his tone of voice a notch lower than before.

She swallowed. "Yes."

"Do I make you nervous?"

The question for some reason gave him even more physical appeal. Yes, he made her nervous because around him she was starkly reminded that she was a woman with needs, needs that hadn't been taken care of for some time. But to him she said, "No, you don't make me nervous. What makes you think that you do?"

He shrugged. "Umm, no reason."

She met his gaze. There was a reason or he would not have brought it up. She then decided to ask a question of her own, one she'd been wondering about since first meeting him. "Are you here with someone?" She couldn't imagine a man who looked like him vacationing alone.

"No, I'm not here with anyone. Like I told you that day we met, I own a summer home here, but I live in Detroit. After enduring a hellishly cold winter, I was ready to head south for the summer."

She understood the feeling. Minnesota's winters were just as bad, which was why her parents had always come to Hilton Head each summer. She felt a rush of relief knowing she was not extremely attracted to someone else's husband or significant other.

"So, if I don't make you nervous, and you know I'm here on the island alone, can you think of any reason why I can't teach you to play tennis?"

Shane's words recaptured Faith's attention. Oh, she could think of plenty of reasons, but none she wanted to share with him. So she answered his question the only way she could. "No, there's no reason as long as we maintain a professional relationship."

A smile tilted his lips and made that dimple in his chin definitely noticeable. Too noticeable. "We will, while on the courts. Beyond that I won't make any promises."

She knew she had found a loophole and that now was the time to say *Thanks, but no thanks,* that she didn't need their professional relationship extended beyond the courts. But for some reason she couldn't make herself say any of that. Around him she had no will to fight or deny what she really wanted. "Okay, fair enough," she heard herself saying.

"Great. We can get those lessons started today and can meet again tomorrow. After the first week, once you get the swing of things, then we can meet twice a week, Mondays and Wednesdays. Will that work for you?"

"Yes, that's fine."

"Good and I reserved a court earlier that we can use today, and you're dressed to play, so we—"

"But I don't have a tennis racket."

"We can rent one at the front desk. Besides, I don't recommend that you go out and purchase one until it's determined what kind is best for you. That will be decided by your stroke form."

Faith nodded. He certainly *seemed* knowledgeable about tennis, and a part of her believed that he was. Her only misgiving was what being around him each day could and would do to her.

And she had an unfortunate feeling that she would find out. Starting today.

11

"*Nice place.*"

Lyle glanced up from scrambling eggs and slanted a smile over at Monique, who'd been taking her own tour of his living quarters. "Yes, I think so. It's nice to take a break from the hospital in Texas every once in a while to go somewhere and teach. Traveling is nice."

She nodded. "That's something I plan to do a lot of one of these days. I already have a list of places I want to go."

Lyle reached across the range to the counter and picked up his glass to take a deep swallow of orange juice. He wished he could get ahold of that list. He would make it his business to make sure she got a chance to visit each and every place she named . . . with him, of course.

For the past couple of weeks he'd been trying to get her used to his presence with them jogging together every day, reestablishing their friendship. Now it was time to move things in another direction but still at a slow pace, and inviting her to breakfast was a start.

After placing the scrambled eggs into a serving bowl he checked on the biscuits he had in the oven. They were almost ready. He flicked another glance over at Monique. Her back was to him as she stood at the window looking out while sipping a cup of coffee. The view of the Atlantic Ocean was gorgeous from here, but nothing, he thought, was more gorgeous than her. She was simply beautiful. Always had been and in his opinion, always would be.

After their jog, they had gone their separate ways to shower and change. Less than thirty minutes later, she had arrived and he had opened his door to find her standing there, looking refreshed and wearing a pair of capri pants and a tank top with a pair of cute leather sandals on her feet. She had offered to help him in the kitchen, but he wanted her to relax and make herself at home. Besides, from where he was positioned in the kitchen he could see her and he couldn't think of anything more enticing that he wanted to rest his gaze upon.

"So, how are things going with three women sharing the same quarters?" he decided to ask, just to give her a reason to turn around. He wanted to look into her face again.

She turned and smiled. "It's been almost a month, and things have been great so far, but then me, Faith, and Shannon have always gotten along. And now there's Anna, our next-door neighbor, who works as a trauma doctor at the hospital. She's been spending time with us as well. She's nice, and I like her."

Monique was silent for a moment and then said. "Faith, Shannon, and I have a special bond. They are the sisters I never had and even over the years, although we lived in separate parts of the country, we still managed to maintain a close relationship."

He nodded as he took the biscuits out the oven. "Wasn't there another one of you guys?"

He saw sadness cloud her eyes. "You have a good memory, and yes, there was Cely. She died earlier this year."

"Oh, I'm sorry to hear that. What did she die of?"

Monique's eyes got bleaker. "A drug overdose. She committed suicide."

Her response hadn't been what he'd been expecting to hear, and he could tell from the look on her face that she still found the thought of someone close, someone she knew, doing something like that mind-boggling. "I'm sorry to hear that, but you'll be surprised how the suicide rate among African Americans, especially the women, has risen over the years. It's a very serious public health problem."

"The entire thing just baffles me," Monique said, shaking her head. "I remember a time when the thought of suicide in the black community was a no-no, definitely a taboo, something you would never consider—but now . . ."

"Yes, you're right. Suicide is usually the culmination of an individual's battle with depression or the stress of living in today's society. But typically it's depression that's the major cause."

Monique wrapped her arms around her waist, clearly disturbed. "And that's what bothers me the most because neither me, Faith, or Shannon had any reason to think Cely was depressed about anything. The last time I spoke with her, which was only two weeks before, she was doing fine. At least she led me to believe that she was," she said, dropping down on a nearby couch.

Within a flash, Lyle edged around the breakfast bar and sat down beside her on the sofa, placing a comforting arm around her shoulder. "Hey, as close as you and your friend were, you shouldn't take it personal that she didn't confide in you before doing what she did. It wasn't that she thought she couldn't; she just chose not to. It's unfortunate that she didn't realize help is available and that early recognition and treatment for depression are the key."

Monique shook her head, trying not to notice how close they were sitting together or that his dark eyes were boring intently into hers. "I know, but when I think of what she was going through alone," she said, fighting not to let his presence overwhelm her. Her heart was beating frantically in her chest. "And she did leave the three of us letters but didn't shed any light as to what she was going through," she said to get her mind back on the right track. "Instead she pleaded with us to live each day to the fullest and do whatever we want to enjoy life and not live up to others' expectations and standards."

"That was some good advice. Maybe the three of you should take it."

"We are," she said, thinking that his strong jaw, sensuous lips, and sculpted nose were right in her line of vision. "That's why we're here on the island together. This is where the four of us met as teenagers one summer, so it seemed fitting to come back here in her memory."

"Sounds like a good plan."

"Yeah, I think so, too." Monique's words faltered when she saw his head beginning to lower to hers and knew exactly what he planned to do, and the split second before their lips touched, she quickly stood to her feet. "Do you need help with breakfast?"

He smiled as he slowly stood and placed his hands in the pockets of his jeans. "You've asked me that already, and the answer is still no. Everything is ready anyway. All I have to do is set the table and, before you ask, no, I don't need help with that either."

She nodded nervously. "Okay, I guess I'll go wash up, then."

"All right."

Monique quickly moved toward the bathroom, thinking if she didn't escape at that moment, she would definitely be sorry. She and Lyle had almost kissed, and she didn't know how she felt about that. After closing the bathroom door behind her, she leaned against it and let out the breath she'd been holding. No matter what, she would not let herself get attracted to Lyle. She refused to do that.

Shane handed Faith a bottle of iced water and smiled. "Your first lesson went well. You caught on quickly."

She smiled back. "I had a good teacher. Besides, all I did today was practice hitting balls."

"Yes, but developing good stroke form is important. It helps to avoid unnecessary arm injuries later," he explained. "And because tennis involves a lot of side-to-side movement, you're going to need a pair of shoes that's not only cute but also built for lateral stability," he said, glancing down at her feet and grinning. "Don't wear those back tomorrow. They can easily cause an ankle injury."

She nodded. "All right. Anything else?"

"Yeah. I found your outfit distracting."

Faith blinked. Of all the things she had expected him to say, that wasn't one of them. She glanced down at her pastel-pink-and-white V-neck tennis top and matching short tennis skirt, along with her cute pink sneakers. He had already explained why her sneakers wouldn't work, but she couldn't fathom what could possibly be wrong with her outfit.

"And just what's so distracting about it?" she asked, glancing up at him before glancing around at other females playing tennis on the courts. "I'm not the only woman wearing this style."

"Yes, but they don't have your legs."

Again she couldn't believe what he'd said. Did the man say whatever he thought? She lifted her chin. "I thought we were keeping this professional."

He took a huge gulp of water from his water bottle, then went so far as to squirt some on his face. "We are. I'm just being honest. An instructor's concentration is important."

"Then that's your problem and not mine."

"You're right. It is my problem, but I figured maybe you should know."

"Thanks, but no thanks. Maybe I should look for another instructor."

Shane grinned. Damn, but her lips became full and pouty when she got mad. And on top of that, her chest heaved, and a heaving chest did wonders to full, firm breasts like hers. "Hey don't get upset—I merely mentioned it just in case I lose my concentration tomorrow. I'm not asking you to change your outfit for me. I just wanted you to know I found it distracting and the reason why. Like you said, it's my problem and I'll deal with it."

He tossed his empty water bottle in a nearby recycling bin and then, taking her hand, said, "Now let's go grab some lunch."

A part of Faith wanted to snatch her hand away, but she hated admitting it: she found the man as intriguing as she found him handsome. "From where?"

"Hudson's Seafood House. Ever been there?"

"Yes, years ago." The restaurant was known for its tasty seafood.

"Well, I heard they have a luncheon special that's out of this world, and I bet you've worked up an appetite."

He was right. She also knew the restaurant was not in walking distance. "Do you want me to follow you in my car?"

He shook his head. "No, we'll go in one car, and I'll do the driving."

A question suddenly flooded her mind. Could she trust him? Just what did she know about this man other than the fact that he was handsome and she found him intriguing? Not a thing. Hadn't she and Monique recently given Shannon the third degree about going off to meet some stranger? She suddenly stopped walking.

He glanced down at her. "What?"

"Nothing, but I've decided to drive my own car so I'll meet you there."

He stared at her for a moment, slid his hands into his pockets, smiled, and nodded. "All right. Whoever gets there first needs to grab a table."

"Okay."

When she turned to leave, he said, "One more thing, Faith."

She turned and met his gaze. "What?"

"You're a cautious woman, and I like that."

"Thanks, but it wouldn't matter to me if you liked it or not."

She heard his deep laugh as she turned toward the area where her car was parked. And as much as she wanted to look back, she didn't.

1 2

Anna glanced down at her watch the exact moment the doorbell sounded. Leave it to Zach to be right on time. He had called that
morning to say he had arrived on Hilton Head and had checked into
a hotel. Once he got settled he would be coming to take her to lunch
at noon. It was noon and he was here.

Taking a deep breath, she crossed the room to open the door,
hoping the smile on her face wouldn't give her away. She would be
glad to see him, and it would be pretty hard not to show it.

As soon as she reached the door, she stopped and nervously bit
the inside of her cheek. The last time she'd seen him had been
around four months ago at the party her grandmother had given to
commemorate the year she'd been united with the family. She and
Zach had danced together, and each time he'd taken her into his
arms, she'd fallen in love with him even more.

Pulling herself together, she unlocked the door and slowly
opened it. She then gazed at the most handsome man she'd ever met.
He was standing there, casually dressed in a polo shirt and a pair of
khaki trousers, leaning against the jamb and smiling at her.

"Anna."

She loved the way he said her name, and hearing it flow off his
lips sent butterflies fluttering around in her stomach. It took all she
had not to take a lunge for him, but she knew doing something like
that would be completely inappropriate. Instead when he opened his
arms, she automatically walked into them for the hug she knew he

would give her. She and Zach always hugged when they saw each other. Hugged but nothing more.

"Zach," she said, getting wrapped in his strong embrace. His scent, one that could leave a woman breathless, seemed to get absorbed in her skin as well as her nostrils. "It's so good seeing you again."

And she meant every word. This, she thought, was the man that fantasies were made of. Tall, standing well over six feet, with medium brown skin and a face whose every detail any woman would appreciate, especially his dark eyes, the sharp cut of his nose, his firm jawbone, and lips that made you turn to jelly when they turned up at the corners for a smile.

"It's good seeing you again as well," he said, releasing her and staring down at her with those adoring dark eyes. "Have you been taking care of yourself?" he asked, keeping a hold on her hand while stepping over the threshold and closing the door behind him.

She made a face that deepened the smile lines around her eyes. "You're only asking me that because you heard my grandmother say I looked thin that night. Admit it."

He flashed a grin while slowly releasing her hand. "Okay, I admit it. Now are you ready to go?"

"Yes, I'm ready. I just need to grab my purse. Where are we going for lunch?"

"It's a surprise."

She glanced over at him as she picked her purse off the table. "Am I dressed all right for where we're going?" She was wearing a blue sundress that came short of covering her ankles. She'd worn the dress intentionally, since she had found out a while back from his sister that blue was his favorite color.

"Yes, you look fine, absolutely stunning," he said.

She smiled. "Thanks. Come on, let's go. I like surprises."

Zach took her to a restaurant on the pier that overlooked Jarvis Creek. From where they sat, they had a really good view of the lighthouse, and while eating lunch, Zach had brought her up to date on the family.

"I'm sorry to hear about Trey's mother," she said. Her first cousin's mother, the one who'd been responsible for Anna not being found all those years ago, had recently died of a severe case of pneumonia. "I understand the services were private."

"Yes, Trey and his stepfather felt it was best, considering Angela didn't have a whole lot of friends. Unfortunately, she never recovered from her mental illness."

Anna nodded. "And how's Trey and Haywood?"

Zach smiled. "They're doing fine, and it's hard to believe that Quad is two years old already," he said of Trey and Haywood's son, Ross Donovan Fuller IV, named after Trey as well as after his granduncle, who was Anna's father. "You'll see them this weekend at Glendale Shores. They'll be at the Fourth of July celebration."

A part of Anna couldn't wait. She always enjoyed the time she spent with her relatives, and Glendale Shores was even more special. Although she never got a chance to meet her great-grandparents who'd lived there, she had heard a lot about Murphy and Mattie Denison—especially Mattie, who had been blessed with having the "gift."

There was a certain curiosity within the family as to which of Mattie's grands or great-grands would eventually inherit her psychic powers. Anna knew it definitely wasn't her, otherwise, she wouldn't be sitting here trying to figure out what Zach was thinking at that moment. He had gotten quiet as if he was in deep thought about something.

She picked up her daiquiri and took a sip, appreciating how the fruity drink slid down her throat, cooling her lustful thoughts. They would merely be tantalizing thoughts to anyone else but they were lustful to her, mainly because she couldn't ever imagine them being more than fantasies. Secret fantasies that would never become reality.

"So how does your schedule look for the rest of the week?"

Zach's question pulled her thoughts back to earth. "When you called and said when you were coming, I cleared my calendar."

He lifted a brow. "So you don't have to report to the hospital?"

She smiled, shaking her head. "Not for two weeks. That will give me a chance to spend time with you before we head over to Glendale Shores. This is the first time you've been to visit me here since I moved."

Zach nodded and then pretended to concentrate on a view outside the restaurant's window. She was right. Getting her to move from San Diego to D.C. to be closer to her father's people had almost been impossible. But finally she'd given in and took a leave from work to move to D.C., making periodic visits to Richmond, Virginia, where her grandparents and uncle lived.

Because he had been one of the few people she'd known while living in D.C., the two of them had spent a lot of time together, but the media was always there, speculating if perhaps the relationship between the son of distinguished Senator Noah Wainwright and the niece of noted acclaimed attorney Randolph Fuller was more than the "just friendship" they claimed. So much media attention, sometimes downright hostile, had bothered Anna, and she had eventually announced to everyone her decision to accept a job offer at the trauma center in Hilton Head.

When she'd left D.C., it seemed his heart had left with her, and he'd been unable to follow her to the island, thinking that if he did so, he would surely make a fool of himself. But now, he was willing to take the chance.

"Mom and Dad send their love." He decided to glance back over at her. He watched that smile, which could brighten an entire room, touch each corner of her lips. And then there were those dark and mysterious eyes. They were eyes that had the ability to draw him in whenever he gazed into them.

"I meant to call them last week, to see how they were doing but things got rather hectic at the hospital. Now I'll just wait to see them this coming weekend."

"Yes, they'll be there. I flew to Richmond a few weeks ago and visited your uncle Randolph and Jenna." He definitely wouldn't tell her the nature of his visit with her uncle, which was to make his intentions toward Anna known.

He watched Anna's smile widen. "You did?"

"Yes."

Now that's one couple who's truly amazing, Anna thought. Haywood had shared the story of how the two—Randolph and Haywood's mother, Jenna—had met while in college at Howard University back in the sixties and fallen in love, and how that love had survived. There was a time, due to the betrayal of Trey's mother, Angela, when Randolph and Jenna had gone separate ways and married others. But eventually, the two had reunited and ended up remarrying. In Anna's book, theirs was the ultimate love story.

"So what are your plans for this afternoon?"

Zach's question invaded Anna's thoughts. "I don't have any. Are you up to discovering a little Hilton Head Island while you're here? There's a Gullah Heritage Tour that starts in an hour."

"Sounds interesting. I'd love to do it."

Anna smiled over at him. "Then we will."

Monique glanced across the table at Lyle. With great effort she tried to maintain her composure and not think about that moment when the two of them had been sitting on the sofa and he'd been about to kiss her.

Since that time, things had gotten rather quiet between them, and more than anything she wanted to regain that relaxed mode they'd always shared. She released a long sigh. It wouldn't be so bad and she wouldn't be feeling guilty if a part of her hadn't wanted him to kiss her, but she had panicked and stopped it from happening. She didn't want her and Lyle's friendship tarnished by wanton lust—the kind that seemed to be getting to her these past few days. It seemed as if Shannon's comment had opened a can of worms.

"Would you like anything else? There're more biscuits if you're still hungry."

Lyle's words drew her attention back, and she glanced up. His gaze immediately locked with hers. He had settled back in his chair, seemingly enjoying the coffee he was sipping. He sat the cup down, and when he smiled it seemed contagious.

"No thanks, I'm full," she said, pushing her plate aside.

He nodded. "Most people are eating lunch about now. We were late starters."

"Yes, but they're not enjoying what we had. You're a wonderful cook."

He chuckled. "Thanks. Pop taught me all I know. He had to. He was a single father trying to raise three sons so we had to learn to do things early. All of us had our specialties. Logan is number one when it comes to making up beds, and Lance was the one who'd made sure we kept plenty of firewood stacked for the fireplace. Pop was a hardworking man, and we tried to make things as easy on him as possible."

Monique heard the love in his voice not only for his father but for his brothers as well. She leaned back, relaxing in her chair as much as she could. "So, Lance Montgomery, the one who wrote the book on how to be a playa—causing quite a stir with the ladies, I might add—finally met his match, huh?" she asked, grinning.

"Yes, he most certainly did. Asia is just what he needs, and the two of them are very happy together. So I guess there's hope for everyone."

She had a teasing glint in her eyes when she asked, "Does that mean you never bought into any of that playa stuff your brother was writing about?"

He picked up his cup again and took another sip before saying, "No. We all knew that Lance had issues, but there was nothing we could do. He had to work them out for himself. My mother's leaving had done a number on him."

"But not on you?"

He shook his head. "No. Lance was too young to see a lot of the things Logan and I saw when our parents were together. And although Logan and I were young, we understood betrayal. I can remember the time some man had to make a quick getaway before my dad came home and left his shoes behind. I'm the one my mother ordered to toss the shoes out the window to him. She practically threatened me and Logan about ever telling our dad about any of her male visitors when he was at work."

Monique shook her head. That was a lot for a child to have to put up with and deal with, especially from a parent. "You mentioned that there was another wedding in your family."

Lyle smiled. "Yes, my sister Carrie. I'm sure Arnie told you about her."

"Yes."

"Well, she met someone too and got married. His name is Connor, and they are happy together as well."

"Now what about you and your brother Logan? Do you think the two of you will follow suit and tie the knot?"

"I can't speak for Logan, but I wouldn't mind getting married one day."

"Are you seeing anyone seriously?"

His grin was slow, and to Monique's way of thinking, seductive. "Not at the moment, but that can change rather quickly if I were to meet someone that I could love for the rest of my life."

"And you think you can do that?"

He lifted a brow. "Do what? Love a woman forever?"

"Yes."

"Sure I can."

His words sounded so heartfelt and convincing that Monique believed him. "Well, I'm glad, because all men can't do that. I was fortunate enough to marry one that could before I lost him."

Lyle nodded as he studied Monique for a long moment. She was slowly sipping her own coffee, and he wondered if she was reliving memories of all the good things in her marriage. "He's not coming back, you know."

His words, which he was sure were totally unexpected, had her snatching her head up. However, he didn't see the deep hurt and pain in her eyes that he'd assumed would be there. Instead he saw what he felt was acceptance. "Oh, I know that," she said softly. "But I can't help but appreciate what I once had, Lyle. Other women aren't as fortunate."

"Do you think there could and will ever be another man in your life?" he couldn't help but ask. "Someone you can love just as much as you did Paul?"

He could tell by her expression that what he'd asked her had been a question to make her deeply consider her response before making it. For a long moment she didn't say anything, pondering the question, and then she said, "Yes, I believe that I could."

He tried to hide the satisfaction he felt at her words. "I'm glad to hear that because I think you would make some lucky man a wonderful wife."

"Thank you."

The smile that touched her lips sent blood rushing through his veins, and he picked up his cup thinking that he dared not tell her he fully intended to be that lucky man.

13

Faith walked into the restaurant, glanced around, and saw Shane sitting at one of the tables in the back, one that overlooked the Intracoastal Waterways. Since he was sitting there, staring out at the water, he hadn't seen her yet, so she stood still for a moment longer and studied his profile. Even from the side, his features were sharp, distinctive, and irresistible.

An achy feeling erupted deep within her that she was determined to control. There was no need to let overwhelmed emotions overtake her good sense. Shane was an adrenaline booster—that was for certain—but the only time she would need extra energy while in Hilton Head was on the tennis courts. Shane had sure gotten a high degree of workout from her today. She intended to get into bed early to be ready for her next training session.

"May I help you, miss?"

Faith turned. The waiter was probably wondering why she'd been standing there as if she had no place to go. "No thanks. I'm meeting someone here for lunch, and I see him sitting over there."

"Then if you would kindly allow me to escort you there?"

"Thanks."

Maybe it was the creaking of the floor that alerted Shane of their approach. He turned and fixed his gaze on her and stood. That achy feeling increased. "For a moment I thought you had stood me up," he said, favoring her with a slow and seductive smile.

Faith couldn't resist smiling. What woman would be that stupid?

Instead she said as she sat in her chair, "And miss the chance for more free tennis lessons? No way."

He chuckled as he sat back down. "So, your only purpose is to use me?"

Her smile widened. "You made the offer, Mr. Masters. I just merely took you up on it."

"True, so I really can't get upset, can I?"

"I don't see how you can," she said, draping the cloth napkin in her lap. "Have you had a chance to look at the menu?"

"No, I decided to wait on you." He then motioned for another waiter, since the one who had escorted her to the table was now helping someone else.

Moments after their orders had been taken, Shane leaned back in his chair. "So, tell me something about Faith Gilmore."

She waved away his request. "I prefer hearing about Shane Masters."

"It might bore you to tears."

"I'm willing to take my chances." She grinned.

"All right, don't say I didn't warn you." He picked up his glass and took a swallow of water. Setting the glass back down, he said, "Like I told you that first day we met, my family is from Savannah. There are a lot of Masterses still living there, but I moved to Detroit after college. I went to University of Michigan on a tennis scholarship and decided I liked the area. I got both my undergrad and grad degree there and was fortunate to get a job there in the area as well. I owned an accounting firm. When I first went into business fifteen years ago, it was just me and my secretary. By the time I retired a couple of months ago, the firm employed over a hundred individuals."

"Wow, that's a huge increase."

A smile touched his lips. "Yes, but as the economy grows, so does the need for capable accountants."

"And are you, like me, the only child?"

He shook his head, grinning. "Heck no. There are seven of us: three girls and four boys, which includes one set of twins—male and female—the youngest of the brood. My father died thirty-five years ago when I was five. I don't remember much about him other than he was good to his family and provided for us well."

Faith nodded. "Are all your siblings still living in Savannah?"

"No, only one of my sisters and my mom are still living there, along with a bunch of aunts, uncles, and cousins. The rest of us are all spread out. My youngest brother, Quinn, is an attorney out in L.A. He's married to the former Alexia Bennett."

"Alexia Bennett? The singer?" Faith's eyes widened.

Shane laughed. "One and the same. She goes by Alexia Bennett-Masters now."

"Yes, I know! She's my favorite R and B performer."

"I'll mention that the next time I see her. Then there's my brother Grey, who's married to Alexia's cousin Brandy. They live in Orlando."

Faith's eyebrows shot up. "You Masterses like to keep things in the family, uhh?"

He shrugged, remembering the woman he was supposed to meet when he got to Orlando, a relative of Brandy's on her mother's side. "Not all of us. My brother Lake falls between me and Grey in age. He's single and lives in Boston. Then there is Quinece, Quinn's twin. She's married to Kendall, and they live in Arizona; my sister Emily is married and lives in Boise."

Faith raised a brow. "Boise, Idaho?" Since she had a job in advertising and marketing, she knew the percentage of African Americans living there wasn't high at all.

Shane smiled. "Yes, nestled right at the base of the Rocky Mountains with astonishing scenery through every window of her home. She and her husband, Wayne, own a software company and are doing quite nicely. Then there's Paula, the oldest of the clan. She and her husband, John, were living in Seattle for a while, but when their only child, Melissa, decided to go to college in Atlanta, they decided to move back home to be near Mom—so they claim, although we all know otherwise. Especially since my mother is rarely home these days. She likes traveling all over the States to see her grandkids."

Faith said nothing for a moment then. "Do you have any children?"

He shook his head. "No. I'm forty, and I've never been married and I don't have any children."

Faith took a sip of her water, considering him. "A bachelor for life, then?"

He flashed an irresistible smile. "I don't have anything against marriage. I almost married once, but a week before the wedding I found out she was pregnant . . . and the child wasn't mine."

"She actually told you the child wasn't yours?" Faith blinked.

"Yes," he offered somewhat quietly, as if he was remembering that time. "She thought I should know since she and the father of her baby planned to elope that night. But the real kicker was that he was someone I knew, someone I thought I could trust and thought was a friend. It seemed that they ran into each other at some business conference, and I understand things got rather carried away. They planned a few secret meetings after that. She claimed she wanted to call off the wedding but hadn't wanted to hurt me."

Faith blew out a puff of anger. The last thing she could tolerate was a cheating spouse or significant other. "She was actually going to marry you anyway?"

"Yes, but then she got pregnant and rethought that decision."

"Thank goodness for that."

Shane smiled again, wondering if Faith knew how stunningly beautiful she was when she got angry. "That was three years ago, and you're right—I'm glad she called off the wedding. Especially since my generation of Masterses vowed not to marry until we found our perfect mates. I guess I'd been rushing things a bit, because Cherice was far from perfect."

At that moment the waiter arrived with their food, and Faith was glad they had something to do to occupy their time. She wasn't ready for the conversation to shift to her. Shane had shared a lot about himself, but there was no way she could do likewise. Admitting that your husband had left you for another man was not something any woman wanted to boast about.

A couple of hours later, Faith let herself into the house. She had to admit she'd shared a very pleasant lunch with Shane. Unfortunately, the conversation during the meal *had* shifted, but she'd told him only the basics, staying away from any details as to why she and Virgil had divorced. He had been too kind to ask, and she had been spared telling him a single thing.

After going straight into the kitchen, she pulled two notes off the refrigerator that were being held by a magnet. Monique wanted her to know she had gone shopping to buy some more jogging outfits. Shannon's note didn't say where she had gone but not to expect her for dinner and don't be surprised if she didn't come home tonight.

Faith pulled in a deep breath and gazed heavenward and said softly, "Cely, what are we going to do with her?"

It's okay this time. Leave her alone. She'll be fine. Faith whirled around. For a moment she could have sworn she'd heard Cely's voice, speaking to her as if she'd been standing right there beside her.

Faith pulled in another deep breath. It had to be the wine she'd consumed at lunch. It hadn't been enough alcohol to keep her from driving, just enough to get her relaxed . . . and she had felt relaxed with Shane. And she looked forward to her next tennis lesson with him.

She glanced at her watch, knowing what she had to do. Withdrawing her cell phone from her purse, she punched in her parents' phone number.

"Hello," her mother answered as she always did, like she was annoyed about being bothered, especially when *Oprah* was on.

"Mom, it's me."

"About time you called. Your dad and I have been worried sick about you. The only thing that kept us from flying to South Carolina to check on you ourselves was knowing Dr. Ross-Fuller is living next door. Have you met her yet?"

Faith sighed. "Yes, Mom, we've met. I even had her over for dinner a few times. She's nice."

"I told you that she was. So, how are the girls?"

Faith shook her head, wondering if her mother would ever really acknowledge her, Monique, and Shannon as grown women. "They're fine, and we're having a good time."

Before her mother could get all into her business by asking what kind of fun they were having, Faith quickly asked, "Have you started packing for your trip to Europe yet?"

"Yes, and your father insists that I buy all new things—so I'm going shopping again tomorrow."

Faith knew she should be grateful that her parents, even after thirty-five years, were still happily married. Unlike Shannon's parents, hers had been good role models. They would have been perfect if they hadn't been so darn overprotective while growing up. A little sneeze could get her a ride in the ambulance to the hospital. Her father had been a well-known physician in the city, and it hadn't been hard to get others to cater to his whims when it came to his one and only daughter.

For the next few minutes Faith let her mother go on and on about what the *Oprah* show had been about the day before and the day before that. Other than her charity work, *Oprah* was her mother's most consuming pastime.

"Well, Mom, I need to go now," she said, finally interrupting.

"But we just started talking."

"Mom, we've been on the phone for almost an hour."

"Well, wait just a minute. Your dad wants to speak to you."

Before she could say anything, she could hear her mother put down the phone. After a long silence, she heard her father's deep voice: "Faith Nicole?"

"Yes, Dad, and before you ask, I'm doing fine."

"That's good to hear. Do you need anything?"

"No, Daddy, I'm fine. How are you?"

"Doing okay. I've been playing a lot of golf lately. Retirement is great. I met this young man you might be interested in and—"

"Thanks, Dad, but that's okay. Really it is." She knew her father felt somewhat guilty since he was the one to introduce her to Virgil. Now he was trying to erase his whale of a boo-boo by fixing her up with someone else.

"Look, I got to go, Dad. I want to take a shower and get into bed early."

"Don't overdo anything, and stay away from the beach water."

Faith shook her head and rolled her eyes. "Right. Talk to you later, Dad."

Once she hung up the phone, Faith quickly made her way to the wine rack. After talking to her parents, she definitely needed a drink—even if it was a mild one.

"I had a lot fun today, Anna," Zach said, giving her a smile. It was late afternoon, and they were just getting back to her house from their island adventure.

"I'm glad. Would you like to stay for a while?" she asked, setting her purse down on the coffee table.

"What I would like to do," he said, pushing away from the closed door, "is take you out to a dinner and a movie. Do you think you're up to it?"

Anna sat down on the sofa, kicked off her sandals, and then proceeded to rub her sore feet. "Yes, just as long as I can wear some flat shoes."

"You can wear anything you want," he said, coming to sit beside her. He leaned down and shifted her legs to his lap. At her startled expression, he said softly, "Let me do this for you."

Zach could tell from Anna's expression that she didn't know what to say. So she didn't say anything, which was fine with him because he needed this time to concentrate . . . on both her feet and on her. As he began massaging her ankles and heels, he watched her lean back and close her eyes. He knew she hadn't expected this. He hadn't expected it either. But after spending all afternoon with her and part of the evening, he knew he wanted to touch her in some way, and for now this was the safest. Anything else might just push him over the edge, and he planned to do just what he promised his parents and her uncle. He would take his time and go slow. More than anything he wanted to show her they were good together and that as one, they could handle anything, including the media.

"Umm, that feels good," she murmured softly. "You might be in the wrong profession."

He smiled. "I can say the same for you. You have pretty feet. They are small but pretty. Have you ever thought of being a ballet dancer?"

He heard her small chuckle, and the sound set off a quivering in his middle. "No, I never gave that much thought. But I did want to become a movie star after coming to the United States at seventeen and seeing my first Cicely Tyson movie. I thought she had so much style and grace."

"And what about before you came to this country? Did you have any dreams then?"

He watched her eyes slowly open, and sadness appeared in them that he'd never seen there before. He went still when she said, "Yes. I would dream every night that one day my father's family would decide to want me and come get me from that orphanage in Saigon."

A part of Zach wanted to reach out and pull her into his arms to give her the kiss he'd been dying to give her all day—even before today. How about for the *past year.* Instead, he said softly, "They were looking for you, Anna. You know that now. For all those years you were dreaming, they were looking."

She smiled as she met his gaze. "Yes, I know that now, and that what's made everything so special to me, Zach. I was being loved even when I didn't know it."

He nodded. It was on the tip of his tongue to say, *And you're still being loved and don't know it, sweetheart.* He needed to put distance between them before he did kiss her, so he slowly shifted her legs from his lap and stood up. "I'll leave so you can get some rest. Since we had a huge lunch, what about a late dinner and one of those midnight movies?"

"Sounds good to me. Anything in particular you want to see?"

He shook his head as he placed his hands in his trousers, still tempted to pull her off the sofa into his arms. "Whatever you decide is fine with me," he said.

"All right."

She was about to stand when he said, "No, I can let myself out. I'll see you later, in a few hours."

And without giving her a chance to say anything else, he quickly headed for the door.

14

As Adam washed and dried his hands at the sink, he glanced over at his newest acquisition. In just a few days he'd made a lot of progress, but there was a lot of restoring yet to be done. When Kent had said the vehicle had had a rough life, he truly meant it. The previous owner evidently hadn't fully appreciated what a gem he'd possessed. But no matter, Adam was the new owner and he would give this *baby* the respect it deserved.

Talking about respect . . .

Not for the first time he couldn't stop his thoughts from turning to Dr. Shannon Carmichael. The proverbial spoiled little rich girl who grew up to become the spoiled and rich woman, she was used to having her way in all things, even in her selection of men.

After she'd left the other night, he had gone up to his apartment and instead of immediately taking a shower, he contacted the guy who handled investigative work for his family's law firm. In a matter of hours, Adam had been given all the info he needed on the good doctor. She had been telling the truth about how she viewed things in life. She'd never been married and, according to what he'd read, it didn't seem likely she would be doing so anytime soon or ever. And although she wasn't a celebrity by any means—definitely not in the same ranks as a Paris Hilton—because her parents were such well-known educators in this country, the media had evidently found her social life interesting and had pegged her with the nickname of "The Prize." It seemed a lot of men wanted her, but she was too discriminating for any of them. According to the report, to say she was nit-picky was an understatement. But the one thing that seemed constant was that she preferred dating professional men, especially those with titles behind their names. If you didn't have one, then save yourself the trouble.

Adam remembered how she had shown up unexpectedly that one night. After his brash behavior, he was certain that he had seen the last of her, since it had been a week already and she hadn't shown back up. For women like Shannon, a bruised ego was something they didn't get over. One part of his mind thought, *Good riddance.* But another part—the part that had kept him walking the floor at night with a hard-on followed by a cold shower every morning—could just imagine what he'd rejected. Maybe he'd been a fool to turn down what she'd so blatantly offered.

And it hadn't help matters that he'd found the scrap of silk panties he'd practically ripped off her on the floor next to his car that following morning. If anything, as a true Tennessee gentleman, he should have offered to purchase her another pair. But then when it came to her, he didn't quite feel like a gentleman. He wanted to be the roughneck she assumed he was, the type of person that she evidently wanted firsthand knowledge of—right between her gorgeous legs.

Adam went over to the refrigerator and pulled out a beer. He needed it. Today he had helped Kent get a customer's classic '68 Malibu ready for a race in a few weeks at the newly opened Savannah River Drag Way, an event Adam intended to travel the forty-five minutes into Savannah to attend.

Clicking off the lights, he was about to turn toward the stairs to go up to his apartment when he heard a sound. He glanced over at the window, thinking his mind was playing tricks on him. He saw her standing outside the window as she had done the last time he saw her.

He lifted his dark brows in surprise. It seemed the good doctor's bruised ego hadn't kept her from returning after all. In fact, knowing how the human mind worked, especially the female mind, he would bet the classic 1965 Corvair that was parked in his garage in Memphis that there was a purpose behind her visit. Some women, he'd discovered, didn't take rejection well, and he had a feeling she topped the list. No doubt she had something in store for him, something he might not be able to resist a second time, given his present horny state.

And for the first time since meeting her, he had a feeling that he was in big trouble. But still, he intended to do things his way. And it would be a way she wouldn't easily forget—and he hoped like hell it was one she wouldn't be quick to regret. If she wanted the raw, unrefined side of him, then tonight she would get it.

If Shannon hadn't seen Adam through the window before he'd turned off the lights, she would not have been certain he was inside. But she had seen him, and she knew he'd seen her.

She nearly jumped when the sound of the huge garage door rising startled her. Since he hadn't turned the lights back on, the entranceway looked dark and spooky. She waited a few moments for him to appear, and when he didn't, she drew in a deep breath, wondered just what kind of game he was playing, and walked over the threshold into the darkened garage.

The sound of her high-heeled shoes crossing the cement floor was loud, and she decided that if Adam wouldn't turn the lights back on, then she would . . . once she figured out just where the light switch was. She stopped and glanced around. Everything was dark, and she forced her nerves to relax. As soon as they did, she nearly jumped out of her skin once more when the sound of the garage door being lowered made her jittery all over again. With great effort, she tried to regain her cool. She had never liked the dark.

Having had enough of Adam's foolishness, she said out loud, "Aren't you too old to be playing games?"

"Is that what I'm doing?"

She nearly leaped out of her shoes. The deep masculine voice had spoken from directly behind her, and before she could move, he settled his body right smack up against her butt. He felt hot, male, and huge.

"Why did you come back?" he asked, leaning closer and whispering the question gruffly in her ear.

She was about to give him some smart-ass response when he reached around and flattened his palm against her bare stomach to pull her back even more firmly against him. His touch sent blood quickly rushing through her and heat pooling between her legs.

"What the hell are you wearing?" he asked, almost growling. "Or should I be asking what the hell aren't you wearing?"

"Why don't you turn on the lights and see," Shannon growled back. Her outfit, at least what there was of it, undoubtedly had caught his attention the moment he'd touched her bare belly. She had intended to be bold tonight, and she certainly was. When she discovered that Frederick's of Hollywood was having a grand opening on the island, she'd been ecstatic. The moment she had walked into the store she had seen the perfect outfit, one that would raise Adam Corbain's temperature up a few notches.

"I think I'll keep the lights off for now. You can model this outfit for me later. Right now I want to touch you all over."

His hot breath made her shiver when he leaned closer to her shoulder and nibbled her there and then again when his hand moved from her bare belly up to her lacy bralette and he slipped his hand underneath to gently rub his palm over her breasts. She couldn't stop the moan that poured forth from her lips. And when she automatically settled her tush even closer to fit against him, he seemed to grow larger.

She closed her eyes as he stroked her breasts with his hands, massaging the tips of her nipples and sending her pulse racing.

"You picked a bad night to come back," he said, whispering the words hoarsely in her ear even while grinding his groin against her backside.

"Why do you say that?"

"Because I'm horny."

His words, raw and jagged, turned her on instead of turning her off. She decided the first time she'd met him that he took the term *bad boy* to a whole other level, and he was proving her theory right.

"Your being horny doesn't scare me, Adam," she whispered, excited.

He slowly moved his hands from her breasts to slide them down past her bare belly to the waistband of the lace thong, which had ties on the side. "And if I go further and slide my hand lower, beneath the waistband of this concoction here, what will I find?" he asked, while easing his hand lower.

"That I'm as horny as you are."

Adam managed to hold himself in check to keep from laughing. Just where did this woman come from? When it came to being sexually blatant, she could hold her own with any man. She was definitely more ballsy and brash than any woman he'd ever had the pleasure of meeting.

"You think so," he countered.

"More than likely," she purred.

"Umm, let's see."

Pulling her even closer back to him, he fitted his knees between her legs, opening them wider. He then traced a path lower beneath the waistline of thong. When his fingers reached their mark, they suddenly went still. "The curls?"

Shannon knew what he was asking, not that it was any of his business. But she decided to respond anyway. "I went to the spa a couple of days ago and decided to get a bikini wax."

"I like hair," he rumbled in her ear.

"Then grow some."

Her smart-ass reply evidently got to him—if his responding growl was any indication. And then to prove his point he snatched her around and devoured her mouth, exploring her insides greedily with the insistent thrust of his tongue.

She hadn't had time to catch her breath. All she could do was wrap her arms around him, breathe in the manly scent of him, and match his mouth play for play. She felt her entire body flaming, and when he shifted her body to give himself access to the heat between her legs, she released a deep moan.

His fingers went to work, just as they'd done the last time and she wasn't sure what was worse: his tongue in her mouth or his fingers in her center. He was driving her mad, and she felt a pull in the lower part of her body that seemed ready to explode.

Seconds later it did.

She screamed when an orgasm hit, and he soothed the sound with gentle kisses along her face and neck. It seemed to take her forever to recover, to come back down off the high he'd sent her on, but when she did, she found herself swept off her feet and into strong arms. Then she noticed they were moving.

"Where are you taking me?" she asked, barely able to get the words out.

"Upstairs to my bedroom, into the light," he answered matter-of-factly. "I want to see just what the hell you're wearing."

The moment Adam placed her on his bed, Shannon glanced around. The efficiency apartment was neat, tidy, but her scrutiny of his living quarters came to an abrupt end when he came to the bed and stood over her. He had turned a light on the moment they had stepped over the threshold, and he was standing there, looking down at her, getting an eyeful. She couldn't recall ever giving any man such liberties before.

"I like it."

His words surprised the hell out of her, and what shocked her even more was the mere idea that she was actually glad that he approved. He then leaned over and lifted the short lace skirt that covered her thong. "Now I understand the reason for the bikini wax."

She started to tell him that she didn't care if he understood or not. What she did with her body wasn't any of his business. And she was about to tell him just that when he reached down, captured her hand, and pulled her to her feet. Before she could ask what he thought he was doing, he showed her, tilting her face up to him and inserting his tongue into her mouth, just as unceremoniously as he pleased. And when he began thrusting that tongue back and forth inside her mouth—right, left, up, down, all around—she began to experience sensations she'd never felt before. This man was actually breaking down every nut and bolt of her sexual system.

He slowly broke off the kiss and pulled back, and his dark eyes searched hers a moment before he said in a deep, husky voice, "You're going to have to work for it."

She blinked, and then her eyes darkened. "Work for what?"

He placed her hand on his crotch. Let her feel the size and the hardness. "For this."

She snatched her hand back and placed them on her hips. "And why should I? I've already had my pleasure for tonight."

He smiled and his gaze became even more intense. "There's a hell of a lot more where it came from."

"Might be, but as a rule I'm only good for one a night."

He brushed her hair off her shoulders and said as casual as you please, "I beg to differ. Care to prove me wrong?"

Shannon's eyes narrowed. He was trying to be in charge again. "Yes, I beg to differ, and I don't have any problems proving you wrong. Some women's body aren't equipped for multiples and mine is one of them."

Adam found what she'd said amusing. "You actually believe that?"

Shannon tilted her head back and stared at him without a trace of a smile anywhere on her face. "I actually know that."

"Okay, then, I'll prove you wrong after I get some work out of you."

She frowned. "What kind of work?"

"In the kitchen on the counter are the headlights to the car I'm working on downstairs. I need them cleaned with the glass cleaner that's sitting next to them."

Shannon almost told him what he could do with both his headlights and his glass cleaner, but she held her tongue. She knew this was a challenge. Although he thought he could push her over the edge again tonight, she knew that he couldn't. But she was thinking about another night in the future. The orgasms of the last time and tonight had spoiled her, and she didn't want to do anything to ruin the possibility of a three-peat. She fully intended to come back.

"And what are you going to do while I'm cleaning those headlights?"

"Take a shower."

Shannon met his gaze. "All right, but if you take too long, I'm leaving."

He let out a sensuous laugh. "You're not going anywhere. You got to prove me wrong tonight, remember." And then he went into the bathroom and closed the door behind him.

Despite her determination to maintain her cool, Shannon practically held her breath until she heard the sound of the shower going. Adam was right. All she had to do was to remember what she'd experienced with his skilled fingers to know she wasn't going anywhere. Especially when he seemed so convinced he could do the impossible. He seemed so certain of it, so downright confident in his abilities. She'd always detested men who thought they knew her better than she knew herself, and she always took pride in her ability to keep them guessing.

But not with Adam Corbain.

It was as if he were privy to her every thought and emotion, and she resented her inability to resist him. There had never been a man to walk this earth whose power of persuasion she couldn't withstand, even the son of that wealthy sheepherder in Australia who'd wanted a black woman to add to his collection of what he considered exotic harem delicacies. He'd gotten pissed that his plan of seduction hadn't worked. He hadn't gotten beyond the customary kiss on her hand.

Deciding to get started on the project Adam had left for her to do, she walked across the room to the kitchen. The place was tiny but perfect for one person. Besides, as she'd noticed early, he seemed to be a neat individual.

She was about to reach for the glass cleaner when she noticed the stack of newspapers on one end of the counter. *The Wall Street Journal.* She wondered why a mechanic would spend his money purchasing a *Wall Street Journal* every day. Umm, that was another interesting facet of Adam Corbain. But then, you didn't have to be rich to think rich or to want to be rich. At least it showed he had potential to move beyond what he was presently doing.

As she worked on the headlights, she wondered why anyone would remove the headlights from their car just to clean them. Wasn't that the reason there were car washes?

She glanced up when she heard Adam's cell phone ring and wondered if she should answer it for him. Deciding that she wouldn't, she continued wiping off the headlight. If it was a female calling, she didn't want to cause any problems—but the thought of him and someone else bothered her in a way it should not have.

But then, while they were having their affair, she had no intentions of sharing. There were too many health risks involved with that happening. That was something she intended to talk with him about after his shower.

Noiselessly, Adam leaned in the bathroom doorway and watched Shannon. She had finished wiping off the headlights and settled down at the small table to read what he guessed was today's edition of *The Wall Street Journal.* He wondered if the presence of the papers had her thinking. Probably not, since she was so surefire she knew what he did for a living. Well, he had no intentions of telling her.

When she shifted in the chair, he couldn't help noticing her attire. He shook his head. When it came to certain things, she evidently had no shame, and dressing provocatively was one of them. Here she sat in his kitchen, just as comfortable as she pleased, in lingerie that should be outlawed. The top looked like a lace white bra

but scantier, which only pushed her full, firm breasts into promi-
nence. The matching bottom was a short lace thong skirt that
showed what nice thighs she had barely covered halfway.

He frowned when he suddenly thought of something. "You
drove all the way over here wearing *that?*"

Shannon jerked her head up to find Adam standing in the bathroom doorway, shirtless and in jeans and bare feet. He had that just-
showered look that would make any woman want to moan out loud.
His features were sharp, almost like a hawk, and God, he had a body;
the kind most women would drool over. Overall the man had a sexual quality that would tempt any woman to say, *Yummy!*

"Well?"

His question reminded her that he had spoken but for the life of
her she couldn't recall what he'd said. "Well, what?"

"Did you drive over here wearing that?"

"No, I hitchhiked wearing it," she said in a voice dripping in
sarcasm.

Evidently he didn't like her response, and all of a sudden he
crossed the room and stood in front of her. He wasn't smiling. "This
is not the time to use that smart mouth of yours," he said in a low in-
tolerant voice.

"Oh? Will there be a better time?"

He muttered something incomprehensible before saying, "Just
answer the damn question."

Shannon leaned her head back to stare up at him, wondering
just what was his problem. The temperature between them had
spiked, but for another reason. He was mad, and a part of her was
surprised by that. "And what if I did?" she asked.

She watched him rub a hand down his face as if to say, *God help
me,* before turning blazing eyes back on her. "What if there had been
an accident? What if you'd gotten stopped for some reason by a cop?
What—?"

"Does it matter to you?" she snapped. He was beginning to exas-
perate her, get on her last nerve.

Before she could blink, he had shoved the newspaper she was

reading off the table onto the floor and had pulled her up out of the chair. His touch made her shiver, although she wished otherwise. She glared at him. "Just *what* is your problem?"

He slid a slow glance down her body and then said in a lethal tone, "*You* seem to be my problem."

Shannon swallowed, not knowing what to say to that. All she could do was stare at Adam as a deep feeling of urgency consumed her and she no longer wanted to see the frown etched on his face. She reached out and slowly slid her fingertips along his tense jaw and went further by tracing a long path along his full lips. The urgency inside her increased when she felt the slight quiver in him that her touch had caused. A similar tension raced down her own spine, and a warm rush flooded her most private area.

"Answer me."

Compliance was not one of her strong points, but she knew she couldn't stand firm against him much longer, especially when her knees were beginning to feel weak like this. "No, I didn't wear this over here, Adam," she finally said. "I had it on underneath my clothes. I undressed in the car before knocking on the window." A smile touched her lips, and she continued softly, "I might do some crazy and wild things every once in a while, but give me credit for having some common sense. What I have on was meant for you to see and no one else."

He continued to stand there and look at her, and then he unceremoniously pulled her into his arms and kissed her. Shannon sighed. As impossible as it should be, her body wanted him again. Right now. That had never happened to her before—not in the same night. It was as if her body wanted to take up where they last left off. There was a fire building deep within her, and she knew of only one way to put it out. She knew of only one man who could.

When he broke off the kiss, she took a step back and reached for the zipper of his jeans. Once she had his fly open and noticed the thick thatch of hair, she immediately knew that Adam wasn't wearing any underwear. She used the tip of her finger to trace a path from his chest all the way lower to his firm abdomen, noting the increased difficulty of his breathing. Earlier, he had checked out what was below her waistline, and now it was time for her to check out what was below his.

Holding his eyes with hers, she moved her hand lower and took hold of his erection. She tugged it out, glanced down, and swallowed. He was a lot bigger than she thought. He was huge, masculine, hot. Doing something she'd never done to any man, she took her fingers and explored him, the sound of his deep breathing encouraging her with every stroke.

"Shannon," he said in a low, husky, warning voice. She heard the effort it took for him to speak, so she increased her strokes. "You're asking for trouble," he cautioned through clenched teeth.

"Trouble? Is that what you call this?" she asked, tightening her hand more firmly on him and meeting his gaze again. "Then yes, I'm asking for trouble. I want trouble. Now!"

Before she could take her next breath, he swept her into his arms and crossed the room to the bed. Within seconds she was on her back with her legs parted and raised high on his shoulders. He covered her body with his and within seconds was mere inches from entering her when he stopped and looked down at her.

"Birth control. I got condoms," he said, about to pull away.

Her legs locked around him. "I'm on the pill, and if you're worried about health reasons, I'm safe."

"Good. So am I," he said, and the thought of nothing between them while they made love sent a tremor through him.

"All right, then. If you're safe and I'm safe and I'm on the pill, let's get into trouble."

He gazed down at her. "You sure?"

"I wouldn't be here if I weren't, Adam."

There was something about how she'd said his name that pushed him over the edge and likewise, he slowly pushed into her, feeling how her body stretched to accommodate him, skin to skin. And then he formulated the perfect rhythm for them, giving his thrusts just the right beat, closeness, and impact. He threw his head back. He hadn't planned for this, he hadn't wanted this, but now that he was getting it, he wanted to keep getting it.

He'd never felt this way while inside a woman before. He was giving an all-out sensual assault on her body, claiming it in a way he had never claimed a woman's body before. His thighs strained with every thrust, the firmness of his stomach connected with hers, and he felt himself growing even bigger each time she clenched her muscles to keep him in.

He was losing his battle with control, and at the moment he didn't give a damn. The only thing he cared about was how Shannon was making him feel, and when he felt her inner muscles grip him tighter before her body detonated in one hell of an orgasm, he threw his head back again stretching the veins in his neck as an explosion the likes of which he'd never felt before ripped through him. He called her name as he flooded her insides with his essence, all the way to her womb. And dammit, he liked the feeling of coming apart that way within her.

Later he would get his head screwed back on straight, but for now he was willing to take everything Shannon Carmichael was giving him. And he greedily did so.

"I *thought you* couldn't come more than once a night."

Shannon lay there, not wanting to open her eyes, thinking she didn't have the strength to do so but knowing she had to. And when she did, she looked into Adam's face, looming over her with a smug look on it. And there was a hint of satisfied sex in the dark depths of his eyes.

"Tonight was a fluke," she said, wondering if she would ever be able to walk again. Not only had she come once again but two *more* times after that. Incredible. His desire for her, like her desire, for him had reached a level that was nothing short of madness.

A smile touched the corners of his lips. "It wasn't a fluke. Admit it. We're just good together."

"Think what you want."

"And I will." He settled back in bed and pulled her closer to him. "Do you need to make a phone call?"

She glanced over at him. "To who?"

"Those ladies you're here with this summer. I wouldn't want them worrying about you."

That's considerate of him, she thought. "I left them a note," she replied. "They know where I am and who I'm with, and I've already told them not to worry if I stayed all night. My overnight bag is out in the car."

Adam frowned and pulled himself up in bed. He looked down at her. "You were that sure of me?"

She couldn't help but smile. "No, Mr. Corbain, I was that sure of me. I refused to let you reject me a second time. I intended to lay it on strong tonight. If you didn't do what I wanted, then I knew what I figured was the truth."

He cocked his head. "Which was?"

"That you're not into women."

He snorted with laughter at the absurdness of that. "And what's your verdict now?"

"That you're all into me, and since I am a woman, then you're definitely straight."

"Umm, but maybe I need to prove it again just in case you have any lingering doubts."

And then he was kissing her with an intensity she felt all the way to her toes, and for the first time in her life, Shannon let herself be completely seduced by a man.

15

"*I enjoyed spending* time with you again today, Zach."

"So did I." There was murky moonlight overhead, but nothing could dim Anna's beauty, Zach thought. When he first met her, it had been her eyes, dark and slanted, that captured his attention, but now everything about her was captivating.

"I know it's late, but you're welcome to come in for coffee if you'd like."

Zach thought a moment on her invitation. It was late; almost two in the morning. But he wasn't ready to part company with her yet. All he had to look forward to when he returned to his hotel was a lonely room that would be filled with thoughts of her.

"Are you sure you're up for company at this hour? You've had a full day."

She smiled. "When we're shorthanded at work, I'm known to pull doubles, so yes, I'm fine."

"All right, then." When she opened the door, he followed her in and closed it behind him. Zach glanced around. Her home suited her—just the right mixture of American and Asian flair.

"I'll be back. I'm going into the kitchen to get the coffee started."

"Okay."

He watched her walk off. She had the sexiest walk of any woman he knew. Sighing in deep appreciation, he crossed the room to look at the pictures she had on the fireplace mantel. There was one of the two of them together. It had been taken that first night he'd delivered her to the family, at his father's sixtieth birthday party. Then there was another one of them together, that one taken last summer on the Glendale Shores Fourth of July celebration. He had taken her out in his boat, and when they returned, Noelle snapped their picture. Then there was a third. The one of them together at his father's retirement party from the Senate. She had been his date that night, and before the evening had ended, he admitted to himself that he had fallen in love with her.

There were other framed photographs: a family photo of Trey, Haywood, and Quad; one of his parents; her uncle Randolph and his wife, Jenna; her grandparents; and a glamour shot of Randi, her youngest first cousin, and Randolph and Jenna's daughter. There was also a group photo that included Noelle and her former fiancé, Donald Hollis. The two called off their engagement two months ago, and Noelle wasn't saying why.

He studied the framed photos of him and Anna together, thinking there were three of them compared with only one of everyone elses. Was that some sort of statement? Was there a chance that she cared for him like he cared for her?

Zach shook his head. All the times they'd been together, she'd never given him a reason to think such a thing, but then he'd never given her a reason to think anything either. What if—?

"Here we are."

He turned around. Anna had reentered the room, carrying a tray with a coffeepot and two cups, and she was wearing a smile as bright as the sun had been that day.

He left the fireplace and crossed the room, and instead of sitting across from her in another chair, he joined her on the sofa when she sat down. He watched her pour the coffee, thinking that like everything else about her, her hands were beautiful.

"Thanks," he said, taking the cup she offered him. He leaned back on the sofa. "So, when do you want to leave for Glendale Shores?"

She shrugged her gorgeous shoulders. "When do you think we

should leave? Tomorrow is Friday, and I understand everyone will start arriving Monday. Do you want to wait until then or do you want to go early?"

Zach knew the answer to that. He'd already talked with the family. No one would be arriving before Monday, which meant if he and Anna left sometime tomorrow or Saturday, that would give them a few days on the private island alone. He had gotten his parents' and her uncle's blessings on what his intentions were—and he knew her grandparents would freely give their blessings as well. But there was one other person whose blessings he couldn't dismiss, and that person was her grandmother, Mattie Denison. Although Mattie was deceased, Trey was convinced his great-grandmother had been instrumental in getting him and Haywood together by forcing them to be on the island alone for a few days to carry out the terms of her will.

Born a Gullah with what some would term a sixth sense, more than once, Mattie Denison had made her presence on the island felt to members of the family. Some had even gone so far as to swear to a Gramma Mattie sighting. He didn't believe 100 percent in the supernatural, but he'd been around Gramma Mattie enough times to know she had possessed powers that defied logic. He also knew that she had loved Anna, the great-granddaughter she'd died before seeing, and that Mattie would want what was best for her.

"If it won't cause you any inconvenience, let's leave around noon tomorrow."

She peered at him over her coffee cup. "Tomorrow?"

"Yes. That way we can get some boating time in before the others arrive. And there's that painting of you I want to finish." In his spare time, he enjoyed dabbling in art, his second love. It would not have surprised his family one bit had he chosen a career as an artist instead of an attorney. With Anna as his model, he had begun painting a portrait to add to the others that hung on the Glendale Shores Wall of Honor, located in the foyer of the main house.

"Oh, that's right," she said softly, after taking a sip of coffee. "I had forgotten about that portrait you were doing."

He nodded. "Going early will give me a chance to finish it."

"Then we should," she said, smiling. "It won't take me long to pack."

Tomorrow, Anna figured, she could get up early and pack for the trip. The thought of spending a few days on the island alone with Zach sent sensual shivers down her back.

At that moment, her phone rang, and Zach glanced over at her. "You're on call?" he asked, wondering who would be calling her this late.

She shook her head. "No, but still, I'll let the machine answer it."

He watched her face when a male voice came on the line and floated over the room. "Anna, this is Todd. Give me a call when you can. We need to talk."

Jealousy reared its ugly green head inside Zach. Todd Langley was the man Anna was supposed to marry, the same man who called off the wedding two weeks before it was to take place because his parents couldn't get beyond the fact that his bride was half Vietnamese.

"You and Todd Langley are talking again?" he asked, although he really didn't want to know—especially if they were.

He watched her draw in a deep breath. "As far as I'm concerned, no, we aren't talking. I hadn't heard from Todd in almost a year, and then after it made news that I'm the niece of Randolph Fuller and the goddaughter of Senator Noah Wainwright, it seems that I've suddenly become acceptable to Todd's family, and he's suggested that we talk again to discuss the possibility of us getting back together."

Zach tightened his hand on the cup's handle as he studied the dark, murky liquid inside for a moment before raising his head. He asked Anna, "And is there that possibility?"

A frown appeared on her face before she shook her head. "No. None whatsoever. I have more pride in myself than that. If he couldn't stand up to his family for me as my fiancé, then I certainly don't want him to be a part of my life now or ever."

Zach let out a relieved sigh. He intended to make sure Todd Langley was never a part of Anna's life. He slowly stood. "Thanks for the coffee, but I think you need to get some rest. I'll come get you around noon."

"All right."

"Come walk me to the door." Zach surprised Anna by taking her hand in his. When they reached the door, he surprised her even further when he leaned over and brushed a kiss across her lips. "Good night, Anna."

She blinked, in a daze. "Good night, Zach."

When the door closed, the thought that immediately consumed Anna's mind was that Zach had never kissed her on the lips before.

16

"*Shannon didn't come* home last night."

Faith glanced at Monique over the rim of her coffee cup. She heard the panicked tone of her friend's voice and noted the worried look on her face. "Yes, I know. I told you last night she left a note on the fridge saying a possibility existed that she wouldn't."

"Yes, but I didn't take that note seriously. I can't believe she did that. Shannon really don't know this guy."

A smile curved Faith's lips. "Trust me, knowing Shannon, she's getting firsthand knowledge of everything she needs to know."

Monique dropped in the chair across from Faith after glancing toward the clock. She didn't have to meet Lyle for another thirty minutes for their morning jog. "And you find her behavior amusing? I can't believe you aren't worried."

Faith shook her head. "Shannon is a thirty-three-year-old woman who knows the score, Monique. The last thing she needs is for us to start acting like her mother."

"I know, but—"

"No, buts," Faith interrupted. "And although we haven't met this guy, I have it on good authority that he's okay and is probably what she needs."

Monique leaned back in the chair. "Really? Did you talk to someone who knows him?"

"Not exactly."

Monique leaned forward. "So what exactly? Our best friend spends the night with a total stranger and you're fine with it?"

"No, but like I said, someone told me not to worry."

A frustrated frown appeared on Monique's face. "Who is this someone?"

"You won't believe me when I tell you."

Monique crossed her arms over her chest. Her patience was wearing thin. "Try me."

Faith didn't say anything for a moment, then she said, "Cely. Cely said it's okay."

Monique took a moment to think about what Faith said before asking, "Cely? Our Cely?"

Faith nodded. "Yes, and I know it sounds crazy, but it was the weirdest thing. I was standing here in the middle of the kitchen and had pulled Shannon's note off the fridge and then went into a state of panic—the same way you did when you discovered she hadn't come in last night. Anyway, I could actually feel my blood pressure rising to my head when I could have sworn that I heard Cely, in that calming voice of hers telling me it was okay, to leave Shannon alone and that she would be fine."

Monique waved her words away. "You were imagining things. And you did say you had a little too much wine at lunch yesterday."

"Yes, and you're probably right, but still I was left with this feeling that Shannon has finally met her match, but not in a bad way."

"With the guy who's a mechanic?"

Faith met Monique's befuddled stare and nodded again. "Yes, with him."

"Your friend Faith is right, Nicky. Shannon's a grown woman who's responsible for her own actions."

Monique was standing at the window in Lyle's condo looking

out at the beauty of the early morning sunrise. Out of the corner of her eye she could see him removing his T-shirt, and she couldn't help but breathe in a sigh of female appreciation. This morning they had run a little longer than their usual hour. Unlike the previous mornings, today a cool mist had covered the beach, making running that much more exhilarating. Neither had wanted to stop.

Lucky for her that she had taken him up on his standing offer for her to use his shower, so she had come prepared. She had taken her shower, and he was about to take his.

"I know that, Lyle," she said turning around—against her will—then wishing that she hadn't. He had stripped down to his running shorts, and his body was as solid as any male body could be. A luscious flutter went off in her stomach and, beneath her scoop-neck tank top, her breasts began to feel achy, her nipples straining the lace material of her bra.

"If I recall, Shannon was the youngest of the four of you, right?"

Monique nodded. "Yes, a year younger, and she was always the most outrageous and nothing has changed."

"Well, like I said, I wouldn't worry about it too much." He crossed the room and took her hand in his. "She's a big girl."

Monique's breasts came to life when Lyle touched her hand. She summoned all the control she could muster to say, "I know you're right. I guess I'm nothing but a worrywart."

He smiled. "And a pretty one at that. Give me a few minutes for my shower, and I'll be ready to go."

"All right." They had decided to go out to breakfast at a restaurant not far away.

"And how about dinner this evening?" he said, stepping a little closer. "I need to go somewhere to celebrate the start of the weekend. And speaking of weekends, do you have anything planned?"

Her legs were trembling from his closeness, and she tried to keep her eyes from locking onto his bare chest. What on earth was wrong with her? This was her friend Lyle, for heaven's sake! She cleared her voice and said, "Dinner tonight would be nice, and so far I don't have plans for the weekend, but I'd like to check with Faith

and Shannon first to make sure they haven't made plans I don't
know about yet."

"Fair enough. And I thought we could drive over to Beaufort
and take a tour on Saturday, check into a hotel, and stay until Sunday. Hilton Head is nice, but I'm beginning to get island fever."

Check into a hotel . . . Monique could only assume he meant
with separate rooms. *Of course he does. He wouldn't mean anything
else,* she thought to herself. "A weekend in Beaufort sounds wonderful, and I'll let you know at dinner if I'll be able to make the trip with
you."

"All right. I'll be back in a minute. Make yourself at home."

The moment she heard the bathroom door close behind him,
she let out a deep sigh. Lyle was pushing some buttons that she had
deactivated years ago. She needed to talk to somebody and wished
Cely was there. God, she missed her friend and felt the familiar loss
come over her. She turned back to the window and the warm, light
shining through it was a welcoming sign for another beautiful day.
She wouldn't ruin it by worrying about her intense attraction to a
certain man.

"I like your new shoes."

Faith smiled as she glanced up at Shane. "They aren't as cute as
the ones I had on yesterday."

"No," he agreed. "But much more practical. Ready for lesson
number two?"

"Yes."

For the next hour or so, Shane went into training mode, and
Faith was once again amazed at what a serious instructor he was. Today he had tossed her a few balls so she could get used to the movement of her feet. By the time her lesson was over, she was glad she
had taken his advice on the shoes.

"You did a good job today, Faith."

She smiled, pleased with his compliment. "Thanks, and you're a
great teacher. How did you start playing tennis?"

He grinned. "As a teen, I used to practically live at the park near my home. My mom worked during the day, so we got involved in a lot of the summer programs there. There was this one counselor who'd always wanted to become a tennis player but didn't. So he spent his time showing anyone interested how to play. I was one of those interested."

She nodded. They had reached the clubhouse lobby, and then Shane turned to her. "How about lunch again today?"

Faith drew in a deep breath. Having lunch with him again today might not be a smart idea. "Mmm, thanks, but I'm not all that hungry. What I'd like to do is spend a day on the beach. With today being Friday, chances are the beach will be real crowded tomorrow."

"You're probably right about the crowds. I have an idea."

She raised a brow. "What?"

"My place."

"Your place?"

"Yes, a summer home I purchased earlier this year on a private beach. And it's really quite nice."

Faith could just imagine it was, but still . . . "I'm not sure that's a good idea, Shane."

His eyes held hers. "Why? Don't you trust me yet?"

She had to smile. "Technically, we just met."

"Yes, and more than just technically, I'm trying for us to get to know each other."

"Why?"

"I think that would be obvious, Faith." The look in his dark eyes pretty much said it all. He was man, she was woman, and he felt the chemistry just as she had.

"I didn't come to Hilton Head for an affair," she said as affably as she could.

"Neither did I. And I don't recall asking you to engage in an affair with me, Faith."

She actually had to blush at that. He had definitely put her in her place. "I know that, but—"

"But what? What are you afraid of? I hope it's not me. Is it getting into another relationship after your divorce?"

Faith could hardly believe that such a question had come out of Shane's mouth. She'd mentioned her divorce to him over lunch yesterday. What on earth gave him the idea that she was afraid of putting her heart on the line again? "That's not it," she said brusquely. "I've dated a number of times since my divorce."

"Oh," he said. "Then that could only mean you're questioning my motives as well as my character for some reason."

Faith shook her head. His motives and character had nothing to do with it. It was all that sex appeal. The man was practically oozing it, and she didn't know quite how to deal with it.

"I promise I won't bite."

Faith couldn't help but smile. "You promise?"

"Scout's honor."

She exhaled shakily. Monique had made plans to go shopping after having breakfast with Lyle, and there was no telling when they would hear from Shannon today. The thought of spending the day on a private beach had merit. "Well, as long as you promise not to bite," she said as another smile touched her lips, "then I guess you're safe."

Faith then found herself wondering which of them she was really trying to convince.

"Ready for that swim?"

Faith turned to the sound of Shane's voice and had to clear her throat to speak. "Yes, I'm ready."

He had changed into swimming trucks that left very little to the imagination. He was the perfect male in the body department. She had seen him in denim, khaki, and cotton. Now seeing him shirtless in a pair of short nylon trunks only added to his masculine perfection.

To get her pulse back to normal, she turned and glanced back out the window. "You could have told me what you have here isn't just a house on a private beach. It's paradise," she said softly.

What he hadn't told her was that in addition to a great view of the ocean, it also had a beautiful winding lagoon embraced by lush foliage and numerous tropical plants. And from where she was standing at the huge floor-to-ceiling window in his living room, what she saw left her breathless. But then all she had to do was turn around and admire the spacious house and beautiful furniture to know that the beautifully restored older home was the most pictur-esque place she'd ever seen.

She felt the heat of him even before he came to stand directly be-hind her. She tried quashing the warmth flooding her entire body.

"I thought that the first time I saw it myself. I was fourteen, and my brothers and I had formed this yard service over the summer. The older couple who used to own the house was one of our first clients here on the island." He chuckled. "I think we stood there a full half hour with our mouths open, we were that much in awe. My mom had dropped us off that morning and made the trip back for us that afternoon, and I remember telling her that first day that one day this house would be mine. I clearly remember her looking at me and saying, 'If you can conceive it, Shane, then you can achieve it.'"

Faith turned slightly and took a deep breath. He was standing closer to her. If she turned completely around, their bodies would connect. "And you did achieve it," she said, quickly turning back to the window. "I could stand at this window all day and look out."

"Yes, but then you wouldn't get any swimming in, and you're only allowing yourself two hours to stay here—so let's go," he said, gently taking her arm.

As he led her across the living room and out through a pair of French doors, she had to concede that she was more than mildly sur-prised she was there at all. As she'd told him earlier, technically they were still strangers. Oh, she knew what he'd shared with her that day at lunch and she doubted very seriously that he was an ax-murderer or anything like that, but still, she'd always made it a point to get to thoroughly know the men who asked her out. And although, as Cely would often tell her, you will never, ever know everything because men often had secrets just like women, because of Virgil she'd developed a tendency to be overly cautious. She doubted she could handle another heartbreak.

"Shouldn't I change into my suit first?" she asked him when their bare feet left the last porch step to sink into the beach sand.

He glanced over at her. "You did say you were wearing your swimsuit under that sundress, right?"

"Yes?" She had pulled on a short cotton sundress over the swimsuit, thinking it was more appropriate than the knitted crocheted robe she usually wore.

"Then all you have to do is not be shy and take your clothes off in front of me." He smiled over at her in a way that gave her the impression he was teasing and dead serious all at the same time. An unwelcome shiver raced through her gut, and she noticed his hands were still holding hers. They were strong hands that felt dependable, trustworthy, and capable of bringing whatever pleasure a woman wanted.

Her pulse leaped at the thought.

"So you did hear from your friend?"

"Yes." She hadn't told him the full story, that Shannon hadn't come home last night. It wasn't any of his business. What she had told him was that she was expecting a call from Shannon.

Shannon had called from her cell phone, and the only thing she said was that she was on her way home. Faith couldn't wait until the three of them were together later so they could talk. Although she and Monique never divulged the intimate details of any relationships they were involved in, Shannon was always colorful with information when it came to hers.

"Last one in the water has to cook dinner for the other one tomorrow night."

Shane's statement reclaimed Faith's attention only in time enough to see him head toward the beach. "Not fair!" she screamed. She had to take her dress off first, and he damn well knew it. She quickly pulled the dress over her head and tossed it aside and took off after him, wondering why she bothered, when he was bound to hit the water first. Besides, who said anything about the two of them being together at any time tomorrow for either of them to cook for the other?

"You lose," he said grinning broadly by the time she made it to the water. Okay, she would admit that she was a sore loser. She frowned over at him, trying not to notice how his nylon trunks were clinging to his wet body.

"Nice swimsuit."

"Thanks." She had decided on a floral one-piece, and there was nothing overly sexy or provocative about it. But from the way he was staring at her, she wasn't so sure of that anymore.

"I meant what I said the other day about your legs. You have such a gorgeous pair."

"Thanks again." His fascination with her legs didn't bother her, since he wouldn't be the first man who'd been taken with them. To Virgil they had been just an ordinary pair of legs. She should have suspected something then.

"And as far as I'm concerned, there was no contest," she said, getting into the water. "So don't expect a cooked dinner from me tomorrow."

He smiled. "I'm disappointed."

"You seem to be the type capable of handling disappointments, Mr. Masters."

"And what about you, Faith Gilmore? Can you handle disappointments?"

She thought of all those she'd endured in her lifetime, especially her marriage. "Yes, I've been known to handle a few and still come out kicking. I learned a long time ago to roll with the punches and not to take some things personal. Life is life, and it can't always be a bed of roses. Besides," she said, glancing over at him, "my grandmother would always say that if there's never any rain in your life, then you won't have any reason to appreciate the sunshine."

"Sounds like your grandmother was a very smart woman."

"She was," Faith said, immediately feeling the pang of loss she always felt whenever she thought of her. "I used to wonder if she was my father's real mother or if he'd been adopted. He was always so serious, and I don't think Nana had a serious bone in her body—at least not around me. She made all my visits to her house an adventure."

She glanced over at him, grateful that his body was emerged in water. "What about your grandparents?"

"My maternal grandparents died quite awhile back, but my paternal grandparents are still alive and kicking—and when I say kicking, I mean that literally. My grandmother is on her third husband, and my grandfather is on his fourth wife, with rumors floating around he's already looking for the fifth. I also heard he wants a woman in her fifties this time around."

Faith's eyebrows shot up. "How old is this guy?"

Shane smiled. "He will be eighty-four his next birthday, and so far he's fathered over twenty-five kids from all four marriages."

"He's lived a busy life."

"And a very potent one. He believes in keeping the Masters line growing."

"Evidently."

"What about you? Do you want kids someday?"

Faith sighed. Now that was a dreaded question. If he knew how much she wanted a child, he would probably be surprised. Not to have a child had been Virgil's idea and not hers. He kept putting her off by saying they weren't ready.

Deciding to give him an answer, a honest answer, she said, "Yes, I want kids, and I intend to be a good mother." She quickly added, "Not that my own mother wasn't, but I just want to be a different mother." And that was all she intended to say on the matter. "What about you? Would you want to be a father one day?"

His face was firmly set in deep thought when he answered, "Yes, but I'm forty now, so if I wait too much longer, I'll be attending my kid's high school graduation in a wheelchair. That might have been fine for Grampa Masters, but not for me. So, I guess you can say the next few years will determine if I ever become a daddy or not."

"Then I wish you the best."

"And I do the same for you, Faith."

They ended the conversation on that note and started swimming, making sure they stayed in the not-so-deep section. From the time her parents had begun bringing her to Hilton Head years ago, she'd loved it, even those days she had to sit on the sidelines and watch others in the water because she hadn't been allowed to go in— all because of her asthma.

"Let me see how good a swimmer you are," Shane said, interrupting her thoughts. "I'll race you over to that boat dock."

She followed his line of vision and thought, *Good grief, he's asking for a lot.* "I told you I only started swimming a few years ago, and you can't get to the pools often in Minnesota."

"Then this will be great practice for you," he said. "I'll even be kind and generous and give you a head start."

"Then you're on!" Before he could bat an eye, she'd taken off, refusing to look back. And to her disappointment, it didn't take him long to catch up with her. His solid, muscled body swam past her with ease.

"Show-off," she said, smiling into his eyes when she reached the finish line, where he was already waiting.

"Sore loser," he countered. He then took her hand in his as he led her out of the water. "Come on, let's go take a shower."

When she stopped walking, he glanced over at her, read her mind, and grinned. "Separately, of course."

A few moments passed without conversation, then he said, "You know, you need to stop being so cautious." His eyes said he was teasing her, but the expression on his face said he was serious.

"Wasn't it just yesterday you were complimenting me for being cautious?" she said, steadily taking the steps.

"I complimented you on being just cautious, not *so* cautious. You're going to have to start trusting me sometime."

"Do I?"

"Yes."

It was on the tip of her tongue to tell him that wasn't the way she particularly saw things. The simple truth according to Faith Gilmore's world was that trust shouldn't come easily. She could date a man without trusting him completely, which meant she would always be on her guard. She doubted that she would ever fully trust another red-blooded man with her heart again, and with good reason.

Instead of telling him that, though, she said, "Trust has to be earned."

He stopped walking now. "Then will you let that happen, Faith? Will you give me a chance to prove that I can be trusted?" he asked, his voice, deep, low, and serious.

Faith ignored the quick little sensation that suddenly pulled at her heart. Maybe it was the air they were breathing. Maybe it was the aftereffects of an afternoon spent in each other's company. What-ever it was had her ready to say yes, to tell him he deserved a chance.

Almost.

She knew just how painful a broken heart could be, and that it rendered a person helpless and vulnerable. Trying to keep her voice calm, she tilted her head, forced a smile, and said only, "Be careful of what you ask for, Shane Masters."

She saw that gleam of interest suddenly revive in his eyes. "When it comes to being careful, I know the score."

She nodded, and for some reason she believed him.

17

"*Are you sure* you're okay, Shannon?" Faith asked, eyeing her friend over her box of Chinese food. When she had returned from Shane's place, she had found Shannon taking a nap. Then later, when Monique had arrived and Shannon had woken up and got into the Chinese food Faith had ordered, she hadn't had much to say. In respect for her privacy, they hadn't pushed the issue.

"Yes, I'm fine." Shannon looked at both Faith and Monique and fell into silence, keeping her gaze glued to her box of shrimp fried rice.

Monique shifted uneasily beside Faith on the sofa. Something was wrong and they both knew it. After a few more minutes, she couldn't take a nontalkative Shannon and finally jumped from her seat. "Okay, Shannon, that does it! What did that man do to you?"

Shannon glanced up at Monique. "I beg your pardon?"

"Don't beg me anything," Monique snapped, worried about her friend. "I want to know what he did to you. He hurt you, didn't he? He was too rough. Forceful. A brute."

She began pacing the floor and continued her tirade. "I tried to talk you out of going after this guy, and when Faith told me you had planned to spend the night—with a guy you didn't even know—I knew that meant trouble."

She came to a stop in front of Shannon's chair. "You're hurting. I can feel it. Tell us what happened so we can get you through this. What did he do to you?"

Shannon fought a smile as she placed her box of food aside. Okay she was hurting, mostly sore in a place she'd rather not mention. And she would admit she'd been rather quiet since returning from spending the night with Adam, but there was a valid reason for it. He had stripped her of her safety net, and she wasn't sure how to get it back. She'd never felt this vulnerable with a man before in her life.

Knowing her best friends were waiting on an answer, she sighed deeply and met their concerned gazes. "The only thing he did to me," she began. "Or perhaps I should say the only thing we did to each other was almost screw each other's brains out for more than eighteen or so hours."

Ignoring Monique's openmouthed shock, she added, "And all I can say is that no toy—make, brand, or model—can compete with the real thing when it belongs to Adam Corbain." And as if her statement was not outlandish in the least, she picked up her food and began eating again.

A half hour later Shannon entered her bedroom and closed the door. It was early afternoon yet she felt tired. She was exhausted. She was so sexually satisfied, it was a doggone shame. And she remembered it all perfectly. Every hot-tamale detail. All she had to do was close her eyes to recall each and every thrust, every tongue-licking sensation. When it had come to positions, neither she nor Adam had had preferences. They believed in equal rights and were as unconventional as any two people could get.

All he'd had to do was look at her in that area and her legs would automatically come open. She should feel like a hussy, but all she felt was the epitome of a sexually fulfilled woman. A woman who had definitely gotten what she'd wanted.

And with that came a floodgate of problems—most of which she didn't want to dwell on tonight. At least Faith and Monique had had the decency not to question her any further, and she hadn't wanted to talk about it. What she and Adam had shared was private, special, and meaningful. Well, as meaningful as hard sex could get.

And that, she had to constantly remind herself, was all that it was. He had the stamina of a damn bull, and she had gone along for the ride—and what a ride it had been. He had turned her slow-moving flame into a full-fledged fire, soaring her to a level she'd never been taken before.

She sighed and stripped off her clothes. She would definitely be paying Adam Corbain a few more visits before putting an end to their affair.

"You still aren't worried about Shannon and that Corbain guy?"

Faith cast a glance over her shoulder when Monique, who was dressed for her date with Lyle, stepped out on the patio. Faith had been practicing the swings Shane had gone over with her that day. She could easily tell Monique was still bothered by what Shannon had said earlier, and placing her tennis racket aside, she met Monique's worried expression. "No, I'm still not worried. Concerned but not exactly worried. She's always been the most sexually active of all of us—you know that."

"Yes, but—"

"But nothing, Monique. Shannon is a grown woman. It's her heart she's been guarding all these years, and we both know why. Leave her alone. She's evidently dealing with a midlife crisis at thirty-three. As always we'll be here when she wants to talk. Otherwise, we keep quiet and listen. No advice. No reprimands. And," she added pointedly, "no judging."

"Besides," Faith said moments later, amused, "I don't think I've ever gotten my brains screwed out. I wonder how it's done and, more importantly, how it feels."

Monique placed her hand over her mouth to keep from laughing out loud. "Well, don't expect me to be able to tell you. Things with me and Paul were standard but always good. I prefer the easygoing, nothing wild and crazy."

Then, deciding that she couldn't hold it in any longer, that she desperately needed to talk to someone, she said, "But at this point, I'll take it anyway I can get it. It's been so long for me."

Faith glanced over at her. "Just how long has it been?"

Emotion gripped Monique's throat when she responded. "Three years. Not since Paul."

For some reason Monique had known Faith wouldn't look at her like she'd lost her mind or something. She would think that Monique's sex life and what she did or didn't do with it was her business and no one else's. Monique truly appreciated her friend for that.

What Faith did do was tilt her head ever so slightly and ask softly, "Do you think Paul would want you to deny that of yourself?"

Monique shook her head. "No. Paul was the most unselfish man I knew. He would want me to move on with my life and to find someone who would make me happy. I've dated several times since his death, but I've never felt that connection or attraction to any man to want to go any further than a good-night kiss at the door. At least not until I ran into Lyle."

Faith's lips quirked in a smile. "So Dr. Lyle Montgomery turns you on, does he?"

"Like nobody's business, but I don't want to ruin our friendship."

"You trust him," Faith said, as if reminding her of that. "How could it ruin your friendship?"

Monique shrugged. "It just might if sex is added to the mix. I'm nothing more than Arnie's sister to him. He's nice, mannerly, respectful, and kind. If I were to come on to him, what would he think?"

"Probably what he's already thinking. That you're a very desirable woman. And who says your friendship can't move beyond that? He's single and so are you."

"Yes, but—"

"But nothing, Monique. You worry too much."

Monique smiled. "I probably do." She then said, "He invited me to go with him to Beaufort for the weekend."

"Are you?"

Monique's stomach fluttered at the thought. "You think I should?"

"Why wouldn't you go? You know him. He's evidently a nice guy. And we're here to have fun, enjoy life, and not cater to anyone's expectations of us. Remember, that's Cely's orders. There's no reason for you not to go to Beaufort with Lyle for the weekend and enjoy yourself. And it might give you an opportunity to let him know that you want to escalate your friendship to another level, if that's what you really want to do."

Monique pursed her lips. "What about you?"

Faith raised a brow. "And what about me?"

"You and your tennis instructor. You like him. I hear it in your voice whenever you mention him. He sounds like a nice guy."

Faith reached over to pick her racket back up. "He is a nice guy and he's been teaching me a lot." *And probably would teach me a lot more if I gave him the chance.*

"Well, you might want to take your own advice: have fun, enjoy life, and not cater to anyone's expectations." Monique glanced down at her watch. "I better get my purse. Lyle should be here any minute."

When Monique turned to leave, Faith called out to her. "Monique?"

"Yes?"

"About the trip to Beaufort with Lyle for the weekend. You are going, right?"

Monique nodded as a smile touched her lips. "Yes, I'm going." As she breezed back through the house and toward her bedroom to get her purse, she felt good about telling Lyle she would be spending the weekend with him in Beaufort.

18

"*I gather your* friend returned home okay."

"She's back and okay," Monique answered Lyle as he opened the car door and she slipped inside onto the soft leather seat. "I guess I was worrying for nothing."

"She's your friend, so your worrying was for something," Lyle said before closing the door. "True friendship is hard to find these days and should be cherished."

After buckling her seat belt, Monique sat back comfortably and watched while he walked around the front of the car to get in. "There's a place called Stellini that I think you'd like. Italian foods are still your favorite?" He started the engine.

She smiled, surprised he remembered. "Yes."

"Then I think you'll be pleased."

"Thank you." It was on the tip of her tongue to add that she would be pleased going anywhere with him, but instead she merely sat there, staring straight ahead, trying not to glance over at him. When he had arrived to pick her up and she had opened the door, it had taken everything she had to hold back her groan. He looked so good in his white shirt and dark trousers. Lyle was 100 percent male—and then some.

"I got a call from my brother Lance before I left my place to pick you up. He had good news to share with me," Lyle said, glancing over at her when he brought the car to a traffic light. He smiled. "He and Asia are going to have a baby."

"Oh, Lyle, that's wonderful! Congrats on your pending uncle-hood. You're going to love it."

He chuckled. "Will I?"

"Yes, I think you will. I also think that you're going to make a wonderful uncle."

"What about you, sweetheart? Do you like being an aunt? Arnie has three kids, right?"

Monique tried to ignore the shiver that flowed through her body with his term of endearment. He probably hadn't realized he'd made it, but she definitely had. "Yes, he has three, and I enjoy being an aunt. I don't get to see my nieces and nephew as much as I like, but I'll have more time on my hands for a while, so I'll be able to visit them."

"Why's that?"

She glanced over at him, glad his eyes were on the road. "Because technically, I'm presently unemployed. My job downsized a couple of months ago, and I was one of the casualties."

"Sorry to hear that. Major corporations seem to be doing a lot of that these days."

She tucked a strand of hair behind her ear. "Yes, and after six-teen years with them, I tried not to take it personal—but that was hard to do."

"I can imagine. So what are your plans?"

"Don't have any concrete ones just yet. I'm going to take my time before going back into the job market. Who knows, I might de-cide on a whole new career since my bachelor's degree is in Business Administration. I'm even thinking about going back to school and getting my MBA. I'm not in a rush to make any decisions. My sever-ance package was a rather good one, so I'm okay for a while." It was then that she noticed they had arrived at the restaurant.

He pulled into the parking space, cut off the ignition, un-snapped his seat belt, and turned toward her. His gaze was soft, ten-der, and considerate. "But if you were to ever need anything, you would let me know, right?"

Probably not, she thought. Chances were she wouldn't even let

Arnie know. He wouldn't hesitate to come to her aid if she needed him, but he had his own life and family now to worry about. Besides, she'd become self-reliant and independent since Paul's death. Other than Cely, Faith, and Shannon, she hadn't had anyone to confide in during those times she needed to talk to someone. Her father was there if she needed him, but there were some things you just didn't share with your dad. Besides, it was time to see to his needs and not vice versa.

"Nicky?"

It was then that she realized Lyle was waiting for her response. "Yes, I'd let you know," she lied.

The smile that touched his lips was instantaneous and intimate. And the warmth she saw in his gaze touched her deeply. "Good. And I'm going to hold you to it."

"All right."

"Now what about tomorrow? Have you given any thought to spending the weekend with me in Beaufort?"

Her tongue nervously darted out of her mouth to lick her top lip. She knew he really wasn't asking her to spend the weekend with him, at least not in the intimate sense. But still, hearing him state it that way was increasing her pulse rate.

She cleared her throat. "Yes, if the invitation is still out there, I'd love to go to Beaufort with you."

A grin quirked the corners of his mouth. "The invitation is definitely still out there, and I guarantee that the two of us will enjoy ourselves and have plenty of fun."

Monique nodded and released her seat belt. She didn't doubt him.

19

"*Now that we've* unpacked, what's the first thing you want to do?"

Anna glanced around and met Zach's gaze. If she really had a choice, she would boldly walk up to him and give him the kiss she'd been dreaming about giving him for almost a year. But she didn't have a choice . . . and she really wasn't that bold.

They had arrived on Glendale Shores a few hours ago. It hadn't taken long for them to unpack after they had gone walking and taken a tour of the island. It was beautiful, scenic, a lush paradise, the perfect place just to get away. Although she lived within thirty minutes by ferry, she'd never thought of crossing the waterways to visit the island alone.

"I guess we should concentrate on dinner," she said, deciding that kind of chore sounded safest. Besides, they had to eat sometime. They had gotten a late start from Hilton Head, since they had made a quick stop at a grocery store. One thing was for certain, they didn't intend to starve to death.

She watched him nod, flashing her one of those endearing smiles that made her want to love him forever, even if he never loved her back. "Hey, you'll never get an argument from a man when it comes to food," he said. "We live to eat."

"Even if they have to do the cooking?"

He crossed his arms over his chest. "Oh, didn't I make myself clear at the store?"

"On what subject?"

"That when it comes to eating, we share cooking duties."

"Share?"

He grinned over at her. "You didn't learn English yesterday, Anna. Yes, *share*. You know what that means."

She shrugged. "It seems while on this island I tend to have bouts of memory lapses."

He cracked up. "Okay, let's see which gets more intense later. Your memory lapses or your stomach griping from hunger."

Anna playfully groaned. "Okay, you win. So what do we cook?"

"Something simple. I don't feel like messing with the grill, so how about if we steam some shrimp, boil some corn, sauté some fresh veggies, and call it a night."

That sounded good to her. "Nothing to drink?"

"Oh, you'll get something to drink," he said in a deep and sexy voice that rumpled down her spine like a frisson of spiraling heat. "I personally know where your great-grandfather used to store his homemade stash."

Anna flashed him a grin, definitely interested. "No kidding?"

"No kidding."

Anna quickly crossed the yard, grabbed Zach's arms, and tugged him up the steps into the house. "Then what are we waiting for?"

A few hours later, Anna leaned over the table, groaning. "I ate too much."

"Hey, don't blame me," Zach said, smiling at her. "You ate most of the stuff while we were cooking it."

She straightened in the chair and shrugged. "I like fresh vegetables."

"I think that was obvious, Anna."

She lifted her chin as she stood up with their plates in her hands. "Well, buddy, let's see if you get any of the dessert I threw together." She then turned and walked off toward the kitchen.

Moments later Zach followed suit and found Anna standing at

the counter lifting her arms as she tried to put something in a top cabinet. He knew the nice thing would be to offer to help, but at the moment he preferred just standing there staring.

She had a mass of beautiful hair. Usually she wore it back in a ponytail, but today it was loose and hung almost past her waist. It looked rich, luxurious, and thick—and whenever she moved, her hair moved with her, definitely placing emphasis to the sway of her hips. He was tempted, really tempted, to go over to her and run his hands through the strands of hair before gently pulling her head back to claim her lips.

"You plan on standing there, or do you intend to help?"

He blinked. She met his gaze over her shoulder. She'd caught him staring. He shrugged. There wasn't a thing he could do about that now. "You want me to help someone who threatened to deny me dessert?" he asked teasingly, crossing the room at a leisurely pace.

"That would be nice."

"What makes you think I'm a nice person?"

She turned around and smiled. "Your dad."

He came to stop directly in front of her. "My dad?"

At her nod, he asked, "My dad said I was nice?"

"No. I'm assuming you're nice because your father is. You know what they say about the pear not falling far from the tree bit."

Zach hung his head down and guffawed, thinking that was much more polite than being rude and laughing in her face. Even after living in this country for quite some time, she still occasionally got her quotes mixed up. He glanced back up. "It's apples and not pears, and just because my father's nice doesn't mean that I have to be."

"But you are," she said, lifting her head defiantly, something he thought she was very good at.

The first time he'd seen her do that had been when he'd made the trip to San Diego to convince her to return to D.C. with him and claim her rightful place as Ross Fuller's heir. He had probably fallen in love with her then but hadn't known it.

"Think whatever you like, Miss Ross-Fuller. You just better hope you never witness my mean streak."

"If you say so."

He sighed. Standing so close to her was stimulating one of his fantasies, his top one, which was to give her a kiss that was anything but platonic. It was a dangerous and crazy thought, but he couldn't help wondering how she would handle it if he did just that.

"I was putting some stuff away while looking for a small plate to serve you some pie."

Her statement intruded into his thoughts. "I thought you weren't going to give me any dessert."

She turned back around toward the sink muttering, and he could have sworn he heard her say something that sounded a lot like, *I'll give you anything you want.* But when he asked her to repeat what she'd said, to make sure, her response was simply, "Nothing."

He sucked in another deep breath. Had he really just imagined the words? Probably. No more than wishful thinking on his part.

"So do you want any pie, Zach?"

He came to stand next to her. "So you baked a pie, did you?" He wondered what she had cooked while he'd been taking a shower.

"No, I didn't bake anything. It's the microwavable kind. I have it from someone who knows you well that you have a sweet tooth."

Oh, yeah, he had a sweet tooth, all right, and at the moment tasting her was all he was craving.

Half an hour later Zach stood drying the last of the dinner dishes while Anna took her shower. Conversation over dessert had been nice. She'd told him how things had been going with her at work, and he shared with her how things had been going for him— deliberately not mentioning that he was considering going into politics. The people that knew wouldn't say anything to her, so for now his secret was safe. Besides, when she found out, he would be the one to tell her and only after he was convinced she would be willing to be a politician's wife.

After drying his hands on a towel, he grabbed two wineglasses and the bottle of wine he had located in the basement, right where he'd known it would be. He would never forget those summers he got to spend here on the island. The Denisons had been super, and he would always cherish the time he got to spend with Trey Fuller and his great-grandparents, forging a friendship with Trey that would last a lifetime. The two of them kept in touch often, and Trey had been the first person he'd confided in upon accepting his true feelings for Anna.

Going out on the porch that practically wrapped all the way around the huge two-story Southern-style home, he breathed the scent of the nearby ocean, flowering plants, and crisp pines. A few years ago, Randolph had decided to screen in the entire length of the porch to keep out the man-eating mosquitoes that came out in the summertime.

Zach set the wine bottle and glasses down on a wicker table before settling his masculine frame onto a matching sofa. He leaned back against the comfortable cushions, thinking this was just where he wanted to be—alone on a private island with the woman he loved. And he had her for the next two days all to himself.

"I wondered where you had gone," Anna said, coming out on the porch to join him moments later.

He glanced up, flickering his gaze over her. She looked refreshed and as beautiful as ever, and with the light shining through the doorway he could see she had changed into a long skirt and blouse. He wasn't sure just what kind of material the skirt was made of, but all he knew was that when she walked, the fabric had a way of clinging to her curves.

His body tensed, responding to her mere presence. He shifted in his seat. "I'm glad you could join me," he said, watching how instead of coming to sit beside him she chose to sit in a chair opposite him. Maybe that wasn't such a bad idea, he decided. Already he was tottering close to the edge. It wouldn't take much to push him right on over.

"Well, did you find Grampa Murphy's stash?" she asked him, and it was then that he noticed her hair was no longer loose but was in a ponytail.

"I said I would, didn't I?" If only he could lean over and snap whatever was holding her hair together so he could watch it tumble around her shoulders.

"Well, may I have a glass?"

"I guess you may," he said, reaching over and pouring two glasses of wine from the bottle. "Careful, this is strong stuff. You don't want to indulge too much or we'll be sleeping until Sunday."

She grinned over at him. "And miss out on you taking me boating tomorrow? Don't count on it."

He handed her the glass then watched as she took a slow sip. Even the way she sipped her drink was sexy as hell.

"Tell me some more about him," Anna asked in a quiet tone.

Whenever the two of them were alone Anna enjoyed hearing stories about her father, stories Zach's father had passed on to him, since Ross Fuller had died before Zach and Anna were born. A lot of the stuff she had heard before, several times, but Anna never got tired of hearing it over and over again. In a way, he always enjoyed sharing it with her, and it only made his love and admiration for his father and the man who had been his dad's best friend that much greater.

"Long ago there were two best friends by the name of Ross Fuller and Noah Wainwright. They attended Howard University School of Law together and were roommates. They were as close as brothers, and there was nothing one would not do for the other. Their friendship was solid. It was made to last a lifetime."

He glanced over at her, saw the attentive expression on her face and the concentration in her eyes. As usual she was listening closely, taking in every word.

"Our country was embroiled in a bitter war, the Vietnam War," he continued. "We were sending men, some too young to know how to hold a gun, or to fight, to defend our country's honor. And because they loved their country, Ross and Noah decided to enlist after law school. Noah went into the air force and Ross into the marines, and they stayed in touch, those two best friends. Then one day Noah received a letter from Ross letting him know he had fallen in love with a beautiful Vietnamese girl named Gia and that he wanted to marry her. It was by a sheer act of God that Noah was able to be with Ross on the day he and Gia were married."

Zach took another sip of his wine. Now came the sad part, the part that always brought out her tears. "Months later, Noah lost Ross when Ross became a casualty of the war, but no matter what, he was determined to fulfill the promise he'd made to his best friend that if anything were to happen to him, that Ross's family would become his. Those two best friends had made plans for their children's future, you see."

Anna lifted her brow, and Zach knew why. He'd never told her this part before, the one about the plans Noah and Ross had made for their offspring's future.

"What kind of plans?" she asked softly.

"If they were girls, they would be best friends. If both were boys, they would also be best friends," he said, staring deep into her eyes.

She nodded. "And if they were a boy and a girl?" she asked thoughtfully.

"In that case, Ross and Noah figured their son and daughter would grow up, marry, and their love would be the tie that would bind the Fullers and the Wainwrights together forever."

For the longest time neither said anything. Anna finally broke eye contact when she looked down into her wineglass. "Our fathers were something else, weren't they?"

"Yes, they were. I would have loved to have known Ross Fuller."

Anna nodded. "So would I. But there are times when I feel he is with me, especially whenever I'm in a disheartened mood. Those are the times I could swear that I hear him, whispering words of encouragement, letting me know he's there, and that he's proud of me and loves me, and that he loves my mother, too. And I believe even now they are together."

She glanced over at Zach. "Does that sound crazy?"

Zach shook his head because he knew that even in death he would love her as well. "No, that doesn't sound crazy at all. There are a number of things that defy logic, Anna. There are some things that can't always be explained. Have you ever heard of predestination?"

She nodded. "The belief that a person's life is predetermined before they are born?"

"Yes. I think there's truth in some of that."

"Do you?"

"Yes." Now was not the time to tell her that in his heart he actually felt he was placed on this earth to love her. And everything the both of them had ever endured in life was in preparation for the moment they would become one—including his marriage to Shaun. Shaun had been given to him to love but for only a short time, to strengthen his belief in love and to teach him how to appreciate the importance of sharing your life with someone.

"I think I'm going to turn in now, Zach."

It was still early yet, and he wasn't ready for her to go inside, but evidently she was ready to leave. "All right. I hope you get a good night's sleep. We'll be going boating first thing in the morning."

"Okay. Good night, Zach."

"Good night, Anna."

He watched as she quickly went inside and knew that his life, his world centered on this one particular woman.

20

Zach was standing in the kitchen leaning against the counter sipping a cup of coffee when Anna, who didn't appear to be quite fully awake yet, strolled into the room early the next morning. He thought she had a sexy rumpled look, and the midriff-baring tank top and shorts she was wearing weren't helping matters. "Good morning, Anna."

She glanced up. "Good mor—"

Instead of completing the sentence, she rushed across the kitchen and when she came to a stop in front of him, he looked at her questioningly. "I need a sip. Bad," she said in a desperate plea.

He looked at his coffee cup then back at her. "Okay."

He handed her the cup. She took a sip and closed her eyes as if the coffee was exactly what she'd needed. She let out a deep sigh before taking another sip. She then returned the cup to him after smacking her lips. When she opened her eyes, a satisfaction shone in them. "Thanks. I needed that."

He smiled. "No problem." And for Zach it hadn't been a problem. In fact, it had been a real turn-on to watch her drink from the same coffee cup that he had. It made him feel good that she had no qualms about sharing it with him with her lips touching the same spot that his had.

"Do you want me to pour you a cup?" he asked when she walked over to the table and sat down.

"Please. I hate to be a bother, but I didn't get to sleep until a little before dawn."

"Really? Why?"

"The sound of crickets, frogs, and no telling what else. I could hear them as clear as day even with my window down."

Zach walked over to her with her cup of coffee, amused. "Welcome to Glendale Shores. The sounds are always annoying the first night, but then you finally get used to it." He sat down across from her. "Don't you remember how things were the last time?"

She smiled at him as she took a sip of her own coffee. "I was too busy looking through all those photo albums that when I did go to bed, I was out like a light."

He grinned over at her. "You know what that means, don't you?"

She raised a brow. "No. What?"

"I'm going to have to keep you up late tonight so you can sleep."

Anna wondered how he intended to do that. She had plenty of her own ideas, but none was safe to mention. "So what time do you want us to hit the water?"

"As soon as you finish your coffee."

She picked up her cup to take another sip. "But don't you have to get the boat ready?"

He smiled. "It's done. I also packed our lunch already."

"How long have you been up?"

"At least a couple of hours."

"You couldn't sleep either?"

One corner of Zach's lips lifted in a grin. "No, I couldn't sleep either." He didn't add that the reasons were vastly different from hers. Nature had kept him up too, but it had nothing to do with the local wildlife. "Would it make you happy to know Trey's new boat has a cabin below?" he asked.

Her sleepy eyes lit up. "With a bed?"

He laughed at that. "Yes, with a bed."

She grinned with delight. "Umm, you wouldn't think badly of me if the first couple of hours I got into that bed, would you?" she asked, looking at him over the rim of her cup.

Not if you don't think badly of me if I crawl in that bed with you.
"No, I won't think badly of you."

She leaned over and patted his cheek. "Thanks, Zach. You're a sweetheart. What would I ever do without you?"

With great effort he kept his head from turning, even slightly, or else he would have been tempted to kiss the hand she still had resting on his face. "Does that mean you're going to keep me around?" he asked in a low voice.

She released her hand from his face, leaned back in her chair, smiled before sipping more coffee, and said softly, "For always."

For always.

Three hours later Anna's words were still all Zach could think about as he inhaled a breath of cool morning air while keeping the boat on its course around the island. She was down below in the cabin sleeping, and he wasn't two seconds in finding a good spot to anchor and join her in the bed. He couldn't help wondering how she would react if he were to do something like that.

He had gone down to check on her around an hour ago to find her curled up in bed lying on her side and dead to the world. That gave him a chance to study her, thinking he'd never seen her sleep before. Even in peaceful bliss, she was beautiful, the thing fantasies were made of.

This island was also something else fantasies were made of. No heavy traffic and sirens going off. Other than the ruffle of the waves off the Atlantic and seagulls flying overhead, this was a place of calm and peace. Of course there were the occasional sounds of the night, the same ones that had kept Anna awake, but even that couldn't take away from the island's serene magnificence.

"Is it lunchtime yet?"

He turned at the sound of Anna's voice. She looked well rested, gorgeous, and he couldn't help but lean back against the rail and stare at her.

She stared right back. "Well, is it lunchtime?"

"No such luck, woman. It's not ten o'clock yet. Do you think all you're going to do on my watch is sleep and eat?"

"Doesn't sound like a bad thing to me," she said, grinning. Her hair was loose and seemed to be flying in the wind. He liked it that way. He also liked the way she was dressed. She was wearing a pair of black shorts and a white tank top that bared her belly.

With a bigger smile she asked, "Are we going to fish or spend your entire Saturday hunting for the lost treasure?"

Anna tried to stop the butterflies from fluttering around in her stomach. Now that she was refreshed, so were her thoughts, and the main thing they were latching on to was Zach. He was leaning against the rail dressed in a pair of khaki shorts and a white sleeveless shirt that showed off his muscular chest and strong arms. Then there was that wide and sensuous-looking mouth he had. He seemed to be watching her the same way a hawk would eye a mouse before swooping down on it. Was she imagining things or was he actually looking at her differently today? She swallowed deeply, overwhelmed by the mere possibility.

"Oh, you remember our tale of the lost treasure, do you?" he asked.

She turned her gaze to all the water beyond the boat, forcing her body to calm down. "How could I not remember when you and Trey convinced me it was true?"

Zach laughed, and the sound seemed to wrap itself around her. "Growing up, Trey and I always believed it since Grampa Murphy was convinced it was true. But then your uncle Randolph said if it had been true that he and your father Ross would have found it by now, since they spent a lot of their childhood searching the island for it and always came up empty-handed. He thought it was a tall tale Grampa Murphy fabricated to keep them busy and out of trouble during their summer visits."

"But you and Trey thought differently?"

She could tell he was remembering those times, entertaining pleasant childhood memories. "Yes. We were convinced your uncle and father didn't look good enough and that we would eventually find it."

"But you never did."

"No, but the fun is in looking, so whenever Trey comes here, we can't resist looking around again just in case we overlooked something."

She nodded. "Well, I hope you find your treasure one day."

It was on the tip of his tongue to tell her he had already done so. Whenever he gazed at her he saw something so valuable and priceless that he knew he wanted to keep her *for always*.

And he knew that before they left the island she would understand that their relationship had taken a turn, and it would be up to her to decide where it would go from there.

Part
three

*By night on my bed I sought him whom
my soul loveth: I sought him but I found
him not.
I will rise now, and go about the city in
the streets, and in the broad ways I will
seek him whom my soul loveth: I sought
him but found him not.
The watchman that go about the city
found me: to whom I said. Saw ye him
whom my soul loveth?*

—SONG OF SOLOMON 3: 1–3

21

Lyle thought that Beaufort, South Carolina, situated between Savannah and Charleston, exuded much of the same charm as both cities but on a smaller scale. They had made good time, leaving the island by ten that morning. He had driven the scenic route from Hilton Head, and the moment he and Monique entered the city, they could immediately tell the town was rich in history.

The historic district was filled with elegant homes that had been built in the 1700s and 1800s, and the quaint but bustling waterfront shopping district was brimming with numerous stores and a huge assortment of eating places.

He glanced over at Monique when he parked the car on Bay Street in front of a very picturesque old house that had been made into a bed-and-breakfast inn. From the smile on Monique's face, he could tell she was pleased with his choice of where they would be spending the night.

When a strand of Monique's hair caught a breeze off the nearby Beaufort River and blew in her face, as if it was the most natural thing to do, he reached out and pushed it back away from her face, tucking it behind her ear.

"This place is beautiful, Lyle," she murmured, looking at him and then back at the huge two-story inn. "I bet it's as nice on the inside as it looks on the outside."

"I got it from a reliable source that it is, and I was lucky to get two rooms, which surprised me with this being the weekend heading into the Fourth of July. Ready to go inside?" He gave her a slow grin.

Excitement flowed through Monique. "Ready as I'll ever be."

When Lyle and Monique had unpacked, they met back downstairs. He was standing at the bottom stair the moment she descended.

"How's your accommodations?" he asked, tucking her arm in the fold of his and leading her out the door.

"Simply beautiful. Thanks for inviting me here with you."

"You're welcome, and thanks for coming."

"Where to first?" she asked, glancing around when they stepped outside into the sun.

"I thought we would take a stroll through that waterfront park we passed and then grab lunch at one of those sidewalk cafés nearby."

"Sounds like a great idea."

Hand in hand they walked through Chambers Waterfront Park, a pleasant swath of luscious greenery between Bay Street and the Beaufort River. Monique appreciated the wide walkways and swinging benches, thinking it was the perfect place for strolling or for sitting and catching a breeze off the nearby water.

A short time later, while sitting on a park bench enjoying the view of the river, Lyle answered her questions about his seminars and explained whether he preferred being in the classroom versus in the hospital treating patients.

"I prefer being in the hospital treating patients," he said, turning her hand over in his and looking down at how small it was. "But it's good meeting with other physicians and researchers to discuss the latest medical breakthroughs in the area of heart disease. It's not enough that we treat more heart patients but what's really important is that we support research to make sure whatever methods we use are affordable and practical. Health care costs have skyrocketed in recent years."

Monique nodded, fully understanding what he meant. Her mother's medical expenses had been extremely high, and she and

Arnie had appreciated the fact that her father had maintained good health insurance on both him and their mother.

"The reason for the seminar," Lyle was saying, "is education. As physicians we need to return to our communities and work with whatever volunteer groups that are out there to support projects that encourage people to make the right lifestyle choices for a healthier heart."

The overall impression Monique got from listening to Lyle was that he was a dedicated physician. "How did you decide on a career in the heart field versus another medical field, Lyle?" That was something she'd often wondered about.

"My dad," he said simply. "When we were in high school, my father suffered a light heart attack. That episode scared me and my brothers to death. Before then we assumed Jeremiah Montgomery was invincible, made to last forever, and there was nothing that could or would ever get the old man down. That year we discovered differently, and the thought of losing the one person in our lives who was constant and kept things normal sent us into a tailspin."

Lyle didn't say anything for a few seconds, as if remembering that difficult time. "Luckily, he listened to the doctor and made lifestyle changes, but it made me realize that something as fragile as the human heart, and how well you took care of it, was the key to determining your longevity. I decided to dedicate my life to finding out everything I needed to know and to help others who want to live longer to do so."

"And how is your father doing?" Monique asked and then watched as a huge smile spread over his face.

"Pop is doing great. With Carrie happily married, he's finally begun devoting time to himself. There's a lady he's seeing now, and although Logan and Lance don't think it's all that serious, me and Carrie do. Time will tell. As far as I'm concerned, it's about time he gets some real happiness in his life." He released her hand and stood. "Ready for lunch?"

Monique sighed, missing the warmth where his hand had been holding hers and realized they'd been sitting there on the bench talking for almost an hour. She smiled up at him. "Hungry, are you?"

"Yes. Dinner last night was great, but I missed breakfast and my stomach is letting me know it."

She nodded. He was right. Dinner last night was great, and she had thoroughly enjoyed his company. When he returned her back home, he had walked her to the door then kissed her on the cheek before leaving. On the drive over from Hilton Head, she had entertained more than a few thoughts that in time maybe their relationship could move beyond friendship, but now she wasn't so sure how she felt, or if that's what she really wanted. She was attracted to him, that was a gimme, but how did he feel about her? What if the attraction was one-sided?

They stopped walking, and Lyle leaned forward to look into her eyes. "You okay?"

"Yes, why do you ask?"

"Because you've gotten quiet on me."

"Umm, I was wondering about something."

"What?"

"Why you don't have an important person in your life. And please don't give me the excuse of having too much work, because I don't think a man's plate is ever too full for a woman if he's interested."

He chuckled. "Now you sound like the old Lance Montgomery, spouting off some of his playa's theology."

"Well?"

"Well, the truth is that although I date occasionally, I haven't found that particular woman with that certain spark I'm looking for."

She was curious. "What kind of spark?"

"It's hard to explain."

What Monique needed at that moment was an explanation. For some reason, she wanted to understand exactly what he meant. She stopped walking and leaned against a black rail. "But I want you to explain."

"All right, then," he said, lowering his voice a notch. He took a step toward her and reached out and slowly caressed her arms with his fingertips. The sensations his touch was causing were immediately overwhelming, and the eyes staring into hers made them more intensely so. She could feel a light breeze flowing over her skin, but more than anything she felt, all the way down to her toes, the rush of heat flowing through her body from Lyle's touch. The spark.

"Feel it?" he asked, his tone of voice lower still.

"Yes," she said, as if snagged by his steady gaze.

"So can I." He then released her hand and stepped back and smiled. "Now let's go enjoy our lunch."

Monique drew in a deep breath as she walked beside him. Just that quick, with a touch that still had her toes tingling, something had changed, and she couldn't help wondering whether or not she could handle that change.

As far as Monique was concerned, Lyle had opened a Pandora's box that was better left closed. But then she couldn't fully fault him since she *had* asked. But instead of explaining, he had shown her and she could still feel the results.

"You're not eating. Aren't you hungry, Nicky?"

She glanced up, and the moment their eyes met she felt a slight tremor pass through her. Then there was that dimpled smile. And if those things weren't bad enough, the sound of her name from his lips was like a gentle wave washing over her.

"Evidently not as much as you were," she said, eyeing his plate. It was clean. She wondered how he could still have such a hearty appetite after discovering "the spark." As he'd alluded earlier, she had barely touched her food. Finding out a man could cause such havoc within your body with a mere touch was sort of nerve-wracking, to say the least.

His smiled widened at the exact moment he winked. "I have to make sure I have my strength for later."

That got another reaction out of her. "Later? What happens later?" she asked.

"We're going dancing at that nightclub on the corner. Remember?"

How could she forget? Especially since it had been her idea when they'd passed the establishment earlier. "Yes, I remember. Did you bring your dancing shoes?"

"No, but I can handle the slow numbers."

Monique swallowed, wondering if *she* could handle them. Just the thought of being in his arms, barely moving around a dance floor, while their bodies rubbed against each other was too much to think about. She didn't know if she should pretend a headache and stay in her room for the rest of the night or just roll with the flow. She quickly weighed her two options and decided to just roll with the flow. She *was* here to have fun.

"And since we're planning to have a late night, maybe we should go back to the inn and take a nap."

Monique glanced up. She knew he hadn't meant it the way it sounded. They would be taking separate naps, but still his words were rather intimate to her ears. Way too intimate.

Lyle glanced across the table at the woman who was trying to look every which way but at him. She was the same woman who had haunted his dreams for years—at least until he heard she had gotten married. After that he forced thoughts of her from his mind, thinking it wasn't right to fantasize about someone else's wife.

But she no longer belonged to anyone, so he was free to pursue her, and a trickle of anticipation ran through him. He intended to make sure that she understood that this weekend belonged to them, just as he'd made sure she understood she possessed "the spark" he desired in a woman.

It was hard to believe that even after eighteen years there were certain things about her that hadn't changed, things he had fallen in love with. And it had always been more than a physical attraction for him. He always admired her zest for life as well as her keen intelligence. And then there was that degree of loyalty within her that you seldom found in people these days. Her concern for her friend attested to the fact that she was someone who cared deeply for others, especially those who meant something to her.

He looked deep into her eyes. "Ready to go?"

She took a deep breath and blew it out before saying, "Yes, I'm ready." He studied her a moment longer before standing.

She stood up as well. "Is anything wrong?"

He shook his head and chuckled. "No, Nicky, everything is fine."

22

Shannon slept in late, waking past noon. She quickly show-ered and, with nothing planned for the rest of the day, she slipped into a sundress and flat sandals before heading downstairs to see what Faith and Monique were doing.

She still found it amazing that her body was humming in sexual satisfaction nearly twenty-four hours after the fact. Just what kind of lovemaking had Adam laid on her? Not that she had any complaints, mind you. The man was a master at tuning up a woman's body the same way he tuned up cars. Somehow he'd known it was time for her to get a service check, and not only had he tuned her up, but he'd done a great job of replacing her spark plugs as well. It seemed her entire body was now sensitive to the touch, as potent as a magnet, and all revved up for more sexual pleasure of his making.

She frowned when she came back to the thought that had con-sumed her lately: Adam Corbain could become her obsession. No man had ever gotten to her like that. It was up to her not to let that happen. She may become *his* obsession, but hell would freeze over before he became hers.

A few moments later she found Faith sitting outside on the patio sipping wine and reading a book on the wicker sofa, totally en-tranced. Shannon hated disturbing her, but she wanted to make sure Faith and Monique weren't still so worried about her.

"That book's interesting?"

Faith almost bolted upright out of her seat. She threw her hand over her chest as if to calm her heart and said, "Shannon, you scared me to death!"

Shannon smiled apologetically and stared at her friend with interest. "Just what kind of book is that?"

"A thriller. A serial killer who calls himself the Hilton Head Slicer is going around killing women who're vacationing on the island. The lady at the bookstore on the strip recommended it. I've been reading all morning and only have a few chapters left. Do you want to read it when I'm done?"

Shannon strolled over and dropped down into the chair across from where Faith sat. "No, thank you. I have a book of my own that I need to start reading. *A Man Before His Time.* It's a book written in the seventeen hundreds by Alexander Hamilton on the economic problems of their day."

Faith sat back and looked at her. "Do you ever consider reading a book just for pleasure?"

Shannon grinned. "No, reading does not give me pleasure. When it comes to what gives me pleasure, I can write my own book."

Faith chortled, leaning back in her seat. "I'm sure you can if you still have the brains to do it. According to you, they were almost screwed out."

"You make it sound like a bad thing."

Faith said teasingly, "Hey, girlfriend, I ain't mad at ya."

Shannon laughed before saying, "Maybe I should be mad at myself, but I'm not. Too much afterglow for that. But I wanted to assure you and Monique that I am okay. Adam was as much of a gentleman as he could be under the circumstances."

She then glanced around. "And speaking of Monique, where is she?"

"Beaufort."

"Beaufort? What she's doing in Beaufort?"

"She went there for the weekend with Lyle Montgomery. She won't return until sometime tomorrow evening," Faith said.

"Ha!" Shannon exclaimed, bouncing around excitedly in her seat. "I knew it! I just knew something was going on between them and that 'he's just a friend' stuff was for the birds."

Faith gave her a pointed look. "You can't really say that, Shannon. Right now they're just friends, but it could escalate into more if that's what the two of them want. But don't assume it *has* to move in that direction."

Shannon made a face. "I know, I know, but I want her to be happy. Although she's been seeing other men, I don't think she's gotten over losing Paul."

"He'll be a tough act to follow," Faith said, studying the contents of her wineglass and thinking just what a sweetheart Paul Grier had been. Not only had he been a wonderful husband to Monique, but he'd also been a good friend to her, Cely, and Shannon. When it came to the friendship the four shared, there hadn't been a jealous bone in his body—unlike Virgil's. Her ex had envied the close friendship she, Cely, Shannon, and Monique had shared and resented the fact that Faith might be sharing too much information about their personal business with them. In the end, she could understand his concern, considering what she'd found out.

"So what are your plans for this afternoon?" Shannon asked.

"Mmm, don't have any," she said, trying not to remember Shane's invitation to come over to his place again. She would see him for her tennis lessons on Monday, and as far as she was concerned, that was soon enough. Too much of Shane Masters wasn't a good thing. "I might go to the clubhouse and practice my tennis strokes and later take a walk on the beach when the crowd thins out. What's yours?"

Shannon shrugged. "Do like you're doing now and read a bit. I plan to stay in tonight. Adam invited me over to the garage tomorrow."

"They're open on Sundays?"

"I don't think they are on a regular basis, but he's working on this one particular car."

"Are you going?"

Shannon shrugged. "I haven't decided yet. I think he intends to put me to work."

Faith smiled. "It might be fun doing something out of the norm. Doing something wacky every once in a while isn't bad," she said, wondering if she should take her own advice.

Memories flooded Shannon's mind. "Trust me. I've been doing a number of things that's out of the norm with Adam."

23

Anna walked out onto the porch and found Zach standing with his back to her as he looked out over the waterways through the marshland. They had spent most of the day on the water, and when it had gotten too hot, they headed back to shore.

They'd played cards, checkers, and had even watched a DVD movie he had rented before finally throwing something together for dinner. Since then they had showered, and she figured with nothing else to do they would hang out here and enjoy each other's company. Tomorrow she would pose for the portrait Zach was doing of her, which would probably take most of the day—he wanted to finish it before they left the island. And once their families arrived, there wouldn't be any more private time in which to do it.

He evidently heard the sound of her feet on the wooden floor. When he turned, his eyes softened. "Come here. I want you to see something."

She quickly crossed the porch to where he was standing. "What is it?"

"That," he said, pointing toward the marshlands and thick underbrush.

She squinted her eyes and saw it, the setting of the sun, and it was so beautiful that she held her breath. The sun appeared as a huge ball of orangey red fire slowly descending into the ocean. The clouds in the sky appeared to be holding still for this majestic departure.

"Have you ever seen anything so beautiful, Zach?" she asked in a quiet voice.

"Truthfully, I have."

Anna glanced up to find him staring at her in a way that made her pulse race.

"You're more beautiful than a sunset, Anna," he said in a husky voice, reaching out to lift strands of hair away from her face. "You're so beautiful that each time I see you, you take my breath away."

His words played through her mind like notes from a well-strung instrument, softly touching parts of her that had never been touched before. She couldn't believe he had said such a thing and truly meant it. She knew he dated a number of beautiful women, and for him to say she was beautiful to the point of taking his breath away was a compliment she would always cherish.

"Thank you, Zach."

He reached out, and his hands settled on her shoulders as he held her gaze. "You don't have to thank me," he said, before reaching up and releasing the knot that held her hair up, making it tumble wildly around her shoulders.

He smiled as if proud of his handiwork. "I like your hair down this way."

She couldn't break the eye contact even if she wanted to. "I never knew you preferred that I wear it down."

Zach's smile widened. There was a lot she didn't know when it came to him and her. Maybe it was time he spelled a few things out for her.

Slowly the hands he had on her shoulders draped around her neck as he moved closer to her, not able to resist the temptation of her lips any longer. Any willpower he once had was all used up.

Anna saw what was coming and held her breath. It would be just the way she had played it over and over in her mind countless times.

She continued to look at him, to study the darkness of his eyes, the perfection of all his features, but it was his lips, about to be joined with hers, that made heat settle in all parts of her body. She watched as his head lowered, not for one minute thinking she should pull away. This was Zach, the man she loved. The man she said a special prayer for every night before going to bed. The man who filled her nightly dreams with fantasies. The man who at this moment was taking her breath away. Had already done so.

"Anna." He whispered her name seconds before taking her lips in his. The expertness of it almost brought her to her knees, and in her mind everything faded, including the beauty of the setting sun.

Everything was replaced with another beauty. The feel of his mouth gently, slowly, and thoroughly feasting on hers, the way his hands that had been draped around her neck were now wrapped around her in a warm embrace. His hands were firm, strong, and caring. Just from the way he had them around her neck was stirring every nerve she had in her body.

Moments later when he released her mouth, the eyes holding hers almost burned through her, fanning the familiar heat. "Zach," she breathed, needing to speak his name to make sure what was happening between them was real and not another dream she wasn't ready to wake up from.

Instead of answering, he leaned down and captured her lips again, this time with startling possession. The first time was the blissfulness of slow discovery; this time around was the audacious awakening of desire, pleasure that was meant to flare through her body like wildfire.

And it was.

His kiss was more than just physical. It was so generous and selfless that it nearly brought tears to her eyes. No one, not even Todd, had ever kissed her this way, and as if with a mind of their own, her hands moved to his shoulders, then moments later wrapped firmly around his neck as his mouth mated unhurriedly, yet hungrily, with hers.

A shiver passed through her when she felt his body shift, bringing her closer to the fit of him, making her front mesh with his muscular form. She felt him, every inch, the hard form of him through his shorts, but instead of feeling tense, she felt safe, protected and secured in his arms.

When he finally lifted his lips from hers, her head was left swimming in desire, her body was drumming to the beat of a heat she didn't know could exist, and her mind was fully absorbed in sensations she had never felt before. That kiss had unleashed a sensuality within her she had been afraid to expose. Would it be a turn-off when he found out just how little experience she had at thirty-four? Would he be totally shocked to discover that technically she didn't have any at all?

Each and every time they had been together, she had been tempted to take the initiative and kiss him, but she'd been too afraid, too unsure of herself to do so. But he hadn't. He had solved her problem—or it could be that he'd created a new one, because she wasn't sure what had driven him to kiss her. Had it been the heat of the moment, or had it been something else? The big question of the hour was whether or not there could or would be anything more than this, a stolen kiss under the setting sun.

"I've wanted to do that for a long time," he whispered, caressing her bottom lip with the tip of his finger. Blood was rushing hard through his veins.

"How long?"

He smiled gently. Leave it to Anna to ask him that. "Umm, maybe from that first day we met, when I walked into your office and found you all serious and self-protective, ready to do battle to defend your right to use your father's full name as your surname. I admired your spunk, your ability to stand up for yourself and not take anything off of anyone, even the rich and powerful Fuller family."

Taking her hand in his, he continued. "Yet at the same time I felt your hurt for being rejected, and a part of my heart that had been closed suddenly opened and I knew two things. That I would protect you no matter what, and that I had fallen in love with you."

She raised a surprised brow. "Just like that?"

His smile deepened. "Yes, just like that."

She shook her head. "And you've felt this way for an entire year?"

"Yes, but I only finally admitted it to myself within the last few months."

She took a deep breath, inhaling slowly. This was almost too much. "But what about Shaun? How can you make sure what you're feeling is real?"

Zach knew why she was asking him that. There was another man she had believed loved her, but in the end he had turned his back on her when he should have remained by her side and fought for their love to anyone crazy enough to ridicule it.

"Oh, I know it's real, sweetheart, and as far as Shaun, she is a part of my past that I will always cherish, and I know she would be happy to know I was able to find love once again."

Anna tipped her head back as if measuring his words. "And you're sure about this? Your feelings?"

He chuckled. "Trust me, I am, but the question I should be asking is what about yours? How do you feel about me, Anna?"

Anna held her breath. She could easily tell him that she loved him, too, and had loved him for just as long as he'd said he loved her. That she had also fallen in love with him that day in her office when he had sat in the chair across from her desk looking like he had stepped off the cover of a *GQ* magazine.

For some reason that day she had felt she could trust him, and when he had convinced her to travel back to D.C. with him, she believed that no matter how things turned out, he would always be her friend—her true friend. And he had been, easily stepping into a role no one else had held before him.

And if he truly felt the way he said, he would be stepping into another role no one else had filled before, the role of her lover.

"Anna?"

The sound of her name from his lips soothed her. She knew he was waiting for a response but wasn't sure she was ready to tell him what he wanted to know, since the truth could potentially complicate things. But then there was no way she could not tell him.

She said, "My feelings for you are the same as yours are for me, Zach. I fell in love with you that day as well, and yes, I've been keeping my feelings to myself because I wasn't sure they were reciprocated. Even now I'm not sure I'm doing the right thing by telling you what they are."

He smiled and reached out and kissed her lips. The thought that she loved him, too, seemed to overwhelm him. "Why, sweetheart?"

"I can see problems."

"What kind of problems?"

"How our families will feel about an involvement between us? Your parents are my godparents, Zach. Then there's Uncle Randolph and—"

"They gave us their blessings."

"What?" she said in surprise.

"My parents and your uncle gave us their blessings. I talked to them before coming to Hilton Head. And I'm sure your grandparents won't have a problem when we tell them. The reason I spoke to my parents and your uncle was that I knew what my intentions were in coming to see you and wanted them to know as well."

She looked at him curiously. "And what were your intentions?"

"To let you know how I felt." Zach decided he would let her get used to how he felt about her before hitting her with the news that he wanted them to marry and share their lives for always. He also would wait to tell her about his political aspirations. He wanted to take one step at a time, and the most important thing right now was letting her know how much he cared.

"And just in case you've forgotten," he said, leaning in closer. "Let this serve as a reminder." And then he was kissing her again.

Anna closed her eyes, thinking that she could get addicted to this, Zach's touch, the taste of him, and the sensations he was evoking. These were moments she wanted to file away and always remember. And the way his fingertips were caressing her bare arms while his mouth mated deliciously with hers was making everything female inside of her come alive.

While she was in college, the girls she'd roomed with had tried convincing her that it was okay to engage in sex with the guys on campus even if she didn't love them. They claimed making out was a healthy and normal release. She was glad she hadn't bought into that theory. She was also glad she hadn't caved in under Todd's persistence that they sleep together before getting married. Again, she felt like waiting had been the right thing to do.

But now I don't want to wait any longer.

All the sensations that Zach was making her feel led her to believe the next part, beyond kissing, would be just that much more pleasurable. And she wanted to share all of that with him, the man she loved.

She could admit now that she probably never really loved Todd, not to the extent that she loved Zach. If she thought she did once it was because Todd had promised her all the things she'd never had and had always longed for: love, family, and devotion. In the end he hadn't delivered any of those things. He had let her down.

But she believed in her heart that Zach would never let her down. He was a man with high principles. He was a man who could be trusted. He was the man she would gladly spend the rest of her days with.

She opened her eyes when she felt him break off the kiss, but she wasn't ready for things to end. She wanted more. She needed a connection to him, one she'd never shared with another man.

She lifted her gaze and met his. She saw the dark desire in his eyes, the heat, the wanting, and knew he wanted her as much as she wanted him, but he wouldn't suggest it or ask. He was too much of a gentleman to do that, so she decided to do it for him.

Up on tiptoe, she leaned close to his moist lips and whispered, "Make love to me, Zach."

24

Without saying a word, Zach swept Anna off her feet into his arms. He carried her into the house, grateful that he knew his way around—because with every step he took, his gaze was locked on to hers.

This wasn't what he'd planned for their time together on Glendale Shores, but the moment she looked into his eyes, he saw more than desire shining in their dark depths. He had seen her heart there as well, and when she asked him to make love to her, he'd fought the urge to comply, then and there, right out on the porch.

But he knew he was going to touch her soon, in the privacy of a bedroom. He would join his body with hers and make her his in every way that it was meant to be. There were still some things they had to work out, but confessing their love for each other was an important start. Joining as one in the most intimate way was another.

When he reached the bedroom he'd been using, he placed her on the bed and stood back. "Are you sure?" he asked, his voice low and husky.

She nodded. "Yes, I'm sure. I want you, Zach, but I need to tell you something first."

"Okay, what is it?" He was staring at her, waiting. And when he saw that whatever she wanted to tell him was important to her and wasn't easy to say, he went to her and lay down beside her, bracing himself on his elbow. "Whatever it is really doesn't matter, you know. I love you, and there's nothing you can say that can erase my love for you, Anna. And you should know by now that you can tell me anything."

She nodded again. He was right. She had gotten so comfortable with him over the past year. They shared a special kind of friendship. And now it had escalated into a special kind of relationship. But how would he feel about making love to a thirty-four-year-old virgin?

"But this might matter to you," she said softly, remembering Todd's words that men didn't particularly like to be bothered with inexperienced women.

"It won't, but go ahead and tell me anyway, since you think it does," he whispered, inching his body closer to her.

Silence fell, and Zach waited patiently for her to speak, rubbing his fingertips across the back of her hand while holding her gaze. Finally, she began talking. "I—I've never done this before."

Zach blinked, then went still. "Are you saying you've never been intimate with a man, Anna?"

"Yes. Does it matter?"

He reached out, gently cupped her face and kissed her forehead, thinking, *If you only knew how much it matters.* Somehow he had to explain it to her. He made an attempt to smile, but it wasn't easy. His entire being was filled with so much love for her.

"Yes, it does matter, Anna, but not the way you think. It matters because to me that means what you're offering me is yourself. That in itself is truly special, and there must be a reason I was chosen to be the recipient of such a very extraordinary gift. And that's how I look at it, your virginity, as a gift. It's a gift that you believe I'm worthy of, and that means a lot to me. For you to have kept yourself celibate for thirty-four years when society dictated otherwise is truly remarkable."

Touched by his words, Anna leaned forward and met his lips with hers, needing the contact, needing the taste she'd come to know just moments ago. And he obliged her, letting her get acquainted with how to work her way around the insides of his mouth the same way he'd done hers.

Zach closed his eyes and remained still, letting her take the lead, not even following in her wake. He wanted her to feel comfortable with whatever she did to him. He wanted her to know that with them there would be no limitations and no prohibitions. When her tongue insisted that he get involved, he tangled his tongue with hers as a deep and profound quiver shook his entire body.

Opening his eyes, he leaned toward her. He slipped his hands beneath her tank top with a quick flick of his wrist, undid the front fastener to her bra. Her breasts seemed to spring free into his hands, and he ran his thumb over the nipples, concentrating on the hardened tips and hearing her moan deep into his mouth.

He pulled back from her kiss, with an urgent need to taste her breasts. He removed the tank top and bra, tossing them aside before pushing her on her back until he was looming over her. The breasts were firm, well-shaped, delicious looking, and he leaned forward and took a swollen nipple into his mouth. Each lick made her moan deep within her throat.

After tormenting her breasts for a few moments, he traced a path with his tongue down her stomach. When he reached her navel, he pulled back to remove her shorts, leaving her clad in a pair of white lace bikini panties. He thought that he'd never seen such a beautifully shaped woman before in his life, and a degree of possessiveness surged through him.

"Has anyone ever made love to you here?" he asked, stroking her intimately through the material of her panties.

She shook her head, writhing beneath his touch. "No. Todd, wanted to, but I wouldn't let him. I wasn't ready for anything like that."

His eyes darkened even more with desire. "Do you think you're ready for something like this now?" he asked softly, his pulse surging.

"Yes," she whispered.

"And would you let me do it?"

"Yes. I don't want anyone but you to touch me this way."

Her words affected him deeply, and he moved over her on his knees to remove her panties. He tossed them aside to join her other pieces of clothing and then he gazed upon her, specifically that area she had decreed he could claim as his.

And he would.

He was getting all his fantasies fulfilled in a way he hadn't thought possible. "Open your legs some more for me, sweetheart," he whispered as he continued to stroke her, feeling how wet and ready she was for him. "Once I get started and if you decide you don't like it, just let me know and I'll stop."

"All right."

He gently gripped her hips and leaned forward, placing a trail of kisses on her tummy and inner thigh. He felt her body beginning to quiver beneath his mouth, and when he moved his mouth lower, he heard a quiet moan escape between her lips.

When his tongue darted out and touched her, savoring a quick taste of her, and then another, she caught hold of his head in her hands to keep his mouth steady.

He glanced up. "You like this already?"

"Yes, I like this already. Do you like doing this?"

"Oh, yeah, baby, I like doing this. Only to you."

And then he returned his attention to her, tasting the sweet wetness between her legs, absorbing all the sensations he knew she was feeling. For seemingly endless moments he stroked her with his tongue, making love with her this way to let her know just how much she meant to him. And when a climax swept through her, she arched her hips closer to his mouth and called out his name. A long mournful groan followed, and he continued making love to her like that. When he pulled back, she opened her eyes and stared up at him, awestruck.

"Now to put the icing on the cake," Zach said, getting off the bed to quickly remove his clothes. He took a condom out of his wallet and slipped it on, knowing she was watching everything he did. Moments later he was covering her body with his, placing his huge erection at her wet opening.

He looked down at her. "This may hurt a little."

"I know. But I want you. I need this and only from you."

Zach considered her for a moment, saw all the love and trust that filled her eyes. Words weren't needed between them right now. Instead he slowly began easing inside her, giving her body time to adjust to the fit of him as they connected. When he'd gone to the hilt, he leaned over and kissed her forehead, then her cheeks before claiming her mouth.

Knowing their bodies were merged this way sent sensations spiraling through them, and slowly his body began rocking into hers, careful not to hurt her. And when another climax hit and she began moving her body frantically beneath his, he began thrusting into her, soaring on a plane so high, he felt the way she was pulling him into her, making love to him.

Wave after wave of pure ecstasy flooded his mind and body, and as the explosion subsided, he shifted so he wouldn't collapse on top of her and brought her to his side, their joining complete, their bodies still connected.

And as he cradled her in his arms, he felt an inner peace like he'd not felt in a long time. And he knew why. He had connected with his future.

25

"Hey, I thought you didn't bring your dancing shoes."

Lyle had a huge grin on his face as he led Monique off the dance floor and back to their table. "Everyone knows how to do the Electric Slide, Nicky."

She smiled. "Yes, but still, you did real good out there."

"And you didn't do so bad yourself." He glanced around when they sat down. "This is a nice place."

Monique agreed. "Yes, and what I like the most is that it caters to adults our ages and not the younger crowd."

Lyle leaned back in his chair, frowning, "You're making us sound rather old."

She giggled. "Not old but mature. I consider the thirty-something group as the mature crowd."

At that moment a slow song began playing, the first for the night, and Lyle glanced over at Monique. "Just what I've been waiting for," he said, standing and offering her his hand.

She took it, refusing to tell him she'd been waiting for it as well. Ever since they had talked at lunch about dancing together, she looked forward to having his body melded to hers.

"You look nice tonight, Nicky."

"Thanks." She smiled, pleased he had noticed. Instead of taking a nap as Lyle assumed she had, she'd left the inn and visited that little boutique she'd seen earlier on their stroll. She had decided that the dress she'd packed just wouldn't work and wanted to purchase a special outfit for tonight.

She hadn't been absolutely certain about this one, since it was a little more daring than any outfit she'd normally wear, but while in the dressing room trying it on, she could have sworn she heard a little voice sounding a lot like Cely's saying, *Girl, that dress looks good on you so buy it*. She had. And from the looks she was getting, it seemed that Lyle wasn't the only male appreciating the way the material clung to her hips as well as the generous glimpse of her cleavage every time she made a move.

The moment they were on the dance floor, he pulled her closer to his muscular frame and wrapped his arms around her as they began moving slowly in place. "You smell nice, too, Nicky."

She glanced up at him and smiled. "Well, aren't we full of compliments tonight, Dr. Montgomery."

Lyle looked down at her, returning her smile. "And you deserve each and every one of them."

He wished he could give her even more compliments but knew he had to be careful not to make it too obvious how very attracted he was to her. Just having her in his arms would suffice for now because he intended for them to share many more slow dances before the night was over.

The moment their bodies had touched, he knew that he would be her only dance partner tonight. If the other men in the establishment had other ideas, then that was too bad. She felt wonderful in his arms and the swell of her breasts pressing against his chest was sending all kind of sensations through his body. Then there was the way her hips rocked against his as they moved to the slow rhythm.

"You mentioned your sister had called," Monique said.

"Yes, she called the minute we got back to the inn from lunch. She and Connor are flying in the week after the Fourth for a visit."

"That's wonderful. I'm sure you'll be glad to see them."

The smile at the corners of his lips widened. "Yes, I will. Carrie's really happy now that she's married to Connor. He's just what she needs."

"And I'm sure she's probably what he needs as well. It works both ways, you know. What day are they coming in?"

"That Friday, and I would love for you to meet them. And according to Carrie, there's a possibility Logan, Lance, and Asia might be coming as well."

Monique gazed up at him with a curious expression on her face. "Is there some special occasion?"

"Umm, nothing special other than my birthday."

She considered him for a long moment. He'd said it like it was no big deal, and Monique had a feeling that to him it wasn't. But evidently his family was going to make it a big deal and so would she. "And how do you feel about having another birthday?" she asked.

"Good as opposed to not having one. I feel grateful. Glad to be alive. In my profession you deal with so many who wish, almost too late, that they had done a better job of taking care of their heart."

She nodded her head. She could definitely believe that.

Their song came to an end, but before they could leave the dance floor, another slow number began playing, so instead of releasing her, Lyle pulled her back into his arms. He was ready to go another round on the dance floor.

"I had a wonderful time tonight, Lyle. I can't recall the last time I had so much fun."

He glanced down at her. "I'm glad you enjoyed yourself."

When they'd returned to the inn, he walked her to her room and opened the door for her. Being the gentleman that he was, he had asked to go inside to check things out as he'd done earlier that day.

She'd let him lead, following him around the room as he checked in closets and under her bed. She, on the other hand, was checking out something else altogether. Besides his seductive scent, he was wearing a pair of black slacks and a gray shirt. His physical appeal nearly had her panting.

"You've been watching too many of those crime shows," she said sometime later, walking him to the door after his inspection was over.

"Maybe so, but you can't take unnecessary chances these days."

She had to agree with him on that. "What time do you want to return to Hilton Head tomorrow?" she asked. Her mind was still back on the dance floor. Each time their bodies had touched, rubbed against each other, she'd felt the hardness of him pressing against her middle. That had been a dead giveaway that friendship hadn't been the main thing on his mind.

"I'm not in a rush, unless there's a reason you need to get back early," he said.

She shook her head and gave him a soft smile. "No, there's no reason. I talked to Faith and Shannon earlier, before we left to go dancing, and they're doing fine, holding down the fort. They told me to have a good time tonight and I did. Thanks again."

He placed the key back in her hand. "You're welcome. And if you don't mind, I prefer not leaving until after lunch tomorrow. That way we can sleep in late and enjoy a brunch at one of the restaurants."

"Sounds like a good plan." She had a feeling that like her, he wasn't ready for their weekend together to end.

For the longest time they didn't say anything, but just stood there staring at each other; then Lyle cleared his voice and said in a husky voice, "I really like this outfit."

She glanced down at herself. "I thought it would be perfect for tonight."

"And it was." What he didn't tell her was that she looked perfect in the dress and had felt perfect in his arms. Suddenly his heart swelled with love for her. He could hardly stand it—he needed to leave. Now. "I better go before I . . ." His words drifted off when she licked her top lip with her tongue.

"Before you what?" She glanced into his eyes and saw blatant desire there but wanted him to say it, to spell it out for her.

"Do this."

And then he reached out and pulled her to him. His kiss was gentle. It was sweet. It took her breath away when he took her mouth now with a hunger that astounded her. It made her realize that the cool, calm, and collected Dr. Lyle Montgomery could be tempted. But then, so could she.

She felt sparks.

She could imagine his skill in the operating room, but it appeared he possessed another skill, one he was applying pretty thick now. Arousal, quick and immediate, caught her, and she felt herself shivering in his arms. This wasn't an ordinary kiss. This was a kiss of possession, of intent and deep desire.

He slowly broke off the kiss and as if warring with what he'd just done, he took a step back. "Good night, Nicky."

She sucked in a deep breath to calm her racing pulse. When he opened the door to leave, she said, "Good night, Lyle."

26

Shannon sat on a pier with her legs dangling over the edge while she sipped a cup of coffee and looked out toward the ocean. It was Sunday morning. She had surprised even herself at how early she had awakened, and since going back to sleep hadn't been an option, she'd decided to put on some clothes and mosey on down to the beach to one of the coffee shops.

She knew Faith was still asleep after having read her killer thriller novel well into the night. When Shannon got up at midnight to raid the fridge of the leftover lasagna, she had seen the light shining underneath the door to Faith's room.

Shannon stood and dusted the back of her black shorts, thinking that with no plans for the day, it would probably be a boring one. In a way she wished she could do like Faith and read for pleasure, but there was pleasure and then there was *pleasure.*

Despite not wanting to do so, she glanced down at her watch. It was a little past eight. She wondered what Adam was doing. Had he gotten out of bed yet to begin his day? Was he still planning to spend his entire Sunday working on that car?

Why am I even thinking about him? she wondered, feeling annoyed with herself.

But then she knew why. Her body was remembering how it felt to be in his arms, his bed, to be pinned beneath hard muscular legs, to have her body stretched to the hilt while he entered her, and being thrust into, over and over again just in that right spot, dead center, that made you moan, groan, and throb for release. And when the explosion hit, it came and shook your body to the core, making you fight to keep your sanity while absorbing multiple shock waves and fiery sensations that rocked the living daylights out of you.

And yet you still wanted more.

Shannon hugged her arms around her middle, shivering despite her best efforts to control it. She released a long-suffering sigh, getting angrier by the minute at her lack of willpower. She could not get Adam Corbain and his sexual abilities out of her mind.

But that was her problem. She couldn't stop thinking about him because in all her thirty-two years, she had never met a man quite like him. He was a man whose incredible body could turn raw sex into a masterpiece, a work of art.

But then there were those times in between their lovemaking sessions when they had actually talked. To her surprise, he was well versed on economics, probably from all those *Wall Street Journals* he read, no doubt. But that showed he had potential to be a lot more than what he was.

And she didn't like it when he gave orders as if he actually expected her to follow the line, like him mentioning for her to come help him work on that car today. Did he actually think she would show up?

There was no man alive who could make her do anything without asking nicely first. It was time Adam saw that.

"Linc, it's clean, man," Adam said into the phone to his brother, while glancing over at his GTO. "Another three weeks, and this baby will be in excellent running condition."

Moments later he nodded. "Yes, I still plan to stop by D.C. to see Sydney and Tyrone before returning home." He smiled. "Tell Raven that I'm going to hold her to that. A home-cooked meal is right up my alley. Okay, I'll see you soon. Give Grant and the folks my best, and tell them I'm doing fine."

He hung up the phone and sighed deeply. Hell, he wasn't doing fine. His mind, his thoughts, his entire being were wrapped in the memory of a woman with an incredible mouth. But that wasn't all Shannon Carmichael had.

She had a face with the beauty of an angel, a body that made a Coca-Cola bottle weep, a tongue that was sharp and delicious at the same time, and inner muscles that clenched him better than any pair of pliers when he was inside her. She pulled everything out of him.

She was a sex vixen if ever there was one. A snooty sex vixen at that. And like it nor not, she had gotten under his skin and no amount of washing could get her out.

Damn.

Ever since the last time he'd been with her, he had prowled around like a caged lion pining for his lioness before finally calling himself all kinds of fool. Even this morning he had moped around before finally picking up the wrench to start working on his car. But that hadn't kept his mind from wandering every so often to remember the sound of her moan when he kissed her, the sound of her groan when he entered her, and the depth of her scream when she came.

The raw sensuality of what they shared suddenly had his jeans feeling tight in one particular spot. A hot pulsing ache had him almost bursting out his zipper. Hell. This was as crazy as it could get. No woman had ever affected him this way, to make him perform like a stallion in heat, as uncultured as she actually thought him to be.

And that's what really had him pissed. He didn't expect her to show up today to help him work on the car, hadn't figured she would when he'd asked, but he'd done so anyway, thinking he might catch her in a weak moment. He'd been disillusioned to think that women like Shannon had weak moments. She was as boogie as they came, with an emotionally wrenched heart on top of it. Over the years, someone had convinced her that she was all of that and a bag of chips, and she measured a man's worth by his academic echelon and his bank account. She haughtily believed that she had an automatic right to the best of everything, and anyone she considered less than her equal didn't stand a chance.

And she assumes I am less than her equal.

The very thought should have him rolling on the floor laughing, but he was hard-pressed to find a damn thing funny. In fact, anger seared through him. He could very well do without a woman like Shannon Carmichael disrupting his well-ordered, uncluttered life. She had gotten what she wanted from him, and truth be told, he'd gotten what he wanted from her. Unemotional sex. While she might have enjoyed all the physical pleasures he'd given her, he knew she had inwardly loathed and resented what she thought he represented.

Deciding to dismiss Shannon from his mind permanently, he began getting the tools together that he would use today. Since it was Sunday, most of the businesses in the area were closed, which meant without a lot of noise, he would be able to get some work done.

He felt his muscles tense as he turned around slowly, thinking he'd heard a sound. Although he didn't want it to, intense pleasure gushed through his veins and a deep feeling of heat rushed through every pore. His snooty sex vixen was standing at the window, staring at him.

Shannon had always prided herself on total control, but as her gaze locked with Adam's she suddenly discovered she had none left. Somehow, the man had done something no other man had been capable of doing. He had tempted her beyond reason, given her a taste of what real sexual delight was all about and had brought to life any fantasy she'd ever possessed.

Because of him she was breaking rules she'd never broken before, not thinking logically, throwing common sense to the wind, and shedding certain principles and values that she'd acquired over a lifetime.

On the drive over here, she'd known she'd made a choice. She would sacrifice everything for another night in Adam's bed. And she quickly dismissed the icky feeling that it was more than that. As heat began spreading through her limbs from the way he was staring back at her, she refused to believe this strange attraction could be based on more than just sex.

Don't dismiss that thought, because it could be.

Shannon's chest tightened at the familiar voice that had sounded quietly in her ear: Cely's voice. Thinking she had really stepped over the deep end in more ways than one, she continued to be locked into Adam's gaze. His expression was unreadable, so she couldn't tell if he was glad to see her or not. But through the clear windowpane she couldn't dismiss the look in his dark eyes. Hot, unadulterated desire. Whether he was glad to see her didn't matter. He wanted her. Just like she wanted him. And although she wondered if she'd made a mistake by coming here, some deep womanly instinct assured her it wouldn't be a waste of her time.

Adam stood immobile. Almost glued to the spot. It was hard to believe she was back, and the magnetic pull between them was more potent, fiercer, and more intense than ever. And knowing she needed him to make the next move, he took a step forward, then another as he headed toward the garage door.

He opened it, thinking that today it took longer than usual to go up. While he waited, a prickle of anticipation flowed up his spine, that part of him pressing against his zipper got harder, and he could barely pull in a normal breath. And when the door was finally up all the way and she begin walking toward him, his gaze raked her from head to toe. At that moment he knew that Shannon Carmichael had become his obsession.

She was wearing a pair of black shorts and a T-shirt, hardly an outfit for messing around in a garage, but definitely one that could take his mind off the work he was supposed to get done today. The shorts were almost too short to be considered decent. They showed too much of her legs, legs that could wrap around him, lock him inside her, refusing to let go even when the warm gush of his release flooded her insides. Those long, gorgeous legs carried a sexuality that was more intoxicating than the strongest whiskey.

She was stunningly beautiful, annoyingly confident, and snobbish as all outdoors. But at the moment, the latter didn't matter. It was something he intended to work on. Starting now.

When she stepped over the threshold, she didn't stop there. She kept walking until she was standing directly in front of him. And when he pushed the button to lower the garage door back down, he knew the last thing he intended to do was to ask why she was there. Like the other times, it was clearly obvious. And like before, no matter how much his hormones ached to pick her up and carry her up to the apartment and make love to her all day, he intended to do things his way.

But first things first. He reached out and pulled her to him, and before a gasp of surprise could escape her lips, he had those lips smothered under his, greedily lapping up any sigh she was to make. On instinct, his tongue went deeper into her mouth, moved all around to taste and possess while his hands moved down to her narrow waist, bringing her closer to the fit of him, wanting her to feel the pressure of his desire for her.

Damn and damn all over again. He wanted her. Here and now. His arousal was so intense, he knew if he didn't have her at that moment, he would go insane.

Within minutes he had unhooked his jeans and pushed them and his briefs down past his knees. She had quickly gotten the idea and had removed her shorts and panties, tossing both aside. He surprised her when he flipped her around, and to keep from stumbling she placed hands, palms down, on the hood of his car. And then he was directly behind her, molded skin to skin to the delicious curve of her buttocks while his fingers eased between her legs.

He heard the sound she made deep in her throat the exact moment he touched her wetness, caressing her intimately with his fingers over and over. She whispered his name . . . *his name* . . . between clenched teeth, and the sound pushed him over the edge.

Aroused to the Nth degree, he cupped her bottom in his hands, tilted her hips upward, and on an urgent groan he drove into her from behind. He thrust in and out, frantically stroking her, and her satisfied moans only made him increase the pace. Over and over he pounded into her, felt her clench him, milk him, demand that he let go and explode inside her, and his heart was thumping at the realization that for a minute he'd been able to read her thoughts. And with that another slow, nearly painful realization struck him, one he refused to acknowledge at that moment, one he refused to acknowledge ever. Instead he continued thrusting into her, and when she let out a loud scream of pleasure that almost shook the windows, he exploded, shooting deep inside her womb. He felt it. Thick. Hot. He felt her clench him with her inner muscles, milk him more fiercely while he gave her just what she wanted, what it seemed her body needed.

He didn't pull out of her until there was nothing left to give; then he turned her around and captured her mouth in his, tasting each and every one of her aftershocks, and at that moment all he could think about, although he didn't want to, was the fact that he wanted this, all of it—her—for the rest of his life.

Shannon let out a deep satisfied sigh as she wiped down the leather interior of the car. After making love to her and then delivering such a torrid and passionate kiss, Adam had given her the key to his apartment so she could use his bathroom to freshen up a bit. When she returned downstairs, he had been waiting for her and handed her a cloth and a bottle of leather cleaner and told her what he wanted done.

She glanced out the windshield at him. He had an intense look on his face while he worked on some auto part she wasn't familiar with. Hell, she hadn't known a car had so many parts, and he seemed to know them as well as he knew the parts of a woman's body. He definitely had a way with women, and his expertise spoke of what was probably years of experience. Although she didn't know his exact age, she would figure he was no older than thirty-five.

She then realized of all the things they'd shared, mostly sexual, there was a lot she still didn't know about him and figured since they had a lot of time to kill, now was just as good a time as any to start asking questions. "How old are you?" she called out, getting his attention.

He glanced over at her through the windshield, and the grin that spread across his face was full of sin and sensuality, a deadly combination. She wished it didn't set off this rush of desire spreading through her.

"Old enough to make what we just did an hour ago perfectly legal," he said before turning his attention back to what he was doing.

"I'm sure of that, but just how old are you?"

"How old do you think I am?"

"Umm, around thirty-four or thirty-five."

He threw his head back and laughed.

Shannon looked bemused. "What's so funny?"

"You're off by a couple of years."

"Up or down?"

"Up."

She nodded. "You're thirty-seven then."

He smiled at her. "Bingo."

"You wear your age well."

"Thanks."

"Have you been a mechanic all your life?"

Adam kept his eyes on what he was doing. He knew that now was a good time to tell her the truth, that he wasn't a mechanic at all and that he was a highly successful attorney in Memphis. He could further boast that he came from a family of attorneys and that they owned a very well established, very affluent law firm there and that he was the oldest son of Judge Warren Corbain.

But Adam also knew if her were to tell her the truth about himself and they continued to see each other, he would never know if the reason she'd hung around was because he was someone she considered worthy of her social class or because he was someone she truly wanted to get to know and be with—regardless of his occupation and personal history.

Although he didn't want to deceive her, deep down he knew

there was a reason he was about to mislead her. Shannon needed to learn that you couldn't go around placing people in nice little slots.

"Pretty much," he finally answered, and said, "What about you? How long have you been teaching in the university system?"

"Five years, right after getting my doctorate. I graduated from high school at sixteen and went straight on through and had my doctorate before I turned twenty-five. First I taught at a small private university in Ohio for a few years, and then I got the opportunity to move to Duke. I worked hard and was tenured by the time I was twenty-eight."

Adam nodded. That was impressive. "And how old are you?" he asked.

"Thirty-two. I have a birthday coming up in September." For a brief moment Shannon wondered why she'd even bothered to mention that. It wasn't as if they would still be having a fling then. She then glanced back at him. "Have you ever wanted to do something else?"

He glanced at her and lifted a brow. "Something like what?"

She shrugged. "Anything other than mechanic work. Did you ever aspire to do something different?"

"Yes. At one time I wanted to drag-race cars, but my father put his foot down and my mother was extremely grateful he did."

She nodded. "Both your parents are still alive?"

His smile widened. "Yes, very much so."

"Any siblings?"

Adam wondered where all these questions were leading to. "Yes, I got two brothers and a sister. I'm the oldest. Everyone is married except for me and my brother Grant." Adam thought she didn't particularly seem to be impressed with that information.

"When will you be through repairing this car?"

Again Adam found himself amused and bit down to keep from laughing out loud for a second time. "This car is not getting repaired."

"Oh? Then what are you doing to it?"

He glanced back at her. "I'm restoring it. There's a difference."

"Oh, I see."

He shook his head, knowing she really didn't see at all. "Tell me about your parents," he said, suddenly wondering about the couple who'd given life to her and how much they contributed to her attitude about a lot of things.

"What do you want to know?"

"Are you close to them?"

He heard when she drew in a shaky breath before turning her face away from him. Evidently the subject of her parents was a rather sore one. But she'd asked him about his, and so as far as he was concerned, it was fair play to inquire about hers. "Shannon?"

She turned her attention back to him. "I'm their only child, so in a way we're close but my parents are and have always been dictators. I think the only reason I was born is because they felt it was logical for them to have a child, and my parents are very logical people."

He nodded. "Why do you say they're dictators?"

"Because they are. For as long as I can remember, they told me what to do, how to dress, how to act, who to become friends with, who not to become friends with, who to date, who not to date, what career to choose . . . so on and so forth."

"You never felt the need to stand up to them when you got older?" Adam asked. His parents hadn't been that way. He, his parents, and siblings had a close relationship, and he couldn't imagine it being any other way.

"Yes," she said coolly. "But then with my parents, you learn not to rock the boat. That's why them living in Connecticut and me living in North Carolina is the best thing. We get together for the usual holidays when I'm summoned to come home, but that's about it."

"What about—?"

"I don't want to talk about them anymore. In fact, I suggest we stay away from getting too personal with each other."

"All right." Adam knew what she didn't say: *Except when we get physical.* And that was as personal as it could get. It was obvious to him that she was trying to keep him at a distance, not wanting him to get involved in the personal side of her life. As far as he was concerned, that was too damn bad—because he intended to get as up close and personal as he could.

27

Zach was intense and greatly intrigued with the subject matter he was painting. And he was deeply in love. They said beauty was in the eye of the beholder and if that was true, he thought he'd never feasted his eyes upon a more breathtaking sight.

Anna sat demurely still, in the center of the room in a high wing-back leather chair of a neutral beige color. The sunlight pouring in through an open window seemed to bathe her in a sort of radiant glow. He was determined to capture that glow with every stroke he made.

Her hair was down, flowing around her shoulders, just the way he liked, and the light pink dress she wore gave all new meaning to femininity. Her feet were bare, which was fine, since he didn't intend to show anything past her waistline, an area he had gotten to know pretty well last night. Even now, shivers ran through him when he remembered everything about their intimate time together, especially her innocence and how she had entrusted him with a gift he would cherish always.

It was Sunday, a little past noon. They had awakened early and made love again before getting up for breakfast. They had been sitting out on the porch, eating pancakes with bacon and eggs and sipping coffee when the sun came up, as stunning as it had been when it went down yesterday. And all the while he'd sat across from Anna, watching her eat and slowly drink her coffee, he had felt this intense love as well as an extreme desire for her. And it didn't help matters to know this would be their last day alone on Glendale Shores.

The rest of the family would start arriving tomorrow at different times, and because he and Anna wouldn't want to be caught un-awares, it would be safer for them not to share a bed tonight. Not that he was trying to keep their relationship a secret—to him it was a matter of respect.

When he placed the paintbrush aside to step back and study his work, he let out a satisfied sigh, extremely pleased with the finished product. He had done a good job of capturing Anna's beauty on the canvas. She could be a model for any magazine cover. She had a beau-tifully shaped face with a cocoa-colored skin tone, dark almond-shaped eyes, full lips, and a straight nose. He thought now the same thing he'd thought the first time he saw her. She was heavenly.

"Are you finished?"

He glanced up and smiled. "Yes, sweetheart, I'm done."

"May I see it?"

"Yes."

He watched how she rose gracefully from the chair to come and stand beside him. "So what do you think?" he asked.

She turned to him with tears in her eyes. "Oh, Zach, you make me look . . ." It was if she was looking for the right word to say.

"Look how?"

"Beautiful."

He laughed. "Anna, you *are* beautiful. Why is that so hard to be-lieve?" He knew such compliments were hard for her to take.

"Because while growing up, the other Vietnamese wanted the children like me to feel that way. Most of them hated Americans and disliked the Eurasians as well because of our mixed blood. They made us feel like ugly outcasts."

Familiar anger raced through Zach at what she had needlessly endured as a child while her father's family and her father's best friend had tirelessly tried to find her to bring her home.

"Well, no matter what you were told then, I'm telling you now. Again," he said, reaching out and pulling her into his arms, "that you're beautiful and I love you."

"Thank you, Zach, and I love you, too. I love you so much, it scares me."

He lifted a brow when he felt her shiver. "It scares you in what way?"

She released a somewhat shaky breath. "I know you talked to your parents and my uncle about us, and that you believe my grandparents will be fine with it, but what about others?"

He pulled back and studied her face and actually saw the worry lines there. "Others like who? Trey and Haywood? My sister Noelle? Randi? Who?"

"No, none of them. I was thinking more of the people you associate with in Washington. Your friends. I can't help but remember what happened when the media thought we had a thing going before when we actually didn't. What will they do when they find out that now we really do? They can be mean and hateful."

"Yes, but we have to keep in mind that what we do and how we feel about each other is nobody's business but ours. Reporters want to sell newspapers, so sometimes they print stuff that's more speculation that proven truth. Our love has to be strong to survive that, and I think it is."

A small smile touched her lips. "You're so positive."

He smiled warmly. "There's no way I can't be. I just discovered within the past twenty-four hours that the woman I love actually loves me in return. I feel like a very blessed man."

He pulled her closer into his arms and captured her lips, kissing her with an intensity that he wanted her to feel too. And when he deepened the kiss, he could feel their shared desire taking over. "Everyone starts arriving tomorrow," he whispered against her lips when he reluctantly ended the kiss. "So this will be our last day alone, and I want to make it special for us. Later today I think it would be nice if we were to have a picnic by the pond."

She smiled. "That would be nice, but you said later today. What do you plan to do now?"

He placed a light kiss on her moist lips and said, "Go back to bed. If I do, will you join me there?"

"Yes."

He took her hand and led her up the stairs to his bedroom.

28

Although it seemed crazy, Monique would swear her lips were still tingling from Lyle's kiss of the night before when she met him downstairs in the lobby. She wasn't quite ready when he'd called, and when he offered to come to her room and wait while she finished dressing, she quickly suggested that he wait for her in the lobby instead.

All last night she'd been restless, barely getting any sleep. Lyle's kiss had reminded her of the sorry state of her sex life, and it had reminded her in a big way. Never had her body felt so sensitive to touch, something she discovered when she'd gotten dressed for bed. Then there were those fantasies that kept floating through her mind: visions of them together, wrapped in each other's arms, kissing . . . making love.

More than just sparks!

That particular memory resurfaced the exact moment her feet touched the last stair and she saw him. Their gazes connected, and she felt an unmistakable air of sensuality surrounding them and quickly drew in her breath. She'd known she was attracted to Lyle, but she'd not known the degree of that attraction until now.

Okay—she would admit there was this charged chemistry flowing between them, but what was she supposed to do about it? The answer was quick: not a doggone thing. She didn't know the first thing about seducing a man. Paul had been the first and only man she'd ever slept with, and until Lyle, she'd not entertained any thoughts of sharing herself with anyone else.

She watched as he crossed the floor to her, and inhaled sharply when he took her hand and laced her fingers with his before leaning over and placing a chaste kiss on her lips.

"You're ready to go?" he asked, his voice deep and sensual.

She was tempted to tell him that she was ready for a lot of things, but decided not to. She'd never been that forward with any man and the way he was looking at her with those dark intense eyes of his was making her heart beat erratically in her chest. "Yes, I'm ready."

He led her out the door, and when they stepped into the sunlight, he turned to her, his expression serious. "About last night . . ."

His voice was low and husky, and she wondered what he was going to say. When he didn't say anything, she prompted, "What about it?"

"Our kiss."

She met his intense gaze. "Yes?"

"Maybe I should apologize, but I won't. It's something I've wanted to do for a long time."

This was news to her, and curiosity made her ask, "For how long?"

"Ever since that first time Arnie took me home with him, which was our first year of med school."

Surprise lit her eyes. "But I was only sixteen."

He nodded. "Yes, I know. You were sixteen, yet so utterly beautiful, I couldn't help but be attracted to you then. If your parents had known how much, they would have asked me to leave. You were sixteen and I was twenty-one. That was a big difference in our ages, although you had a maturity about you that was beyond your sixteen years."

Monique shook her head, not wanting to believe any of what he was saying. How could he have been attracted to her and she not know it? He'd always treated her with respect yet indifference, like he thought of her as nothing more than Arnie's kid sister. "Did Arnie know?"

"Not for a long time, but then I think he began to suspect something when he found that picture of you that I kept in my drawer. It was the one we took together that day when me, you, and Arnie had gone to New Orleans. It accidentally fell out my wallet. He never said anything, but I think in a way he knew."

Monique remembered that day. She'd heard that he and Arnie had plans to go to New Orleans for the weekend, and she begged them to take her along, and they had.

When Lyle didn't say anything for a long moment, Monique had a feeling there was something he wasn't telling her, something he was holding back. And then she wondered if he'd regretted telling her anything at all. What was she supposed to do with such information?

"I hope you're hungry," he finally said.

With those words she knew he was through discussing anything about yesteryears. "I'm starving, actually."

He grinned. "Good. I'm going to feed you, and then we'll head back to Hilton Head," he said, tugging on her arm to lead her down the sidewalk.

"All right."

She wanted them to stop walking so she could tell him that she'd noticed him that summer as well, and that when she'd seen Cely, Shannon, and Faith the following month, she had told them all about him. But at the time she'd thought her attraction was that of a teenage girl finally noticing boys for the first time. She would never have thought in a million years that it was reciprocated.

But it had been, and knowing that only compounded her problems.

Lyle would have liked nothing better than to pull Monique into his arms at that moment and kiss her again, but knew he had to practice control. At least he had told her about his feelings back in the day. No, in all actuality, he hadn't told her about his feelings. He'd only told her that he'd been attracted to her. He'd deliberately left out the part that he had also fallen in love with her then, and that he still loved her now.

As they continued walking side by side, a number of thoughts ran through his mind. This could have been strictly speculation on his part, but he had a feeling that she'd enjoyed their kiss last night as much as he had. At first he'd known that he took her by surprise, but then she returned it, putting as much fervor into it as he had.

It had been hell trying to sleep after a kiss like that, and he'd stayed awake, late into the night, just lying in bed, thinking about her, wanting her, and needing her. He couldn't recall the last time he'd been with a woman. It had been that long ago. He'd been so wrapped up in his work that a love life was something he'd pretty much kicked by the wayside. Lance would tease him all the time about him not getting any—but then would further say not to fret because he was getting enough for the both of them.

Lyle shook his head, grinning, thinking of how the one brother who swore he would never be a one-woman man was now just that. Lance was happily married with a baby on the way, which proved that miracles could happen.

Lyle glanced over at Monique as she walked quietly beside him. He'd always told Lance that he would settle down with a woman once he found one who could make his heart tremble. Monique had done that the first time he met her, and she was doing it now. She was the only woman who could do that.

When they reached their restaurant, he held the door for Monique to step inside. It was then that she glanced up at him and just that quick, that spontaneously, a jolt of electricity shot through him, and although they hadn't touched, he had a feeling she'd felt it as well. Neither of them spoke. They just stood there staring at each other for a long moment before someone else cleared his throat, reminding them that they were blocking the doorway.

Lyle's stomach muscles tightened as he gently took Monique's hand to lead her to an empty table. From his standpoint it appeared that Operation Monique was now under way, and her healing process was going to be one that he would guide as meticulously as he performed any heart operation. He was going to make sure of it.

29

"*This place is* simply beautiful, Zach," Anna said, glancing around at the place they had chosen to have their picnic. They had spread a blanket near a pond that was fed by an underground spring. It was a beautiful spot, picturesque and scenic.

They had returned to bed after breakfast and made love again and again, and each time Zach had filled her body with his, she felt connected to him in a very special way, making her fall in love with him that much more. He was the most considerate man she knew, and he always made sure she got her pleasure before taking his. She'd learned from listening to other women talk around the various hospitals where she worked that not all men were so selfless.

"Yes, it is beautiful, isn't it?" Zach said. "And it has a lot of history."

She smiled, recalling some of that history. She remembered the first time she had come here. It was with her uncle Randolph not long after she'd been united with her family. He had sat on one those tree stumps and told her how he and her father would spend their summers on Glendale Shores while growing up, and would go swimming in this pond all the time, and all the fun they had, just the two of them. She knew from listening to him that he and her father had been as close as any brothers could be, but then she had figured as much from the old love letters her father had written to her mother.

"I know," she said softly. "This is where Haywood and Trey got married." And smiling she added, "And where Haywood says Quad was conceived."

Zach chuckled. "I wouldn't doubt it." He decided not to mention that he'd once overheard his parents say that this particular spot was where her uncle Randolph and his wife, Jenna, had conceived their daughter Randi as well. It would probably shock her to imagine her suave, polished, and debonair uncle and his beautiful and sophisticated wife being so passionate.

He then shook his head, thinking his parents were just as bad. He had walked in on them unexpectedly enjoying a passionate kiss a number of times. His parents' ardent love for each other was something he and his sister had always accepted and appreciated, and after nearly thirty-six years of marriage, it hadn't waned any.

"So how are things back in D.C?"

He tilted his head and looked over at her, wondering if there was any particular reason she'd asked. "Mostly the same. Everyone, especially my father, is hoping the war in Iraq doesn't turn into another Vietnam. So many lives have been lost already," he said.

"I hate war," Anna said bitterly. "It was what took my father away. But then it was also what brought my parents together in the first place. I guess there's no perfect world."

He reached out and took her hand in his. "Sure there is a perfect world and it's here, in this very place. I can't think of anything more perfect than the two of us here together after having confessed our love for each other and consummating that love. In my mind there can't be anything more perfect than that, Anna."

His words touched her and as she gazed deep into the eyes, she felt the love he spoke of and saw it in the dark depths the same way she knew he was seeing it in hers. A shudder suddenly coursed through her, and she knew she wanted to leave their own bit of history in this place as well. It would be something they would always remember when they came here.

She pressed against him, making them tumble back together on the blanket. She then pushed up on her knees, straddled his thighs, and looked down at him. "I love you, Zachary Wainwright, with all my heart and with all my soul."

Zach was so touched by her words that he reached out and cupped her face in his hands. At that moment he wanted to ask her to marry him, spend the rest of her life with him, but he knew to do so now without telling her everything would not be fair. And he didn't want to spoil the moment by announcing that he wanted to run for a public office. So instead, he whispered back to her, "And I love you, Adrianna Ross-Fuller, so much I ache."

And then he brought her head down to meet his, focusing on her lower lip, a place he'd recently discovered as a spot that could drive her over the edge. So after kissing her thoroughly, he gently attacked her bottom lip, licking, tasting, and sucking on it, enjoying the sound of the moans she made, knowing what he was doing was escalating her desire.

When he pulled back, he saw the intensity of the heat flaring in her eyes. "Oh, Zach, I want you so much," she murmured in a voice that was filled with so much yearning, it overwhelmed him. "And I want you now," she said, reaching out and pulling his T-shirt out of his shorts. He helped her by shrugging it off and tossing it aside.

And with desperation he'd never seen in her before, he watched her go to his zipper and with nervous but eager fingers begin lowering it. She then reached inside the opening and tightened those same fingers around him, holding tight. And then she slowly began stroking him. He felt himself grow even larger, get harder, within her grip.

"Let's make our own lasting memories here, in this very place, Zach," she whispered, releasing him but only long enough to whip her tank top over her head and wiggle out of her own shorts, glad she hadn't bothered with putting on a bra and panties.

She returned to him, getting on her knees over him, and immediately leaned down to kiss him. A short while later she pulled back and smiled. "Now where was I before I stopped to take off my clothes?"

She reached for him, taking his erection in her hand again in a firm grip, noticing it hadn't gone down any. In fact, it seemed larger than before. She'd never touched a man this way and was thrilled to do so now. She doubted there was a man anywhere any more developed or well made, and she began stroking him, kneading his thick, hard shaft, watching his facial expressions as she did so. Seeing the effect her touch was having on him made her feel wanton, sexy, and provocative.

"I can't take any more," Zach whispered through clenched teeth. "I want you now."

He tumbled her backward, quickly positioning himself between her thighs. And while looking into her eyes, he entered her, feeling her body stretch wide for him as he buried himself within her to the hilt. He began moving and she began moving with him as they once again established the rhythm, the beat, the cadence tempo they had created the night before. He felt the tremors in his belly with every thrust he made, he heard the sensuous whimpering sounds she began making, and all of it increased the urgency, the craving, the necessity of being overtaken by turbulent waves together.

And then it happened, and she cried out his name when an orgasm crashed into her at the same time one slammed into him. The very air they breathed seemed to thicken with unadulterated pleasure, intense fulfillment, and never-ending desire as he thrust into her over and over again, convulsed in a climax so strong, it nearly took his breath away. He fought to inhale, exhale, as his body started shaking almost uncontrollably.

And he knew that what he had with Anna, what they were sharing, was something he wanted . . . for always.

30

Adam sighed deeply. For the first time in his life his total concentration wasn't where it needed to be while working on one of his cars. Instead of focusing his attention on repairing the GTO's transmission, his thoughts were on the woman who was upstairs taking a nap in his bed.

He smiled, thinking he had definitely gotten a lot of work out of her today. The leather upholstery in the GTO almost sparkled, and so did the dashboard and console. Once she had stopped asking questions and had gotten to work, Shannon turned into one hell of an assistant.

He had ordered in lunch, and after they had eaten, she asked if she could take a break and a short nap. That had been an hour or so ago. Several times over the past hour he'd been tempted to say to hell with working today and go upstairs and crawl in bed with her. What they'd shared earlier that day had been incredible. In his thirty-seven years he'd slept with plenty of women, but he couldn't recall one giving him the level of euphoria that he'd reached while inside Shannon's body.

Hell.

He hadn't counted on this. The memories. The intense arousal that wouldn't go away. The urge to throw his wrench down and go upstairs, wake her up, and make love to her again. If he wasn't careful, she could become addictive, habit-forming, embedded deep into his system. He had to stay grounded, on guard, and watch his own back . . . but then all he had to do was recall all the things she could do to his front. His body hardened even more at the thought, and the memory had him perspiring. She had shown him that she could do a lot more with her mouth than talk sass, and he had come apart under her assault, her ultimate gift of pleasure to him.

He threw the wrench down, unable to work any longer. He knew what he wanted. He knew what he needed, and heaven help him, he knew what he had to have. Now.

He intended to quench all his desires and worry about the risk later. Not today.

Shannon slowly came awake and forced open her eyes. She glanced at the clock on the wall and saw it was late afternoon. How long had she been napping? She smiled. If she'd been a real employee, Adam would have fired her by now.

She hated admitting it, but she enjoyed working alongside Adam on that car. They had talked, and she was surprised about all the stuff he knew about the economy, politics, foreign affairs . . . those things she figured someone in his social class wouldn't bother knowing. She could only assume his reading of *The Wall Street Journal* was the primary reason for it. She couldn't help but admire him wanting to improve himself.

She shifted in bed, thinking she better get up before Adam came looking for her. She pulled herself out of bed, remembering what they'd shared when she first arrived that day. No one had ever taken her on a car before, and just the thought sent her body into a fever. The man took on sex like it was his most favorite pastime.

She recalled the last time she had been in his bed, that time she had spent the night. After a couple of rounds of raw, hot lovemaking, he had toned things down a bit and made love to her slow and easy.

She smiled, thinking she had probably surprised the hell out of him when, while showering together, she dropped to her knees and took him into her mouth, needing to know the taste of him. Greedily, she had explored his erection with her tongue from tip to the shaft, finding it easy to do to him what she'd never done to another man. And when he hadn't been able to take any more, he had pulled her into his arms and kissed her hard and senseless, making her climax just from the invasion of his tongue in her mouth.

Amazing.

Shannon tilted her head back and inhaled deeply. For the first time in her life she felt herself consumed by a situation she couldn't handle with a man—one where it was obvious she was losing control. Some inner struggle was taking place, and she wasn't sure how to proceed. The most logical thing would be to get out of Dodge while she had the chance, before Adam Corbain became her one downfall. He was all wrong for her. *Except in bed.* They had nothing in common. *Except in bed.*

And that's what she had to do: remember to stay focused on that one major point. This was an affair. Nothing more. Affairs weren't intended to last. They were a pleasure boost, and nothing more. In a few weeks she would go her way and he would go his. He would be out of her sight as well as out of her mind. As long as she accepted and understood that, there wouldn't be any risk involved. Satisfied with that thought, she was about to cross the room to the bathroom when the apartment door was flung open. She turned to meet Adam's dark, intense gaze. He stood in the doorway, staring at her.

Seeing Shannon in the brightness of day, with the sun streaming through the window, made his body ache in a way it had never ached before. There was something about her in those damn black shorty shorts.

His hand immediately went to his zipper, and he watched her watch him slowly ease it down. He felt harder, fuller, although he knew such a thing was impossible. He then inched his jeans down his legs and kicked them aside. His T-shirt followed and within seconds, he was standing in front of her completely naked.

Shannon refused to back up. Besides, a wall was practically at her back. She knew just what was on his mind, and immediately her body was ready. And she really hadn't quite grasped the size of him all those other times. Jeez. The man was so well endowed, he should establish scholarships to the Adam Corbain School of Fine Arts.

"I want you again, Shannon," he said, slowly crossing the floor and coming to a stop in front of her.

She tried to keep her breathing under control. "What if I said that I'm not interested?"

A smile touched the corners of his lips. "Then I'll work hard to make you interested."

"Think you can?" she asked.

"I believe so," was his response. "Take off your clothes and prove me wrong if you dare to."

"I think I will."

He stepped back and watched her remove every stitch of her clothing. He'd never seen a striptease act so provocative. He leaned forward and backed her against the wall. "Now for a reminder."

She swallowed hard. "You're planning on giving me one?"

"Several."

She believed him. There was a flash of fire in his eyes, as well as a deep, intense look of desire. She should have known better than to challenge him. There was no way she could stand in front of a naked Adam Corbain and not be interested.

And when he reached out before she could blink and lifted her up and pinned her to the wall, she knew that whatever he did to her, she would not only be interested, but would also be an eager participant.

First Adam went for her breasts, needing to taste them, to feel them in his mouth. They were full, firm, and the nipples were protruding like they were just waiting for his attack. He stuck out his tongue and greedily licked them, sucked on the tips like they might disappear any moment.

He heard her moan, but he hadn't given her anything to moan about yet. He had a firm grip on her forearm to keep her from sink-ing to the floor but placed his knee between her open legs for added support. The moment he did so, he felt her wetness. She was ready for him. But first he intended to do what he'd wanted to do last night.

Make her his meal.

He eased her down so her feet touched the floor and then he got on his knees in front of her and couldn't recall the last time he'd done this to a woman, the last time he'd wanted to. But he needed Shannon's taste on his tongue the same way he needed air to breathe. With a rough, sensuous growl he placed a palm between her legs to widen them, then dipped his head and claimed this special part of her as his. The moment the tip of his tongue touched her, she screamed. But that didn't bother him. There would be plenty more screams before it was over.

For endless moments he continued to taste her like a man who'd been robbed of a meal for days. His tongue absorbed each and every sensation that passed through her, every pleasurable shock that her system endured without letting up, although she was begging him to. But then in another instant she was also begging him to continue, not to stop.

Without wavering he focused only on this, devouring her sweetness, the very essence of her womanhood. She had screamed three more times and still he wasn't through with her. Even the way her nails were deeply embedded in the flesh of his shoulders didn't bother him. His mouth was locked to her, tight, and he refused to let go until he was ready, and he wasn't ready yet. He liked her taste. He was a hungry man, and he intended to get his fill.

In a matter of moments, he felt himself about to come, just from her taste, and knew where he wanted his shaft to be when it happened. Gritting his teeth, clinging for control, he pulled himself to his feet, lifted her bottom, and wrapped her legs around him, and pinned her to the wall just seconds before he thrust into her. But she didn't seem to mind—her muscles began clenching him to pull everything she wanted out of him. It didn't take long for that to happen.

"Shannon!"

The orgasm that exploded from deep within him sent sensuous chills all the way up his spine, his thighs firm and strong, pinned her in one spot while he pounded into her, just like she was begging him to. Her screams of pleasure made any self-control he might have had vanish. Completely. He inwardly cursed her ability to do that to him, to bring him to this. But at the moment there wasn't a damn thing he could do about it.

When she collapsed against him, he felt as drained as she did, and without unlocking their bodies he made it over to the bed. And when they lay side by side with their bodies still locked, he threw his leg over her hip to keep them that way.

"It's getting late and I need to leave," she managed to whisper in a low, ragged breath.

"Not yet," he said, rubbing her back gently before moving his hand to her bottom and gently gripping it. "We're both tired. Let's take a nap together."

She met his gaze and he knew she was fighting whatever this thing was between them. This urgency, this obsession, whatever it was that seeped through their veins when they were within ten feet of each other, making them act sexually crazy.

Suddenly he felt himself get hard inside her. He knew she felt it as well. *Aw hell.*

At that moment he couldn't resist leaning over and taking her lips. He wanted her again. And at the moment he couldn't imagine not ever wanting her.

Adam suddenly came awake when he felt the dip in the mattress. He turned to see Shannon as she eased out of bed. He rolled to the side, lifted himself up on his elbow. It was dark outside. "You're leaving?" he asked when he watched her reach for her clothes that were still on the floor.

She glanced over at him. "Sorry, I hadn't meant to wake you, but yes, I'm leaving. It's nighttime already."

He nodded as his gaze raked up and down her naked body. "Come here for a second."

She looked at him skeptically, not sure she wanted to do that. "Really, Adam, I do need to go."

"I understand, but come here for a second," he coaxed in a low, sexy voice. "I promise not to keep you, and I'm walking you down to your car."

Unable to deny his request, she slowly crossed the room to him. "Closer," he whispered, not moving out of his reclining position on the bed, which brought him eye to eye with her navel. He reached out and brushed his knuckles against her belly. "Umm, I think I missed a spot." And then he leaned forward and took his tongue and swirled it around her navel while the palm of his hands eased between her thighs to caress her there.

"Think of me tonight," he said, giving her something to make doubly sure that she did. A shiver passed through him at the thought that now he knew her too well. He had her taste down pat. He knew how she felt when she came, whether he was inside her or not. When he came inside her, the explosion that would rip through him, made him want to bury himself between her succulent thighs forever.

"I got to get dressed and go, Adam," she said in a tone of voice he thought wasn't the least bit convincing. But he knew he had to let her leave in order to regain his control and, most important, his common sense.

He reluctantly pulled back. "Okay, I won't hold you up any longer. I want to ask a favor of you, though."

She inhaled deeply and glanced down at him. "What?"

"I'm going to a drag race on the Fourth in Savannah. I want you to go with me."

Shannon shook her head, and he could imagine what she was thinking. Sleeping with him was one thing, going on a date with him was another. That thought sent anger surging through him when she said, "I can't, Adam. That wasn't part of the deal."

A curse slipped past his lips as he pulled himself up in bed to sit.

"We never got around to making any deals, remember. We've been too busy getting our groove on."

She backed up, still shaking her head. "But I can't."

He met her gaze. "Can't or won't?"

She tossed her hair over her shoulder and glared at him. "Same difference."

"Maybe it's the same difference in your book, but it's not in mine. If you change your mind, be here the morning of the Fourth at ten."

She didn't say anything, and he watched as she raced into the bathroom, closing the door behind her.

Part four

Apply your heart to instruction, and your ears to the words of knowledge.

—PROVERBS 23:12

31

"*Well, it certainly* sounds like the both of you had a wonderful time," Faith said, smiling over at Shannon and Monique as she poured glasses of wine.

"Yes, but I feel bad that we left you here all alone," Monique said.

"Hey, don't feel bad. It was a lazy weekend for me. I finished one book and began another. This one was a romance novel that came highly recommended. I also practiced my tennis strokes and walked on the beach whenever the mood hit. I missed having you guys around, but it was okay."

What Faith refused to tell them was that while reading the romance novels and coming across several hot and explicit love scenes, she had reached for the phone ready to take Shane Masters up on his offer to spend some time over at his place, but her willpower had always won out and she hadn't. There had been times where things had gotten lonely and little too quiet, but her novels had pretty much kept her entertained. She had even gone next door to visit Anna and discovered her neighbor had gone away for the weekend as well. She then remembered Anna mentioning a few days ago that she would be spending the Fourth of July on that island her family owned.

"What do you want to do for the Fourth?" Faith asked. "Have the two of you made any plans?"

"No," Shannon said quickly, looking into the glass as if studying the contents of her wine. She remembered Adam's request that she go to a drag race in Savannah with him, and like she'd told him, there was no way she could do that. "I don't know about Monique, but I haven't made any. In fact, I plan to just hang around here and get some reading in."

Faith and Monique glanced over at each other. Since Shannon read so much with her regular job as a college professor, she detested sitting still and reading anything when they were together. They couldn't help but wonder if there was a particular reason for her wanting to do so now.

"No, I'm free on the Fourth, although Lyle mentioned he would like for us to do something together later that day. There's going to be fireworks somewhere on the island, and if possible, I'd like the two of you to meet him."

Shannon eased closer to the edge of her seat, interested. "Why? Are things serious between you two?"

Monique smiled. "No, he's still just a friend, but since I'm spending a lot of time with him, I want you to meet him."

Later that night, when Monique slipped into bed, she thought of what Shannon had asked earlier, and what she, in her opinion, had answered truthfully. She and Lyle were friends and nothing more—although she doubted friends had a tendency to lock lips the way they had while in Beaufort. After brunch they'd walked back to the inn to check out, and once they were on the road, they had easily slipped into conversation. When he stopped to gas up the car, she had gotten out to stretch her legs and had been standing by the car when he returned from paying the gas station attendant.

And without any type of warning at all, he'd touched her arm and leaned over and kissed her. And when they reached Hilton Head and he brought her home, he kissed her again before she'd gotten out of the car. He walked her to the door, too.

She couldn't dismiss from her mind the other thing he'd shared with her, the part about him being attracted to her when she'd been younger, and that the only thing that had kept him from making his move had been the difference in their ages. The five-year age difference didn't matter anymore, and she couldn't help wondering how he felt about that now.

Another thing she wondered about was how she was going to react when they jogged together in the morning. As she fluffed her pillow to settle down for the night, she couldn't wait to find out.

Faith glanced over at Shannon. "You aren't sleepy?" Usually of the three of them she was the first to retire for the night.

Shannon leaned back in her chair and smiled. "No, I'm fine," she said, deciding not to tell her about the long nap she'd taken over at Adam's place. "I really had fun working on that car with Adam today. I didn't think I would, but I did."

Faith nodded as she studied Shannon. "If you thought you weren't going to enjoy yourself, then why did you go?"

Shannon didn't say anything at first and then leaning forward, she placed her wineglass on the table. She thought about Adam and felt a gentle tug at her heart. She knew she shouldn't have gone there. What was there about him that made her mind go topsy-turvy where she threw sense, good common sense, out the window? Was the sex really that good that it should make her lose herself that deep?

"Shannon? What's going on with you? Do you need to talk?"

Shannon glanced over at Faith and considered her question. She then settled back in her chair, appreciated Faith giving her time to get her thoughts together. "Yes, I need to talk," she said softly. "I have a question for you. How can something that starts off totally sexual end up in a different way?"

Faith's brow furrowed, assuming Shannon was asking for a particular reason. "I don't think it's hard for physical attraction to be the dominant factor when two people meet for the first time," Faith said, thinking of her situation with Shane. "It's natural for a woman to be attracted to a man or vice versa at the first meeting and sometimes it's the only reason for the meeting. Sexual attraction is a very powerful thing."

She took a sip of her wine before continuing. "But after the two of you spend time together, you discover it might not be the only thing. Especially if it's someone you could grow to like." She thought again of Shane Masters. He was definitely someone she could grow to like if she hung around him, which was the reason she tried to keep their relationship strictly professional.

"But what if you don't want to like him? What if you know he is all wrong for you?" Shannon asked, frustration deep in her voice.

Faith shrugged. "In that case, you should cut your losses and move on."

"But what about the chemistry, the great sex, the desire to be with that person in or out of bed?"

"So it's not only about taking the edge off your sexual neediness?"

Shannon smiled. "No. I'd proved that's not as big a deal as I thought," she said. "I hadn't mentioned it to anyone but Cely, but I took an oath of celibacy more than a year ago and had walked the straight and narrow path until I met Adam Corbain, and then it was like I was making up for lost time. The sex with him is off the chain, hot-hot-hot, crazy and torrid as hell, but then I'm discovering something else."

"What?"

"It's not just the Penis Syndrome that has me caught in its grip. I really like him. He's different."

"Umm, in what way?"

"Well, he certainly isn't my usual type, and before you start on me about how I feel about that, just hear me out for a second."

Faith nodded. "All right."

"Okay, I might be what one could consider a snob, but that's just me, okay? I admit it. And I've been this way for so long, it's part of who I am and the way I am. But with Adam, I can still feel naughty in the bedroom and somehow feel like we're on the same level out of the bedroom—when I know we're not."

Faith nodded slowly. "Could it be that levels don't mean anything with the two of you?"

"But it should!"

"Yes, but it seems it doesn't. You're beginning to like him for who he is and not for what he does, and only you can decide if that's enough. This is just a summer fling, right?"

"Yes."

"Then why are you so concerned about it? It's not like you're going to see him again once you leave this place."

"I know, but . . ."

"But what?"

Shannon shrugged. "But nothing. Maybe I'm getting worked up about it for all the wrong reasons."

"Or you could be getting all worked up about it for all the *right* reasons." Faith stood. "Go to bed and sleep on it, and I believe that the answers will eventually come. My advice is that if you like this guy—and I mean really like him—then nothing else matters because fling or no fling, you, Shannon Carmichael, will make things work. I've never known you to back down from a challenge, and with that last comment I'm turning in."

Shannon smiled up at her. "Thanks for listening."

"Hey, that's what friends are for. I wished Cely was here. She was the one who was good at giving advice."

"That might true, but evidently she didn't take any of her own. She would never have let us contemplate doing what she did," Shannon said bitterly.

Faith heard the anger in Shannon's voice and understood it. Cely had been a friend and a confidante to all of them, but to Shannon, Cely had always been her voice of reason, the one who used to give Shannon a good bitch reading when she needed it. "I don't think we'll ever fully understand why Cely did what she did without turning to us, and it hurts because the four of us were so close. But it comes a time when we have to accept things as they are, let it go, and move on."

"It's hard," Shannon said, wiping a tear from her eye.

"I know, but I feel her presence, especially here. It's like she's missing from our midst physically but not in spirit. I truly believe whenever we gather together like this, she'll always be with us. Good night."

After Faith left and Shannon found herself alone, she poured another glass of wine. Faith was right. Cely was there with them in spirit.

32

"Good morning."

Monique glanced up at Lyle's greeting. Everything appeared as usual for their early-morning jog: the beach was empty except for those individuals wanting to walk or run along its shores, which weren't too many.

Although the scenery was the same, she and Lyle were different, and she could immediately feel it. This past weekend they had crossed a line in their relationship, and she was still trying to figure out just where that line was . . . and, more important, what were the expectations.

"Good morning," she replied, smiling.

Then like it was the most natural thing to do, he leaned down and kissed her. And it wasn't a brotherly kiss, either. It was a replay of the ones from yesterday but this had even more tongue play. When he pulled away, she had to almost fight for breath.

He smiled down at her. "You okay?"

"Kind of. I guess I'll survive."

He chuckled. "And I'm going to make sure of it. Ready to start jogging?"

"Yes, but we need to talk." She was certain she didn't have to tell him what about.

"Okay. We're having breakfast together this morning, right?"

"Yes."

"Then we can talk then. Come on, let's start our run before it gets too hot out here."

And as they began jogging together, Monique was sure things would be fine. They just needed to get a few things clarified.

"Okay, Monique, let's talk."

"All right," she said after taking a deep swallow of orange juice. It seemed that Lyle didn't intend for them to waste any time to get down to the business at hand. After their jog she had used his bathroom to shower and change and then had joined him in the kitchen.

On this particular morning, he had prepared sausage and biscuits. They had decided that on Wednesdays she was the one responsible for getting in his kitchen to prepare breakfast. One thing she had discovered was that the two of them worked well together.

She placed her juice glass down and met his gaze. "We were friends."

He smiled warmly at her across the table. "I hope we still are."

She nodded. "But we kissed this past weekend. Several times, and not in a way friends would kiss."

"That's true," Lyle agreed.

"Now I'm confused."

"Don't be." He leaned closer to her over the table and captured her hand in his. "I was honest with you in Beaufort when I told you that I was attracted to you that first summer. But I didn't tell you everything."

Monique wondered what else was there to tell. What he had told her had taken her by surprise. Was there more? "What didn't you tell me?"

He held her gaze steady when he said, "That not only was I attracted to you but that I had begun developing feelings for you as well."

A shiver ran up Monique's spine. She cleared her throat and asked. "Feelings? What kind of feelings?"

"The kind a man would have for a woman he cared seriously about."

She had another question. "How serious?"

"Real serious."

Monique blinked, not sure she comprehended what he was saying. So she decided to ask. "Are you saying that you thought you were in love with me?"

"Yes, that's exactly what I'm saying. You acted mature for your age, which was one of things that attracted me to you."

"Okay." Monique drew in a deep breath and slowly blew it out. "So when did you get over those, ahh, feelings toward me?"

He looked at her seriously and said, "Who said I'm over them?"

Monique sighed deeply. "Lyle, be serious."

"I am serious. I'm as serious as a heart attack. I am also being totally honest with you, Monique, which is only fair. I fell in love with you that summer, and I never stopped loving you. I thought I had after Arnie called to let me know you'd gotten married, since it wasn't good to yearn for another man's wife. But when I saw you again a couple of weeks ago, I realized that deep down I still cared for you."

"But—but there were those summers before I met Paul, and you never came back to visit, not even to call when I got older before leaving for college."

"Yes," he said sadly, "and there's a reason for it."

Over the next twenty minutes, he told her about his sister Carrie and went into more details with her regarding the situation than he had with Arnie. He wanted to make sure Monique understood that although his time and attention had been given to his sister, his heart still belonged to Monique. But her marrying Paul had made it too late to do anything about it.

"I never knew," she said sadly, holding her head down. She couldn't help but admire Lyle, his father, and his brothers for sticking by his sister the way they had and for the role they played in making sure Carrie felt safe and secure. Monique also regretted not knowing about Lyle's feelings for her.

She then thought of Paul and the five good years they'd shared and said, "I loved Paul, Lyle. I don't regret any of the years I spent with him."

"And I wouldn't want you to, Nicky. I believe he was placed in your life for a particular reason, and I'm sorry for your loss. But you're alive, and so am I."

Monique took another huge swallow of her orange juice. Her body suddenly felt tense, nervous. "Why did you decide to tell me all of this?"

"Because you said we needed to talk."

"B-but—"

"And the reason you wanted for us to talk," he said, ignoring her interruption, "was because I had started kissing you and you were confused as to why. The reason I'm being so brutally honest with you and telling you everything is because I believe honesty is the best policy. I'm not like my brother Lance used to be. I don't know how to work a woman or play games with one. I deal with openness and directness. That's the doctor in me. You ask a question, and I will answer it as sincerely as I can. Whether or not you're ready for the answers I give is not my decision to make. It's yours. I just didn't want you walking around thinking I was coming on to you, kissing you every chance I got, because I couldn't control any male urges and saw you as an easy and convenient mark. That's not it at all."

Monique nodded, knowing she would have eventually assumed that. "Thanks for explaining things to me."

He leaned back in his chair. "You're welcome. Now I have a question for you."

"What?"

"How do you feel knowing that I'm in love with you?"

Monique wasn't sure how to answer that. So instead she said, "This is rather complicated."

"It doesn't have to be. I'm not rushing you into anything, Nicky. And I can certainly understand if you're not ready to get seriously involved with anyone just yet. But I am asking that while we're here on the island together that we continue to spend time together, get to know each other all over again, and go from there. If you decide when your summer here is over that I was just a fond memory, then that's all well and good and I'll survive. I've done it before where you're concerned and I'll do it again if I have to. My work has become my other love, and if it has to be, it will continue to be so."

He then leaned in and added, "But if you think there's a chance you might grow to love me back, then I'd like to know that as well. I know my way to Louisiana; in fact, I'm just a few hours from where you are. I can handle a long-distance romance if you can."

Monique shook her head. "I don't know what to say."

"Don't say anything for now. Just let me continue to do what I've been doing."

She lifted a brow. "Which is?"

"Trying like hell to capture your heart."

3 3

"Did you enjoy your weekend?"

Faith consciously crossed her fingers beneath the tennis racket she was holding and smiled up at Shane, knowing she was about to tell an outright lie. "Oh, yes, I had a wonderful weekend. How was yours?"

"So-so, but it could have been better had you come over. I had a lot of things planned for us to do."

She could just imagine, but a part of her wanted him to tell her anyway. "Things like what?"

"Grill some ribs, watch a movie, play a game of cards, Jet Ski—"

"Jet Ski?"

"Yes."

"Shane, I just recently learned how to swim. Surely you didn't think you would have gotten me out on the water trying to do something like that."

He chuckled. "Sure I did. I have a gut feeling you'd be good at anything you set your mind to doing."

Faith wasn't so confident about that as he seemed to be. She held up her tennis racket. "Well, can we take just one thing at a time? Right now I want to put my concentrated efforts on learning to play tennis."

And for the next hour or so, she did exactly that, determined to capitalize on those practice sessions she'd done over the weekend.

"You're getting better and better," Shane said, wiping sweat off his brow with a towel. "You're doing an excellent job with your strokes."

"Thank you."

"Any plans for this afternoon?"

She slipped her racket into the cover and glanced up at him. "Why do you ask?" *Like I don't already know.*

"I thought that you might like to take advantage of my private beach again."

"Sounds nice, but I've already made plans. Thanks for the invite."

"Anytime. Come on, I'll walk you to your car."

"You don't have to do that."

"I know, but I want to."

She didn't say anything while they walked side by side to the parking lot. He commented about a recent news event, and she listened, adding her thoughts only occasionally. She enjoyed listening to the sound of his voice. It had a sexy tone, one whose tempo could caress every part of her body. She wondered if he ever thought of being a disc jockey. He would definitely croon a lot of women to sleep every night.

They had gotten a few feet from her car when she heard someone calling her name. She turned to find Shannon walking toward her.

"Someone you know?" Shane asked, and it was then she realized how close he was standing to her.

"Yes, one of my girlfriends who I'm here with for the summer." When Shannon came to a stop in front of them, Faith raised a surprised brow. "Shannon, what are you doing here?"

Shannon smiled brightly. "Looking for you. I wanted to see if you're interested in going shopping with me." She then glanced over at Shane, and her smile widened when she said, "Hi." She offered him her hand.

"Oh, sorry," Faith quickly said. "Shane, this is my good friend Shannon Carmichael. Shannon, this is Shane Masters, my—"

"Tennis instructor," Shannon finished for her. "Nice meeting you, Shane. I've heard a lot of good things about you."

"Thanks."

Shannon turned her attention back to Faith. "Well, what about it? Do you want to go shopping? I looked for Monique, but she left to go jogging and hasn't returned."

"She's probably having breakfast with Lyle," Faith said. "Sure, I'll go shopping with you, since I don't have any plans for this afternoon." *Oops.* Too late Faith realized she'd been caught in a lie. A quick glance at Shane let her know he'd been the one who caught her. She had told him just minutes ago that she *did* have plans for the afternoon.

Their gazes locked and held for a moment, and then he said, "I'll let you ladies go enjoy your afternoon. I'll see you next week, Faith, for another training session."

She nodded. "All right." And then she watched him walk away, feeling lower than low.

"He's gorgeous."

"What?"

"I said that he's gorgeous. Gosh, look at his tush. Maybe I should be taking tennis lessons."

Faith frowned, not liking Shannon's interest in Shane. "You already know how to play tennis."

"Yeah, but if all the instructors look like him, then . . ."

Faith's eyes reflected annoyance. "All the instructors don't look like him, and he's not really an instructor. He's just someone I met who offered to teach me how to play."

Shannon looked surprised. "Why would he do that? I'm sure there's more on this island for a gorgeous hunk to do than to teach someone to play tennis."

Faith shrugged. "In that case, maybe I should feel lucky."

"Maybe you should." And seemingly as an afterthought, Shannon added, "And there's only so much you can get from pleasure reading, Faith. Especially, when it's a romance novel. Once in a while, you'd want to try things out for yourself."

Before Faith could comment, Shannon said, "Come on, we can take my car."

—————

Five stores later, and Shane was still on Faith's mind. She could only imagine what he thought of her. Although it had been a little white lie, a lie was a lie, and she knew he was a man who appreciated honesty. She had determined that fact after he'd shared with her what his fiancée had done to him just weeks before the wedding.

"Okay, what's going on? You're too quiet."

Faith glanced over at Monique. She had joined them after getting the message Shannon left on her cell phone. Shannon was in the dressing room trying on several more outfits that she had picked out. "Shane Masters caught me in a lie."

Monique's brow rose. "What kind of lie?"

"He invited me over to his place to enjoy his private beach again, but I told him I'd made plans for this afternoon. That was before Shannon showed up and asked me to go shopping with her. Right in front of him, I told Shannon that I'd go because I didn't have any plans for the afternoon—a direct contradiction to what I'd told him earlier."

"Ouch."

"Yeah, I know," Faith said, putting a dress back on the rack after deciding it was way too small for her, although the tag said it was her size. "Now I don't know what to do. He probably got the impression that I don't want to spend any time with him."

"Do you?"

Faith glanced at Monique over the row of clothes. "Yes. No. Hell, I don't know. He's scares me."

Monique frowned. "Scares you in what way?"

"I can see him as someone I could really start liking, someone I could get close to, want to sleep with . . . so on and so forth."

"Is that a bad thing?"

"No, not exactly but we only have so many weeks on the island and—"

"Aren't we supposed to have fun, enjoy ourselves, not live up to anyone's expectations but our own?"

"Yes, but—"

"But nothing, Faith. If you like him, then what's the problem? What are you holding out for? An engagement ring?"

"Of course not!"

"Okay, then."

Faith glanced over at Monique. What she'd said made sense. "Who made you an expert on issues of the heart all of a sudden?"

A slow smile touched Monique's lips. "Trust me, I'm far from being an expert. I have my own issues to work out." And then knowing she needed to tell someone and Faith was the one she wanted to tell, she looked past Faith's shoulder to make sure Shannon wasn't coming and whispered, "This morning Lyle told me he's in love with me."

Faith blinked. "What? He said it? Just like that?"

"In a way, yes. I thought it was time we talked, considering what happened between us this weekend."

Faith's eyes widened. "What happened this weekend? Did the two of you sleep together?"

"No, but we kissed, plenty of times, and they weren't the friendly kind, either. They were the type that's usually followed by the taking off your clothes."

Faith swallowed. "But things never got that far?"

"No. Lyle was able to keep things under control. But still, I wanted to know why things had shifted between us. I kind of figured we were attracted to each other a little, but I hadn't figured on the explosion I got in Beaufort."

Faith nodded. "So, how do you feel about him wanting to be more than just a friend?"

Monique let out a frustrated sigh. "That's just it. I don't know how I feel. I never thought of loving any other man but Paul."

"Yes, but even you said that Paul would want you to be happy."

"Yes, but in my mind being happy meant going out occasionally, having a good time. Falling in love means something altogether different. People who love each other want permanency. Forever after."

"And that scares you?"

"Yes," she said, lowering her voice even more. "I had that before, and I lost it. I wouldn't want to go through the pain of that happening again."

"Oh, Monique, things won't necessarily be that way. But then you know as well as I do that life's a gamble."

"Yes, and that's what has me too afraid to take a chance with my heart again."

34

Randolph Fuller glanced over to where the group of young people were presently involved in a serious game of volleyball. His heart swelled with love and pride for all of them. There was his own son, Trey, and his stepdaughter, Haywood. The two had decided a few years ago that they were in love and had gotten married. Then there were his biological daughter, Randi, as well as Zach Wainwright, whom he considered a godson; and his niece, Anna.

Anna.

Had it been only a little more than a year ago that they had finally found her after a thirty-four-year search, a search that he and Noah refused to give up on even when others said they should.

"You're okay, sweetheart?"

Randolph turned and met his wife's curious expression. Jenna was the woman he had fallen in love with the moment he'd seen her on Howard University's campus so many years ago, and she was the only woman he'd loved since. She was and always would be his one and only. She was his soul mate.

He smiled and reached out and opened his arms for her. "Yes, I'm okay. How's Quad?" he asked of their grandson, who would be celebrating his second birthday in about six months.

Jenna smiled as she walked into his arms. "He's fine, but he fought sleep all the way." She glanced over to the spot where Randolph had been staring earlier. "How's the game going?"

He shook his head and chuckled. "Real serious about now. The guys have the advantage and they know it, but then so do the girls. See how they're dressed."

Jenna did and laughed. Both Haywood and Anna were wearing cutoff shorts and midriff tops that showed a lot of belly. Evidently they thought they had a chance of winning if they made themselves the center of attention rather than the volleyball. "I bet what they're wearing was the scorekeeper's idea," she said of their twenty-year-old daughter, Randi. When it came to fashion, Randi Jenna Fuller was as daring as they came.

Randolph grinned. "You're probably right. And you were right about something else as well."

She lifted a brow. "What?"

"Zach wasn't going to waste any time letting Anna know how he felt."

Jenna nodded. "Do you think he's told her about his political aspirations yet?"

Randolph shook his head. "No. He said he was going to wait to do that. He wanted to give her time to adjust to his feelings for her first. He wants to marry her, and how she feels about him entering politics will determine if he throws his hat into the ring or not. He really loves her, Jenna. Did you see that finished painting of her?"

"Yes, I saw it. It was beautiful."

"That painting was done through the eyes of a man in love."

She smiled. "I can tell that, too. Leigh and I had that figured out that night he brought her to you and Noah and we were all sitting in the study asking questions, trying to figure out why it took thirty-four years to find her. He was so protective of her, so caring. I knew then it would just be a matter of time."

Randolph pulled her closer into his arms. "I know that Ross and Gramma Mattie are overjoyed at the thought of a Wainwright marrying a Fuller. I can feel their presence, even now."

"So can I."

A few minutes later he said, "How about if we leave the big house to the young folks tonight and spend the night in our favorite place," he said, staring down at her. Whenever he brought her here, he wanted to spend time totally alone with her. She knew the place he meant. It was their special cottage, located a few miles from the big house.

"I think that's a wonderful idea," she said, snuggling closer into his arms. "When will Noah and Leigh arrive?"

"Tomorrow. Around noon."

"Good. I can't wait to visit with Leigh."

"I hope you ladies know you only won by default," Trey Fuller said, grabbing his wife and bringing her to him for a kiss.

"By fault or default?" Haywood asked, wrapping her arms around his neck. "Now is not the time to be a sore loser. You should have been paying more attention to the game."

Trey glanced over at Zach. "I don't think they played fair. Maybe we ought to take them somewhere and ditch them."

Zach chuckled. "I'm all for taking them somewhere," he said, taking Anna's hand in his and bringing her closer to him. "But I don't know if I want to ditch them, though. It would be nice if we were to take them on a treasure hunt tomorrow. What do you think?"

Trey's eyes lit up. "In search of the lost treasure? Hey, why not."

Haywood frowned. "Don't Anna and I have anything to say about it?"

"No," both men said simultaneously.

Haywood glanced over at Anna and winked. "In that case, we might as well make the most of it and go along."

Anna laughed as Zach pulled her closer into his arms. She wasn't sure what Haywood had up her sleeve, but she knew her friend had something. And whatever it was, she was game. She was glad that no one seemed surprised that she and Zach were an item. Instead everyone seemed really pleased about it.

"I'm going to miss having you in my bed tonight," Zach leaned down and whispered for her ears only.

She looked up at him. His face glowed with an invitation to sin of the worst kind. "Are you?"

"Yes," he said, smiling. "But your aunt and uncle have to go to sleep sometime."

A sensuous shiver raced up her spine at the thought of him sneaking into her bedroom. "You wouldn't."

He laughed. "Trust me, sweetheart. I would."

3 5

Faith sat in her car for a few minutes, gathering her courage. She was parked in front of Shane's house, and she had come to apologize.

After returning home from shopping and having dinner at a restaurant with Shannon and Monique, she knew what she had to do couldn't wait until she saw him again next week. She needed to do it now and get it over with. The man had been nice to her, a real gentleman, and she didn't want him to think she wasn't interested in him—because she was.

And as she'd told Monique, that was the problem.

She hadn't known how much what Virgil had done had affected her until now. She'd gotten over a lot of it, but there were still issues she had regarding men, and that wasn't Shane's fault.

Getting out of the car, she slowly strolled up the long walk to his front door, wondering what she would say. She inhaled deeply, gathered up more courage, and rang the doorbell. It was getting dark, indicating an end to another day, and tomorrow she and Shannon had decided to make it a lazy day. All that shopping had worn them out.

She almost jumped when Shane opened the door. He was wearing reading glasses, and it seemed strange for him to look at her over them. "Faith?" he said with surprise in his voice while he removed his glasses.

"Shane. May I come in?"

"Sure."

He stepped aside to let her enter, and the moment she walked over the threshold, she turned around while he was closing the door behind her. When he glanced up at her she said, "I owe you an apology."

"Do you?" He leaned back against the closed door, and she wished he hadn't done that. He was wearing shorts and a T-shirt, and his feet were bare. He definitely looked comfortable and at home. And it was hard to get past his nicely built chest with rippling muscles, a trim and flat tummy and powerful thighs.

"Yes. I told you a lie, but there was a reason for it."

He gave her a wry smile. "You had a reason to lie? This should be interesting. I was always taught to believe that it pays to be honest with people."

She nodded, knowing he wasn't going to make things easy for her. "I was taught that as well, which is why I'm here. Is there somewhere we can talk?"

He nodded. "Yes, let's sit in the living room."

She followed him through the foyer into a huge room that overlooked the ocean. Being in his house reminded her of the last time she was here and what a perfect gentleman he'd been and the fun she'd had with him that afternoon. "I hope I'm not bothering you."

He glanced back over his shoulder at her. "You aren't. I was finishing up a novel I've been reading over the past couple of days."

"Oh? What's the name of it?"

"The Island Massacre."

Faith nodded. It was the one about the serial killer. "I read it this past weekend and enjoyed it. But it kept me looking over my shoulders."

He motioned her over to the sofa. "I know what you mean. Please have a seat."

When they sat down, she didn't say anything, and then he cleared his throat and said, "You wanted to talk."

Faith nodded. Was it just her imagination, or was Shane looking at her strangely. She shrugged self-consciously and said, "About today. The reason I didn't want to plan an afternoon with you was because . . ."

When she didn't complete what she was about to say, Shane asked, "Because what?"

"Because I'm not interested in getting involved with someone, and I think that you are."

He gazed at her intently, before saying, "I believed we've had this conversation before or one pretty close to it and we left with the understanding that you would stop being overly cautious and start trusting me."

"I do trust you, but I'm not ready for what you want."

"And what is it that you think I want?"

"The same thing most men want," she all but snapped. "A willing woman in your bed."

"And you think that's all this is about, Faith? Trying to get you to sleep with me?"

Faith stood, angry with herself. Things weren't going the way she wanted them to. She looked over at Shane. "I don't know what to think, Shane."

He nodded slowly. "Is there a reason why you're so very cautious?" he asked quietly.

"Yes, there is a reason," she admitted softly. "Remember when I told you that I was divorced after being married nearly three years?"

"Yes, I recall you saying that."

"Well, what I didn't tell you is that I found out my husband had been unfaithful."

Shane frowned. "I'm sorry to hear that."

"With another man."

His frown deepened. "That's rough."

"Tell me about it. I'm the one who found them in bed together. I came back early from one of my business trips. They were in our house, our bed, and had been drinking our wine."

"I know that must have been hard on you."

"It was. But he made the divorce easy, since he didn't want me to air our dirty laundry."

Shane gave her a cynical chuckle. "I can imagine. And now you don't trust another living male."

She stared at him disbelievingly, wondering how he figured that. "No, that's not it. I've dated since then."

"Okay, then it must be me. Do you think I'm one of those down-low brothers or something?"

She shook her head. "No, that hadn't crossed my mind."

"Okay, then, what is it? There has to be some reason why you prefer not getting involved with me."

"There is," she said, sitting back down.

He stood and crossed the room until he was standing directly in front of her. "Do you want to share that reason?"

Not really, she thought, but she knew she owed him an explanation. "I feel things with you that I haven't felt in a long time."

He met her gaze. "What kind of things?"

She shrugged. "All sorts of things, but especially a funny feeling in my stomach whenever we're together."

A smile played at his lips. "It could be indigestion."

"I doubt it."

"Okay. You should know your body."

"Trust me, I do."

With the mention of her body, the air surrounding them suddenly became charged. She felt it, and knew he felt it as well. "See what I mean. I didn't want this to happen."

He sat down in the seat beside her. "Some things are inevitable," he murmured.

"But I'm not ready."

His hand came up to cup the side of her face, the tip of his finger tracing over her lip. "Then maybe it's time for you to get ready."

He leaned closer, brought his lips closer to hers, but refused to go any further. He wanted her to make the next move.

And she did.

With a strangled sigh, she leaned forward to fit her mouth over his, and the moment she did so, her body went on full sexual release. And when he parted his lips, she slipped her tongue inside and trembled at the sensations swirling around in her body.

The kiss seemed endless, and when he took it over moments

later, she heard a moan from deep within her throat. She didn't come over here for this. She came to apologize. But since this is what she was getting, then . . . oh, well.

She moaned again when she felt his hand moving from her face to reach down between them and cup her breasts through her sundress. "Tell me to stop," he whispered against her moist lips when he pulled back.

Instead she said, "No, don't stop."

He stared at her for a moment, and then as if he'd made up his mind about something, he dropped his hands and stood, stopping anyway. "I want you to be sure, Faith. A few minutes ago you said you didn't want to become involved with me, and I don't want to make love to you when there's a chance you're going to regret things afterwards. I suggest that you go home and think about it and be sure before we move any further. Whether we share a bed or not isn't the most important thing with me. I want you to first believe that I would not hurt you the way your husband did."

"Shane, but—"

"No. Think about things. Think about whether there can be an 'us.' I'm not someone who routinely gets involved in flings. If we decide to move forward, that's what we'll do, move forward with no time frame or limitations."

Faith nodded. "All right."

"And another thing. I need to cancel our lessons. My brother Grey is giving my sister-in-law a surprise birthday party in Orlando and I'm going. I won't be back until late Sunday night."

His words echoed in her head, and immediately she latched on to the fact that she wouldn't be seeing him for a few days. It made her realize how she'd gotten accustomed to his being around. "Thanks for letting me know, Shane. Please have a safe trip, and I'll see you when you get back."

And then she quickly turned, not waiting for him to walk her to the door, and left.

3 6

Monique smiled as she gazed upon the beautiful floral arrangement that had been waiting for her when she returned home from shopping. Lyle had said he wanted to capture her heart and he was doing a good job of going about it.

"Your guy definitely has taste," Shannon said.

She smiled over at Shannon. "*My guy* certainly does."

Shannon chuckled. "So now you're going to claim him as yours?"

Monique nodded, remembering everything else Lyle had told her earlier that day over breakfast. "Yes, I'm going to claim him as mine."

"And no more 'he's just a friend' stuff?"

Monique smiled warmly. "He *is* a friend, but a very special friend." She wanted to call and thank him for the flowers but recalled that he was meeting with a few of his colleagues tonight to plan the next seminar and wouldn't return home until late. She would just have to thank him properly when she saw him again.

Later that night when she crawled in bed, she thought it was a blessing to have been loved by two very special men in her lifetime. Not too many women could boast of having that. Paul had been good to her. He had been the best. But now he was gone, and she had to move on as he would have wanted her to do.

She then thought of Lyle. He was good to her, too, by not rush-ing her into anything and making sure she understood that his feelings were genuine by confessing his love for her. Yes, Lyle was a good man in all the ways that mattered.

And he loves me.

Emotions were swirling inside her. Emotions she hadn't felt since losing Paul. Could she be falling in love with Lyle as well?

A short while later, as sleep began claiming her, she hugged her pillow thinking that yes, she *was* falling in love with Lyle Montgomery.

Monique wasn't the only one snuggled in her bed having thoughts of the man she loved. Across the waterways, Anna lay on her back, staring up at the ceiling, thinking that today had been special.

Her uncle and aunt had arrived early that morning, and everyone else followed shortly thereafter. Zach's parents would arrive sometime tomorrow, and his sister, Noelle, as well. Whenever there were gatherings such as this, she felt so much a part of the family she had been denied for so long that all she could do was to thank God for uniting her with them.

She always enjoyed the friendship she had developed with Haywood. And it was plain for anyone to see just how much in love Trey and Haywood were. They were a beautiful couple with a beautiful little boy, who represented so much of the love they shared.

And Anna knew she wanted that for herself and for Zach. Although he hadn't mentioned marriage, she hoped that one day he would. She truly believed that he loved her, but did he also see her as someone he wanted to marry? What if he wanted to run for political office like the newspaper had claimed during the time she was living in D.C.? Would she be more of a liability to him than an asset? Would his constituents expect him to marry someone American born? Would they be accepting of his marriage to a part Vietnamese, or would they denounce her as Todd's family and friends had done?

She sighed deeply. Was it wrong to want to be the woman he

came home to every day, the one who bore his children? . . . And she wanted his child something awful. She would be a good mother. The best. Just the way her mother would have been to her had she lived. She would make him a good wife. She knew that she would. But she wouldn't let him sacrifice a political career for her. She loved him too much for that.

She closed her eyes and decided to have a conversation with her parents. It was moments like these that had helped her during some rough stretches in her life. The belief that, no matter what, her parents were always near gave her the encouragement to go on when she felt like giving up.

"Mom, Dad," she whispered into the darkness. "It's me, Adrianna. I'm okay. In fact, I couldn't be better. Zach loves me, and to me that's the best thing to ever happen in my life. After reading all those letters you would write to Mom, I know how it feels to have a man love you deeply, Dad, and I feel that same depth of love from him. And you would like him, Dad. He's just like the man you wrote Mom about in your letters, Noah Wainwright. Zach is so much like his father. He's honorable, respectful, loving, and caring. I couldn't have asked for a better friend or a more devoted lover. Be happy for me, please, because I believe I have finally found what the two of you had. A very special kind of love."

Anna wiped the tears from her eyes and shifted her body in bed. She never knew her parents, but she had always felt their presence and the love they shared for each other and for her, their unborn child, through her father's letters. Also in those letters he would always speak highly of his best friend, Noah Wainwright, and of his brother, Randolph. And after meeting and getting to know both men, Anna understood why.

Anna blinked when she thought she heard a sound and raised herself up in bed to see her bedroom door opening slightly. "Anna?"

She smiled upon hearing the low tone of Zach's voice. "Yes, I'm here in the bed," she whispered back, pulling to sit up.

"Just where I want you," Zach said, coming toward her.

Anna had hoped he would come. "Where's Uncle Randolph and

Aunt Jenna?" she asked when she felt the weight of the bed shift as he joined her there.

He reached out and took her into his arms. "They aren't spending the night here. They decided to stay at their cottage and won't be back until breakfast in the morning."

"So we're all alone?"

Zach chuckled again as he reached out and turned on the lamp next to the bed, bringing soft lighting into the room. "In a way, yes. Trey and Jenna are down the hall, and Randi has a bedroom downstairs. But enough about them. I want to concentrate just on us. I love you."

"And I love you, too."

Bracing himself on his elbow, he captured her face in his hands and leaned down to kiss her. And then he was touching, thinking how soft she felt through the silky material of her nightgown. But he wanted to be skin to skin with her. He wanted to make love to her tonight in a very special way.

He had decided that he didn't want to wait any longer. He wanted to ask her to be his wife, and whether he sought a career in politics or not didn't matter. The most important thing was having her in his life forever.

"We have on too many clothes," he whispered, and pulled back to remove his. And then moments later he was in the bed removing hers, tossing her gown aside.

He reached out and captured her breasts in his hands. "You're beautiful," he whispered softly. "These are beautiful," he added, running his thumbs over the nipples, loving the way they felt in his hands.

He leaned down and took one deep into his mouth and watched how Anna threw her head back and how her eyes closed. He feasted on one and then the other, liking the sound of her moans while he did so.

He pulled up and gazed deep into her eyes. "Tonight," he whispered. "We're going to take this slow and easy." He grinned. "Might be less noisy that way."

She smiled at him, remembering the other times he had pushed her over the edge and how the sensations had ripped through her. "Yes, it just might, but I can't guarantee it."

He found her smile a total turn-on and needed to kiss her. So he did, slow and easy, making her moan some more. Kissing her felt sensual, and it was a physical pleasure he wanted for the rest of his life.

But it was time to deepen the pleasure, and he lowered his hands to the area between her legs and began stroking her there. When her moans got a little louder, he whispered in her ear, "Shh, remember we aren't here alone anymore. There are other guests in the house."

And then he left her mouth and began tracing downward to taste her sweetness. When he got to her belly, he took his tongue and drew circles all around her navel, and just loving her this way made him that much more aroused. And when he got to the area of her he sought, he went in for the gusto, determined to give her the most intimate kiss that a man could give a woman.

Her thighs that cuddled his head began shaking, and he knew it was only a matter of time for her, and he wanted to be inside her when the explosion hit. He pulled up and placed his body over hers and guided himself unerringly to her.

"I love you." He said the words the moment he entered her and watched her face when she began to reach a climax. He felt her muscles clench him, and when she was about to let out a scream, he leaned down and latched on to her mouth, absorbing the sound deep in his throat. The sensations caused by her orgasm were so profound that he broke off the kiss and threw his head back and squeezed his lips together to kill his own scream.

When the explosion had passed, he shifted their bodies, holding her tight against him. Never had he experienced anything so earth-shatteringly magnificent. When their breathing had slowed and they could talk, he asked her the question that had been burning in his heart for months.

He leaned on his elbows and gazed down at her. "Anna, will you marry me?"

He saw the tears that suddenly sprang to her eyes and said, "Before you answer, I want you to know something. I'm thinking of pursuing a political career, but only if that's what you want, too. I want you more than a political career, and I want you to know that. If that's not what you want, too, then I'll do without it, but I won't do without you."

She reached up and cupped his face with her hand. "Oh, Zach, more than anything I want to marry you, but I'm not sure I'd make a good politician's wife. What if the people don't like my mixed heritage? There are still those who still remember Vietnam and—"

"You'll make a wonderful politician's wife. You are everything I want in a woman, the total package. There are those who admire what you had to endure for all those years and how you grew up to make something of yourself without the Fuller family name. You're a fighter, Anna. I knew that the first day I met you, and that's what captured my heart: the fighter in you. And you're the type of woman I need by my side."

Another tear fell from her eye. "I don't want to disappoint you."

He smiled with all the love in his heart. "Trust me, you won't, sweetheart. But like I said, I want a political career only if it's something you want, too. Otherwise, I can continue doing what I'm doing now."

She nodded, but deep down Anna knew for him even to be considering a political future meant he really wanted one. Could she be the wife he needed?

Suddenly, a particular letter her father had written to her mother came to mind. In that letter he told her that he had ask for leave to bring her to the States where he wanted their child to be born. He didn't care what anyone thought about his marriage to a Vietnamese. The most important thing was their love for each other because together they would be able to handle anything.

And she believed that in her heart. Together she and Zach would be able to handle anything. Emotions filled her entire being, and she reached out and cupped his chin and said in a soft voice, "Yes, Zach, I will marry you. There's nothing in this world that I want more than to be your wife and the mother of your children."

37

A smile touched Monique's lips the moment she saw Lyle. "Good morning."

He leaned over and brushed his lips against hers. "And a good morning to you, too."

"Thanks for the flowers. They're beautiful."

"Just like you," he said, reaching out and pushing a strand of hair back from her face. "Ready to go jogging?"

"Yes."

After jogging a couple of miles along the shore as they usually did each morning, they walked hand in hand back to his condo. He told her about the meeting he had attended last night and that he'd been asked to come back next summer to host another six-week symposium.

"Think you'll do it?" Monique asked quietly while walking by his side.

"Next summer is a long way off, but I'm really thinking about it," he admitted. "I like it here. This place has a tendency to grow on you." He then looked at her, smiled, and winked. "But then you being here had a lot to do with it, too. I enjoyed sharing breakfast most mornings with a beautiful woman."

They sprinted up the brick steps to his apartment. Today would be her day to prepare breakfast while he showered. And when he was getting dressed, she would use his shower. But today things would be different, too. She had done a lot of soul searching last night and had made a number of decisions. She knew her feelings for him were real, and if he was willing to go the distance and establishe a solid relationship, then so was she.

He unlocked his door and stood back to let her in. "Do you have a taste for anything in particular this morning?" she asked when he closed the door behind them.

"As a matter of fact . . ." And then he pulled her into his arms and kissed her, and it seemed his kisses were becoming hotter and hotter, and the moment their tongues began to tangle, her desire for him escalated.

"If you don't go ahead and take your shower, you're going to be late for work," she said, reluctantly breaking off the kiss and whispering across his moist lips.

"Oh, I forgot to mention that I don't have a class today. Since tomorrow is the Fourth, they gave everyone an extra day. I was going to ask you to spend the day with me."

Monique immediately thought the cancellation of his class worked nicely into her plans. "Umm, I'll have to see. I thought about going shopping with Faith and Shannon again today," she lied. "Now go take your shower so I can feed you afterwards."

He gave her another quick peck on the lips before turning to walk off toward his bedroom. He hadn't made it to the door when his mobile phone on the table started ringing. "Will you get that for me?" he tossed over his shoulder, not breaking his stride, before going into the bedroom and closing the door.

She shrugged. If he didn't have a problem with her answering his phone, neither did she. She quickly crossed the room to pick it up.

"Hello."

There was a pause.

"Hello," she said again, certain someone was on the other end.

"I was trying to reach Dr. Lyle Montgomery," a feminine voice said.

Monique would be a fool to think other females didn't have Lyle's number, but the woman in her wanted to know why this particular one was calling. "He's busy at the moment." And to get her point across, she added, "In the shower. Would you like to leave a message?"

There was another pause, and then the woman said, "No message. Just let him know his sister called."

His sister! "Carrie?" Monique asked tentatively.

"Yes?" The woman seemed surprised that Monique knew who she was.

"This is Monique, a friend of Lyle's. He and my brother Arnie went to med school together."

"Oh yes, he's mentioned Arnie several times. And how are you, Monique?"

"I'm fine, and congratulations on your marriage."

"Thank you. I just wanted to let Lyle know our flight plans for next Friday."

"He told me you were coming in to celebrate his birthday," Monique said.

"That's right, and I hope to see you when I get there. I look forward to meeting you."

"Same here, and I'll let Lyle know you called."

"Thanks. Good-bye."

"Good-bye." Monique smiled as she clicked off the phone. Like her brother, Arnie, Carrie seemed very protective, a good sister.

She lifted her head when she heard the shower going and decided that now was the time to let Lyle know of her decision.

Lyle lifted his face to the shower head to let water flow over it. He always enjoyed taking showers after jogging. And today he felt full of energy, filled with life, and so much in love.

Monique hadn't said anything about their conversation of yesterday, although she had thanked him for the flowers he'd sent. He wondered what would be her reaction to discover a bunch would be delivered to her almost every other day. He intended to do whatever it took to get his point across.

He turned when he heard the shower door opening and blinked, then taking his hand, he wiped the lathered water from his face to make sure he was seeing straight. Monique was standing there, totally naked. His gaze did a swoop of her body and zoomed in on the perfectly shaped shoulders before moving downward to her firm, thrusting breasts with the hardened nipples, moving lower still to her flat stomach, small waist, and shapely hips and legs that had him losing his breath. But what his gaze was fixed on more than anything was the dark triangle in her center.

He forced his gaze away from that particular spot to her face and saw her smile softly. "I decided it would save time if we showered together this morning. Do you mind?" she asked.

He swallowed and forced himself to speak. "No, I don't mind."

"Good." She held out her hand and when he looked at it like he'd never seen a hand before, she grinned and said, "The soap, please."

"Oh."

The moment he placed the soap in her hand, their fingers touched, and she felt the spark at the same moment he did. Monique watched as his eyes darkened and she heard his breathing suddenly become labored. But what really gave him away and proudly announced the magnitude of his desire for her was the way his erection was growing, right before her eyes. *Oh my.*

"Do you need help?" he questioned in a low, sexy voice. "Do you want me to lather you?"

She gave a small sensual laugh. She intended for him to do more than just lather her. "Only if you let me lather you."

"Whenever you want."

She smiled and handed him back the soap and watched as he lathered some in his hand before reaching up and, meeting her gaze, began gently rubbing the soapy substance onto her chest, caressing it onto her skin. She gave a sensual shiver when his hand touched her breasts, bathing them in soft bubbles around her hardened tips. The confined space had the fragrance of the scented soap that he continued to lather into her body, leaving his imprint everywhere he touched.

"You okay?" he questioned softly, when he saw her eyes close.

She nodded. "Yes, I'm okay. Just don't stop."

"I won't."

And then he was leaning down to lather lower, moving toward her waist, reaching around and massaging soap into the curves of her butt, all over her hips, and slipping his hand lower to lather the area between her legs.

When she made a deep sound in her throat, he glanced up and saw her eyes were no longer closed but were looking at him, focusing hard on his enlarged erection.

"Are you ready for me to lather you now?" she asked in a voice that sounded so sexy, it made his heart pound hard in his chest.

"Yes," he said, forcing the words out through clenched teeth. "I'm ready."

She took the soap from him and instead of starting with his chest the way he'd done her, she went straight to the area below his waist, reaching out and gripping him in her hand. But instead of lathering it, she just held it for a moment, stroked him, cupped him, and slowly begin sliding her fingers up and down him.

"Do you know what you're doing to me?" he asked, backing up against the shower wall as if his legs couldn't support him any longer.

"No, what am I doing to you?" she asked innocently, like she didn't have a clue.

"You're driving me crazy. You make me want to take you here and now."

"Then do it."

He didn't have to be told twice, and leaning down, he captured her mouth with his at the same time that he lifted her off her feet, and she automatically wrapped her legs around him. He turned slightly and backed her against the shower wall while water cascaded over them. She gripped his shoulders when he nudged her legs apart, and before she could catch her next breath, he drove into her, locking their bodies tight. For a moment he didn't move, just continued to kiss her with a hunger that sent waves of pleasure all through her, and when he began moving, thrusting back and forth inside her, she let out a loud scream.

That same orgasm that had torn into her ripped into him, and he began moving faster, going deeper, groaning out her name over and over again. And then he switched positions where he was the one whose back was against the wall. He sagged against it for support with her body still locked to his, refusing to let her go. And they stayed that way for long, glorious moments while getting their breathing under control, while she tucked her face into his neck.

When he pulled back, he met her gaze. Smiling, he said, "That was some shower."

She giggled. "Yes, it was."

His expression then turned serious. "Why?"

She knew what he was asking. "Because I'm ready to move on with my life, and I want you to be a part of it. I've fallen in love with you, Lyle."

"Oh, sweetheart." And then he was kissing her, and Monique believed with all her heart that everything would be all right.

38

Shannon stood at the window in her bedroom and looked at the sky. The sun was coming up, and it was a beautiful sight. Today was a special day, the birthday of the nation, and already her nose picked up the scent of charcoal. Evidently several residents in the community had decided to fire up their grills early.

Monique decided to spend most of the day with Lyle and wouldn't be back until later when it was time to view the fireworks from the pier. Faith, who seemed rather quiet last night, mentioned that she had picked up another book at the grocery store and intended to hang out on the beach and read.

Shannon wasn't sure what she would be doing, although Adam's invitation weighed heavily on her mind. He wanted her to go to Savannah with him, to a drag race, of all places. But then she figured that's probably what a mechanic did on his days off: go somewhere to inhale more nitrogen and carbon monoxide. Why on earth did he think she would want to tag along? Did she even closely resemble a drag racing babe? If Adam Corbain thought for one minute that she would show up at his place today, then he had another thought coming.

But then when she should have been satisfied with that decision, a gentle stir seemed to vibrate under her skin. And suddenly the feel of Adam caressing her body came to mind. She quickly gathered her defenses, not willing to fall under the Corbain spell, but she couldn't help it when an ache took over her.

The feeling was highly unexpected, and something she couldn't explain. The only thing she knew was that she had to act on it. Moving away from the window, she went to the closet and began getting dressed. She didn't understand any of it. All she knew was that she wanted to spend the day with Adam, no matter where he planned to go.

Later she stopped only long enough to scribble a note to place on the refrigerator for Faith and Monique. Then she quickly headed for the door.

A smile touched Adam's lips as he hung up the phone. The Fourth was not only the birthday of the nation, but it was also his father's birthday, and he had just finished talking with his parents. They were excited about becoming grandparents, and he had listened while they went on and on about how long they had waited for such an event.

He checked his watch, giving up all hope that Shannon would show up. He'd figured she wouldn't but had held out that maybe, just maybe, she would. He turned around, wanting to punch something. The woman had gotten under his skin in the worst possible way.

He glanced up when he heard a sound. She was standing there by the window. Surprise and pleasure filled him, and he quickly crossed the floor to let the garage door up. She strolled in and looked at him. Tossing her hair out of her face, she said, "You said to be here by ten. I'm here and ready to go."

The breeze coming in through the SUV's window did little to cool off the inside of the vehicle as they headed toward Savannah on Highway 278. With little traffic off the island, it would take less than an hour for them to make the trip.

Shannon settled comfortably into the leather seat, feeling she was where she wanted to be and for the time being she wouldn't question things.

She glanced over at Adam. Why did he have to be so darn handsome? Why did his mere presence cause shivers to run down her spine? He glanced over at her and caught her staring, and the grin that spread across his face was full of sin and sensuality: a deadly combination. She wished it didn't set off the rush of desire that began spreading through her.

"You okay?" he asked in that sensuous voice of his, reaching across the seat to place his hand on her thigh.

No, she wasn't but she wouldn't tell him that. "I'm fine, but don't you think you should have both of your hands on the steering wheel?"

He threw his head back and laughed. "But I like touching you."

"I gathered as much."

"And you like me to touch you."

"Yes," she admitted, deciding to be truthful about that at least. "But there's a time and a place, and driving down the highway while doing seventy miles an hour isn't the time or the place."

He removed his hand from her thigh and placed it back on the steering wheel. "I'll agree with you on that."

"Thank you."

When he laughed again moments later, Shannon looked over at him. "What's so funny?"

"I was just remembering you helping me work on my car that day."

"And that made you laugh?"

"No, not the work you did, since I've never seen the inside of a car so clean, but what happened later in my bathroom."

"Oh," she said, understanding why he'd laughed. She had dashed off to his bathroom to put on her clothes instead of doing so in front of him. Somehow she'd gotten locked in the bathroom. Instead of helping her to get out, he had threatened to hold her hostage unless she let him make love to her one more time. She had countered his offer by agreeing only if they did so without completely removing all their clothes. The end result was creativity at its best.

She glanced over at him and smiled. "You liked hearing me beg, didn't you?"

He shook his head. "Not while you were standing on your feet and three inches of wood stood between us. I prefer hearing you beg when I have you flat on your back beneath me and we're skin to skin. It's even better when I'm buried deep inside you to the hilt."

"You enjoy talking dirty, don't you?"

His hand eased back to her thigh. "Who's talking dirty? That's clean. Now if you want to hear dirty, listen up."

She barely had time to blink before some god-awful filthy words came tumbling out of his mouth, rolling off his lips and painting one hell of an erotic picture. She felt herself get embarrassed and turned on all at the same time. "You're a bad influence on me, Adam Corbain."

"And you, Shannon Carmichael, are a good influence on me." A few minutes later he said, "You never did tell me why three women decided to spend their summer together at the beach."

"Is that a crime or something?"

"No. I know women do stuff like that."

"Men do, too, when they go on hunting trips and such."

"That's true."

She turned and glanced out the window for a second, and then she glanced back at him. "There is a reason we're here together, though. It used to be four of us, and we would spend every summer on Hilton Head together since we were teens. Me, Cely, Monique, and Faith were as thick as thick could get."

He lifted a brow. "Were?"

"Yes, Cely died earlier this year." She then slowly added, "She committed suicide."

He glanced over at her. "Sorry. Did any of you know she was in that frame of mind, that she was going through some sort of depression?"

"No. We didn't have a clue. She was the most together person that we knew. Even now we haven't completely gotten over what happened. But in her memory, we decided to come back here this summer. We hadn't been here together in a few years, and although

Cely isn't here in body, I believe she's here with us this summer in spirit."

For some reason Shannon felt good talking to Adam about her friendship with Cely.

She wasn't surprised when he reached out and took hold of her hand. "And if you truly believe that, Shannon, then she is here with the three of you."

Hours later, Shannon wondered if her ears would ever be the same again with all the loud noise that came from the high-performance cars she'd seen racing that day. It had truly been an educational experience for her.

Just from conversing with the people sitting around her in the stands, she'd discovered that drag racing originated in the United States and that it had since grown in popularity in other countries.

All she had to do during any race was to glance over at Adam to see the excitement in his eyes to know that it was a sport he enjoyed. At first she hadn't seen anything exciting about two modified cars racing against each other over a set distance to see which would cross the finish line first—especially when the driver didn't have any turns to negotiate or opponents to defend against. Once she got into it, she discovered that what made it exhilarating was the nature of the race, which in essence tested the vehicle in terms of acceleration and top speed. And she had to admit that she'd never seen cars run so fast.

Adam had been patient in answering her questions and making sure she understood everything about each race, even if she still didn't fully comprehend what he'd told her about a car's engine capacity, the number of cylinders, or whether the vehicle in question had either a turbocharger or supercharger installed.

"You want to grab something to eat before we head back?"

Shannon shook her head. "No thanks. I've eaten too much junk food to think about eating anything else for a while. But if you're hungry and want to stop and get something, that's fine. I could always grab a diet soda."

"Are you one of those women who assume they can eat whatever they want and wash the calories away by drinking a diet soda?" he asked.

She teasingly glared up at him. "And what if I am?"

Adam laughed and wrapped his arms around her shoulder, pulling her closer to him as they walked toward the exit. "Nothing. I personally like the way your body looks both in and out of your clothes," he leaned over and whispered for her ears only.

And he had definitely seen it plenty of times without her clothes, she thought, remembering just when and how. She felt a shiver pass through her at all the recollections. "I thought we would be meeting up with some of your friends today here," she said when they reached the parking lot and moved toward the SUV.

"I never told you that we would."

"No, but I assumed it. Had I not come, you would have been all alone?"

He smiled down at her. "Possibly."

She wondered if that was his way of letting her know that another female would have been glad to have been his date today? Refusing to let him know his response had bothered her, especially when she didn't understand why it did, she said, "Well, I had fun, and I'm glad I came."

"I'm glad you came, too."

The drive back to Hilton Head seemed to go a lot quicker than the drive they'd made to Savannah, and much too soon they were back at the garage.

"Are you in a hurry to leave?" Adam asked when they got out of the SUV. He closed the driver's door and walked around the vehicle to where she was standing.

"Why?" she asked, deciding they should have had enough of each other for one day.

"I want to show you something."

She raised a brow. "What?"

"Something."

She crossed her arms over her chest, wondering if he was running a line on her in an attempt to get her up to his apartment. "Something like what?"

Adam laughed. "It's not what you evidently think. In fact, if you wait here, I'll go and get it."

"Yes, you do that," she said, still not convinced there was anything behind him getting her up to his apartment. She watched as he sprinted up the stairs, thinking that whatever he had to show her, he was certainly excited about it.

Shannon glanced around the garage and had to admit it was probably a lot cleaner and neater than most, but for the life of her, she couldn't understand why someone would want to spend their life working in such a place day in and day out. It was obvious to her that Adam had the potential to do more with his life. He was so well versed on a number of things. So what was his problem?

She shrugged, deciding it was *his* problem and not hers. At least there was one thing she knew for a fact that he was 100 percent motivated to do, she thought, smiling.

She then thought about his persona. He had a good attitude and was genuinely friendly with people he met. That was obvious by how he had carried himself that day, chatting with those sitting near them in the stands. And then there was that time when they had passed by a booth a group of women had set up near the ticket gate, asking for a contributions to help build a youth center in the area. It still amazed her how Adam had reached into his wallet and pulled out a hundred-dollar bill to give to the group. Shannon was certain he didn't make that much as a mechanic, yet he had willingly shared what he had.

She glanced up when she heard him returning, and he stopped when he came to stand in front of her. "Here."

She took what he was offering her and cast him in a sidelong glance. "Okay, what am I supposed to do with this?"

He chuckled. "Do you know what it is?"

She rolled her eyes. "Of course. It's a toy car," she responded.

He leaned back against a work counter, grinning. "No, it's a miniature replica of a '69 Pontiac GTO. What do you think?"

She glanced down at the item she held in her hand. *I think men are boys who still likes to play with toys.* But to him she simply said, "I think it's cute for an older car."

He grinned again. "Cute?"

"Yes, cute. I like the color, since red is one of my favorite colors, and I like the tires. It's cute." She then glanced up at him curiously. "Was there a reason you wanted to show me this?"

"Yes," he said, smiling brightly. "That car over there will look like this when it's finished."

She glanced over at the car she'd seen him working on many times and back to the miniature replica she held in her hand. Although the car looked in much better condition than it had the first time she'd seen it, she just couldn't see it. She then tried visualizing it through his eyes and still she couldn't see it. There was a lot of work yet to do to accomplish that. Didn't he know there was more to life than fixing or restoring cars? "And after working on cars all day, you still want to work on that car in your spare time?"

It was on the tip of Adam's tongue to say his spare time was all his time, but instead he said, "Yes. I get the most work done after the shop closes and then sometimes I'm working on it well after midnight." At least that much was true. In the daytime when the shop was open, there was usually too much activity going on for him to do his best work.

"Well, thanks for sharing with me. I can tell pulling this off means a lot to you," she said.

"It does."

Shannon wasn't sure how she knew, but somehow she knew it really did. "For some reason, Adam Corbain, I think you can do anything you set your mind to doing." Then, leaning up on tiptoe, she pressed a kiss against his lips.

That evidently wasn't enough for Adam, and he pulled her into his arms and kissed her the way he figured she needed to be kissed. She thought it had to be one of the most erotic exchanges that had ever been performed on her mouth, the way he sucked her lips between his and then took his tongue and tortured her lips until they tingled. He was slowly but thoroughly arousing a deep hunger within her.

"Stay with me for a little while," he whispered against her moist lips when he broke off the kiss.

She was tempted to tell him that yes, she would stay, but she knew a little while would extend to a long time and she would end up spending the night.

With all the control she could muster, she pulled back and shook her head. "I can't. I shouldn't. Besides, on the note I left for Monique and Faith, I told them that I would try getting back for the fireworks." It was on the tip of her tongue to invite him, too, but she stopped herself from doing so.

The truth of the matter was that around Adam she tended to get a little crazy and was quick to forget things she should be remembering. She backed up a little, knowing she needed to leave while she had the chance. Her willpower with him wasn't the strongest.

"Thanks for taking me to Savannah. I've got to go." She turned to leave.

"Shannon?"

She turned back around. "Yes?"

"When will I see you again?"

His question made her stand there a moment, thinking of a response. She wished she hadn't done so when he slowly walked over and gently touched her shoulder, then took that same hand and cupped the side of her face. "I want to see you again soon. I *need* to see you."

She breathed in deeply and then leaned in for his kiss while thinking that she wanted and needed to see him as well. A shudder passed through her body the moment their mouths touched again. The merest brush of his lips against hers set her body aflame.

"Go," he murmured softly moments later, taking a step back. "Go while I have the mind to let you."

39

"Lyle's a cutie," Faith whispered to Monique when Lyle had walked off to get them some bottled water.

Monique smiled. "Thanks, I think so, too."

Faith didn't have to ask if the two of them were intimate. The glow on Monique's face said it all. "Shannon should be here soon. She left a note saying she decided to go to Savannah with her mechanic."

Monique then studied Faith. "What about you and your tennis guy?"

Faith sighed deeply. "Shane left town to spend time with his brother's family in Orlando. He'll be back Sunday night, but it doesn't matter. I think I blew things."

Monique lifted a brow. "Why do you think that?"

"Because I did. He's tried getting something going with me and I balked him at every turn, even when I told him I would give him a chance. I ended up telling him about Virgil, though."

"Really? What did he say?"

"Not much, but it felt funny telling him."

"You know what that means, don't you?"

Faith shook her head. "No, what do you think it means?"

"You trust him."

Faith shrugged. "I told him I did, but I don't think he believed me."

"Then when he gets back, you're going to have to prove it to him," Monique said.

"Hey, everyone, am I late for all the fun?"

They turned when Shannon walked up. "No, you're just in time," Faith said. "I was hoping you were bringing your guy. Monique and I want to meet him."

Shannon narrowed her eyes. "He's not my guy. He's someone I'm having an affair with, no biggie." Shannon nearly swallowed her lie. It *was* a biggie and was turning into an even bigger biggie all the time. "So where is your Dr. Montgomery?"

"There he is, coming back with our bottled water."

Shannon glanced over in the direction where Monique was looking. She let out a low whistle. "He's gorgeous. You did good."

Monique couldn't help the smile that spread across her face. "Thanks, and like I said, I plan to keep him."

Faith had just gotten into bed when her cell phone rang. She glanced at it and didn't recognize the caller but decided to take the call anyway. "Hello."

"Did you enjoy your day?"

Faith distinguished Shane's sexy voice immediately. She couldn't believe he had bothered to call her. She snuggled deeper in the bed. "Yes, it was nice. How about you?"

"It was good seeing family again but I missed you."

"Really?" His words sent a warm feeling through her.

"Really. Had I known I would miss you this way, I would have asked you to come with me." When she didn't say anything, he asked, "So, did you go to the fireworks display?"

"Yes. It was nice."

"I went to the one here in Orlando, but I missed seeing them shoot out toward the ocean like they do in Hilton Head, so it wasn't the same."

"Yeah, I can imagine."

"Well, I don't want to hold you. I just wanted to let you know that I was thinking about you."

"Thanks, Shane. That means a lot."

"Does it, Faith?"
"Yes."
"I'm glad. Good night."
"Good night, Shane."

40

"How soon can we get married?"

Anna's laugh was warm as Zach wrapped his arms around her and brought her close to his side. That morning at breakfast they had made the announcement to everyone, and then when Zach's parents and sister arrived later that day, they'd told them the news as well. Everyone was so happy for them.

Anna smiled, remembering how Zach had barely let her out of his sight all that day. They had walked around the island making plans. She would have to put in a transfer at work for her move to D.C. One good thing was that she had enjoyed working at the hospital where she'd worked before.

They also talked about the media and how they would handle them. Zach assured her again that she would make a good politician's wife and that he would be proud to have her by his side.

They had grilled ribs and steaks and a number of delicious treats, and when everyone had sat down for dinner, her uncle Randolph had told the history of the Gullah people, which made her proud of her heritage all over again. Then later they all sat on the porch and watched the fireworks display from both Hilton Head and Savannah. It was beautiful how the explosion of lights seem to erupt into a beautiful ball of shimmering fire over the ocean.

"I talked to Grandmother Julia before the fireworks started," Anna finally said, smiling. "And she made me promise not to set a date until she can contact a wedding planner. I have a feeling she wants to go all out for our wedding."

Zach nodded. "And how do you feel about that?" he asked, bringing her closer to his side.

Anna shrugged. "All I want is to be married to you, Zach. How we go about doing it really isn't all that important to me. I was to have a big wedding with Todd and it never happened and—"

"I'm not Todd, and it will happen for you this time, sweetheart. And maybe a big wedding isn't a bad idea. I'll stand before the entire nation if I could and let them know how much I love you."

She turned and rested her head on his shoulder. "Oh, Zach, that's so sweet."

He leaned over to kiss her when there was a polite clearing of someone's throat. They turned to find his father and her uncle standing there. "Sorry to interrupt things," Randolph Fuller said, smiling. "But Noah and I wanted to talk to the both of you about something."

Anna heard the seriousness in her uncle's voice and glanced at Zach. He merely looked at the two men and nodded. "All right."

Taking her hand, Zach led her over to the wicker sofa and they sat down side by side while he held it. Anna recalled the first time she had faced the two men in Noah Wainwright's study. On that particular night as well, Zach had set next to her holding her hand just like this.

"Is something wrong?" Zach asked, his voice strong and sturdy.

Noah smiled warmly. "No, son, Randolph and I believe that everything is completely right, which is why we want to talk to you. But first I want to say how extremely happy we are for the two of you, as well as to tell you how happy you've made this family. I can just imagine how elated Ross is about this union."

He leaned against the porch rail and continued by saying, "I was blessed in my lifetime to have three men that God placed in my life who were truly men I can consider as my best friends. First there was Leigh's brother, Zachary, my childhood friend who was killed in the line of duty as a police officer, and the person for whom you're named. And then there was Ross Fuller, a man I met my first day at Howard University. Both men touched me at different times, but their presence in my life was more profound than I can ever say."

He was quiet for a brief moment before glancing over at Randolph. "And then there's Randolph, who I consider as my best friend. He was the one who stuck by me in my quest to find you, Anna, and during the thirty-four years that it took, we've developed a rather close relationship. I trust him more than I trust any other man. That's why it means so much to me for you and Zach to join our families together by your marriage."

Anna nodded. She'd always known Zach's father's relationship to her uncle was a close one.

"I didn't come out here to say all of that," Noah then said in a deep voice filled with both emotion and the sheer exuberance of a spokesman. "But I think in saying that, the two of you will understand just how important this moment is for us."

It was then that Randolph came forward. "The last letter I got from your father, Anna, told of his plans to bring your mother home to us that January and present her to the family as his wife. They had gotten married at a small church somewhere in Saigon and by an almost miracle, Noah was able to be there as Ross's best man. That day your father presented your mother with a small, inexpensive wedding band, just something for the occasion. To give her anything expensive at the time would not have been wise because she was still living among her people, and the paperwork hadn't been completed for her to be sent to the States. It was always his plan to purchase a more expensive ring for her later. One day while on a short leave in Paris, he did so. A particular ring caught his eye, and he purchased it and had it shipped to me for safekeeping."

Randolph took a step back, and Noah took up the story. "It was Ross's dream that he and Gia have another wedding once they got here in the States and that would be the ring he placed on her finger. As the two of you know, none of that took place because Ross lost his life in the war and Gia died months later while giving birth to you, Anna. But Ross's ring to her has been in my and Randolph's possession since that time, and considering the occasion, I think Ross would have wanted us to give it to the two of you."

Noah pulled a small white box out of his pocket and handed it to Zach. "I brought it with me because I felt that you would be asking Anna to be your wife soon."

Zach took the small box out of his father's hand and slowly opened it up. He heard Anna's gasp the exact moment he sucked in a deep breath. The ring Ross Fuller intended to give his wife was simply stunning and beautiful in every sense of the words.

"It's breathtaking," Anna said, wiping a tear from her eye, knowing such a gift would have made her mother happy.

"Yes, it is, and now it belongs to you and Zach."

Zach met Anna's eyes as he took the ring out of the box, the diamond's brilliance shone brightly for all them to see. He then reached for Anna's hand and slipped the engagement ring on her finger, knowing very soon the wedding band would follow.

"I love you, Anna, just as much as Ross loved his Gia," Zach said, leaning down and kissing her lips.

His words were too much for Anna, and she began crying. Zach pulled her into the comfort of his arms and held her while murmuring more words of love to her.

Noah glanced over at Randolph, and the two men nodded. They both knew that somewhere Ross, Gia, and Murphy and Mattie Denison were extremely happy. It was a joyous time for the Fuller and Wainwright families, which was fitting after so many years of betrayal and bitterness. Now it was a time of love, devotion, and peace.

41

"You're quiet, Shane."

Shane glanced up at his brother, Grey, who was younger but almost just as tall as he was. And Grey, a former FBI agent, was very observant. "I don't have a lot to say, Grey."

Grey chuckled. "All right, then let me ask, what's your opinion of Brandy's cousin?"

Shane took a sip of his drink as he glanced across the room at the woman who was engaged in conversation with Grey's wife, Brandy; Quinn's wife, Alexia; Brandy's mother, Valerie; and Brandy's cousins, Taye and Rae'jean. He then looked at his brother. "Do you want my honest opinion?"

"Yes, that would be nice," Grey said, taking a sip of his own drink.

"She surprised me by being a looker, I'll give her that. But she has one major flaw."

"Which is?"

"She talks too damn much."

His words, spoken so candidly, straight to the point and direct, had Grey bursting out laughing. The group of women across the room turned to stare at him. He gave them, especially his wife, an apologetic smile. "Do you have to be so damn blunt, Shane?" he asked.

"Hey, you asked."

"Well, for a man who always fancied himself as marriage material, I don't see you making any progress."

"Trust me, I'm working on it."

"Working on what?" his other brother, Quinn, came up to ask, along with his other brother, Lake. "We heard Grey laughing and wondered what was so funny."

Grey smiled. "Shane thinks Brandy's cousin, Linda, talks too much."

Both Quinn and Lake were amused. "He's not far from hitting the mark. She talks just as much as Valerie, and that's scary." The four men who had gotten to know Brandy's mother all nodded.

Quinn Masters then turned to Shane. "You never said what you were working on."

Shane smiled as he took another sip of his drink. "Giving Mom another daughter-in-law."

Lake Masters stared at Shane. "You've met someone?"

"Yes."

"In Hilton Head?" Quinn asked curiously.

"Yes, but she's from Minnesota."

"And you want to marry her?" Grey asked. Everyone knew that although Shane had always been marriage material, his last engagement had soured him.

"Yes, although it will take some time to work up to that point with her, since we met less than a month ago. But I'm past the age of wanting a chase. I'd rather go straight for the capture, and she's trying to be difficult at the moment. But then you know how I feel about difficult women."

"A lot better toward them than a talkative one, evidently," Quinn said, grinning.

Shane glanced down at his watch. "Do you think Brandy would get upset if I left early to return to Hilton Head?" he asked Grey.

Grey was surprised by the question. "How early?"

"Just as soon as I can pack."

Grey smiled in understanding. "No, not after I explain to her the reason why."

"Thanks." He then looked at his brothers. "Wish me luck."

Lake tipped his wineglass up to him. "You're a Masters. You don't need it. Just pull out that Masters charm."

Shane nodded as he walked off. He intended to do just that.

42

Shannon glanced up from the book she was reading when Faith entered the room. A smile touched her lips. Now that things had heated up between Monique and Dr. Montgomery, Monique spent more time over at his place than she did here with them, but they weren't complaining. They were happy that another good man had entered their friend's life.

"You're staying in again tonight?" Faith asked, flopping down on the sofa across from her.

Shannon drew her brows together sharply. "Yes. Do you have a problem with it?"

"No, I'm just curious as to what happened to you and that mechanic. You haven't mentioned him lately."

After a brief pause Shannon said, "It was just a fling, Faith, nothing more. We had a good time, and now it's over. Flings aren't meant to last."

Silence settled between them again for several moments, and then Shannon said, "What about you? What happened to you and that tennis guy?"

"Nothing happened. We were never involved."

"Umm, what a waste."

Faith shook her head. Leave it to Shannon to think that way. "But not for long. I've decided to engage in a serious relationship with Shane before leaving here."

Shannon looked shocked. "Really? How serious?"

"As serious as he wants it."

Shannon placed her book down. "When did you decide all of this?"

"Rather recently."

"And where was I?"

Faith gave her a pointed yet teasing look and said, "Somewhere getting your brains screwed out, I guess."

Shannon glared at her as she picked her book back up. "Be serious, Faith."

"I am." Then when Shannon's glare deepened, she said, "Oh, all right. I decided this a few days ago, but Shane is out of town now." What she didn't say was that he was giving her time to think her decision through. But there was nothing to think through. She wanted an involvement.

"I can't believe it," Shannon said, shaking her head.

"What can't you believe?"

"You and Monique's plans for this summer. None of them included finding a man, but you found one anyway."

Faith nodded, seeing her point. "Maybe because unlike you we didn't go out looking for one to become a victim. Now if you were to ask me what I want, I would give you an answer in more specific terms rather than general."

"And what would that answer be?"

"I want a man who will love me for me. A man I know I can trust and a man I believe I can count on when the going gets tough."

"And what about security?"

Faith raised an arched brow. "What security?"

"Don't you want someone on the same level as you? Who can provide for you?"

"I can provide for myself. Besides, the size of a guy's bank account isn't everything. I learned that the hard way with Virgil. When my father introduced us, he assumed he was securing my future. Boy, was he wrong." Faith stood. "I guess we shouldn't expect Monique back tonight," Faith said.

"No, I guess we shouldn't," Shannon said, thinking about what

Faith had said. When Faith left the room, Shannon momentarily closed her eyes, and the face that suddenly came in view stirred her heart. She had been fighting the truth, but couldn't any longer. She had fallen in love with Adam Corbain.

She threw her book across the room and stood up, knowing something like that was not supposed to happen. Emotions had no place in a fling. Sex was sex and nothing more.

But it had been more than sex, the greatest she'd ever experienced. It had been a touching of her soul as well. Even without trying, Adam had left his mark on her, and she wasn't sure what to do about it. How had he gotten to her so quickly? How had he gotten to her at all? Why had that guard she usually kept up lowered just for him, giving him an in she never meant for him to have?

Just like Faith, if anyone were to ask her now what she as a woman wanted, she would have to tell them she wanted a man who provided her with true love, regardless of what he did for a living. She wanted a man who would supply her not only with all the love she could handle but with hot, satisfying sex, emotional intimacy, and the willingness to let her be herself in the bedroom. A man who, when she was in his arms, made her forget the world existed. There was only one man who she knew could give her everything she wanted.

She glanced over at the clock. It wasn't late, just a little past eight. Was Adam still up working on his car? It had been a few days since she'd seen him, trying to deny in her heart what she now knew as the truth.

Deciding she needed to see if there was the slightest chance her feelings were reciprocated, she went into the kitchen and scribbled a note for Monique and Faith—mainly for Faith. Chances were Monique wouldn't be returning tonight, since it was the night Lyle's family was coming into town to celebrate his birthday.

She headed for the door, hated to leave Faith alone again. *She'll understand.* Shannon stopped within a foot of the door and turned around. She could have sworn she'd heard Cely's voice. She shrugged. Again she'd been hearing things.

Adam put the Wall Street Journal article down and leaned back in his chair. He couldn't get Shannon off his mind. He hadn't seen her since the Fourth of July. For the past few days he'd had no sense of direction, no desire to do any of those things he'd always wanted to do.

Today was the first time he hadn't worked on his car. Instead he had hung out in his apartment, practically doing nothing but drinking a beer every now and then, eating only when his stomach demanded it and taking unnecessary naps. At one point he thought about driving to D.C. just to get away for a while to visit with Sydney and Tyrone. But he couldn't get up enough energy or any real interest to make the drive.

He hadn't been able to sleep through the night, waking up a dozen or more times just to gaze out the window whenever he thought he heard a sound downstairs. It finally dawned on him that she wasn't coming back. Their affair was over, and she'd made a clean break.

And I wish like hell that I could do the same.

But instead his mind was playing over and over the intimacies that they had shared. He'd had sex with other women, but none of them ever came close to making him feel the way Shannon had. What was it about her that was so different, so intense, so downright unforgettable?

Was it her snappy attitude? Or was it the way she could hold her own against him or the way she could give just as good as she could take? Probably all of those things. He had enjoyed their time together—their little fling, as she called it—and he knew when he returned to Memphis in a few weeks that she would dwell in his mind for days and months to come.

Dwell in his mind as well as in his heart.

Adam sucked in a deep breath, almost daring himself to breath when it suddenly hit him why he felt so strongly about Shannon. Why he'd been in such a piss-awful mood since he'd last seen her.

She had been wrong. It hadn't been all about sex. At least for him, it hadn't been. For her it was the challenge of doing a mechanic, but for him it was something else all together.

He hit his hand on the table in denial but knew it hadn't done any good. The truth was the truth. And speaking of truth . . . he hadn't told her his true profession, because he had wanted her to accept him for who he was and not what he was, but she hadn't been able to do that.

He turned when his cell phone began ringing. He wondered if it was Kent calling or a member of his family. He started to ignore it since he wasn't in the mood to talk to anyone, but then decided what the hell. He crossed the room and picked up the phone. "Hello."

"I'm downstairs. Will you let me in?"

Adam went still at the sound of Shannon's voice. His muscles tensed. He tried to swallow but couldn't.

"Adam?"

He snapped out of his daze and said, "Yes, I'll let you in. I'll be down in a second."

Although he was glad she had come, he knew why she was there. She wanted unemotional sex, but he had news for her. There was no way he could be emotionless where she was concerned. She would not be making any more booty calls, at least not with him.

Shannon watched the garage door go up, and the same adrenaline that had been working a number on her since leaving the house was at its peak. She could only stare beyond the opened door as her pulse escalated alarmingly. And then Adam was there, and she quickly moved toward him.

"Hi," she said, hearing the garage door lower behind her. The moment their gazes locked she felt an intensity of emotions she'd never felt before.

"Shannon," he acknowledged, a deep, throaty sound that seemed to caress her skin. "Why are you here?"

She swallowed nervously. Wasn't he glad to see her? Was he upset that she hadn't contacted since the Fourth? "I needed to see you," she said softly.

"Do I need to ask why?" he asked dryly.

She studied his face. This wasn't exactly the reception she had hoped for. But then with all things considered, and what she said the last time they had seen each other, what did she expect?

She inclined her head. "Aren't you going to invite me up to your apartment?"

He slowly raked his eyes over her, making her pulse that much more erratic. She was dressed in a pair of jeans and a regular blouse, probably the most clothes he'd ever seen cover her body.

When his gaze returned to her face, she knew he was trying to fight her, fight whatever it was that always pulled them together, that strong sexual chemistry they could never deny. And the question that lodged in her mind was, Why was he even trying?

Before she could wonder any longer, he swept her up into his arms.

He hadn't intended to touch her, definitely didn't intend to make love to her, refusing to put himself through such torture and pain. But the moment she looked into his eyes and asked if he was going to invite her upstairs, any resistance to her died then and there. Every step he took defined a weakness in him for her that he could not fight. He could no longer focus on what was right or wrong about their relationship, or about the lie it was based on. The only thing he could concentrate on was how much he loved her and wanted her in his life, although she would want no part of the things he wanted.

Loving her was a lost cause. He knew it but loved her anyway. The only things that would sustain him during the lonely months ahead would be the memories of the weeks they shared together; especially tonight. It would be one he intended for her to remember for a long time. Then after tonight it would be over, and he meant it.

In the morning he would pack up and go to D.C. for a few days and then return to Memphis. He would pay one of Kent's top mechanics to finish restoring his car, since doing so no longer held the thrill that it once had. The next time Shannon came looking for him, he would be gone, and he'd give Kent strict instructions not to tell her where if she asked.

Once inside the apartment, he placed her on the bed, stood back, and reached for the zipper to his jeans. "Wait, Adam!"

He blinked. "Why? Isn't this what you came for?"

"Yes. No." She swung her legs on the side of the bed and sat up. "We need to talk."

Surprise lit his eyes. "Talk? What do we have to talk about? Besides, I don't feel like talking."

Shannon frowned and braced back on her hands and glared up at him. "Well, I do."

"Fine, then talk," he snapped, leaning back against the wall and crossing his arms over his chest.

Shannon decided she didn't like his attitude. She stood. "I'm leaving."

She turned toward the door, and he reached out and touched her arm. She met his gaze and suddenly felt it, something other than the sexual chemistry they shared. And before she had time to dwell on it further, he gently pulled her into his arms.

She couldn't deny herself this, another chance to be held by him, kissed by him, touched by him, and so she went willingly, locking her arms around his neck just when his mouth came within inches of hers. As if he knew this would be a kiss to savor, he took the tip of his tongue and slowly outlined the fullness of her mouth, licking it like it was the best thing he'd ever had the pleasure of tasting. Her body shuddered as sensations rammed through her, and when he captured her bottom lip and began gently sucking on it, she felt a relentless tug that began in her stomach and moved down with aching leisure to the area between her legs.

She wondered if he knew how much he was torturing her. Did he care? Evidently not, because then he took his hands and began caressing her back, slowly moving his hands down to her backside, and the moment he pulled her to him, to let her feel the magnitude of his desire for her, he captured her mouth like a hawk bearing down on its prey.

She felt him easing her back on the bed as she became engulfed in heated desire. She knew she had to talk to him and make him understand; otherwise, what they were doing would end up being just another roll between the sheets, and she couldn't end things with him that way.

She pushed at him. "No, Adam, get off me. We do need to talk."

Adam pulled back, hearing the desperation in Shannon's voice, and something broke within him, a flood of intense love he could no longer contain. He reached out and took her hand in his and caressed it lightly. He didn't want what they both wanted to end up being just another sex-intense coupling. She was right. They needed to talk, and although he was certain what they had to say would be vastly different, they needed to hear each other. She probably wanted to reemphasize what she saw as the depth of their relationship so there wouldn't be any misunderstandings.

He would let her go first, and then he would tell her how he truly felt, exactly what was in his heart. When he walked her to the door, he would ask that she not come back.

He gently pulled her up to sit beside him on the bed. "Okay, let's talk," he said in a quiet voice, still holding her hand.

Shannon didn't say anything for a long moment, not knowing where to begin. So she started at the beginning. "This fling was to mean nothing to me," she whispered emotionally.

"I know that," he said, trying to keep the pain and despair out of his voice.

"All I wanted to do this summer was to find a man to put at the top of my to-do list," she said, glancing down and studying their hands. "I hadn't counted on him being *you*. You were all wrong from the beginning. You lacked a lot of things I look for in a man, a lot of things I felt were important. But then on the other hand, you had a lot to offer that I hadn't counted on, and they began outweighing all those things you didn't have."

She looked up at him, hoping she wouldn't fall apart and turn any more emotional than she already was. "I liked being with you because you were you. I enjoyed making love with you because you were you. I began to know you as Adam Corbain the man and not Adam Corbain the mechanic. Suddenly, what you did for a living didn't matter," she said quietly. "I simply enjoyed spending time with *you*."

Adam struggled to hide his emotions. Was she saying what he thought she was saying? What he hoped she was saying? He needed clarification. "Are you saying that for you this fling has turned into something else other than a 'wham, burr, thank you, sir'?"

She nodded slowly. Although she'd never heard it phrased quite that way, he had the gist of it. "Yes. I know things weren't supposed to turn out this way, and I thought you should know. I'm not asking for anything in return, but I couldn't walk away without letting you know."

Adam stared at her. "So my being a mechanic doesn't matter?"

She shook her head. "No. We were all born with special gifts, and yours evidently is in your hands," she said, remembering all the things he could do with those hands in addition to working on a car. "I don't expect anything to develop from this, and I don't want you to think I expect my feelings to be reciprocated—because I don't. I just wanted you to know the stakes for me have changed."

Adam studied her face for long seconds, and then he stood and his heart swelled with the force of the realization that she cared for him. But he had to be sure. "Are you saying you're in love with me, Shannon?" he asked in a low, husky voice.

She swallowed hard and lifted her head to meet his gaze. "Yes, that's what I'm saying." She then forced a smile. "But like I said, I don't expect you to feel the same way, and that's okay."

"But what if I told you that I do feel the same way?" he asked softly. "What if I told you that I loved you, too? And what if I were to go even further and say that I'm not what you think I am?"

Shannon's head began spinning. All his questions were coming at her all at once. "If you told me that you loved me," she said, meeting his gaze, "and truly meant it, I wouldn't know what to say since I know I'm not the easiest person to love."

"No, you're not," he agreed truthfully.

"But I don't know what you mean when you say you're not what I think you are. I meant it when I said that what you did for a living doesn't matter to me anymore."

"And if I want to pursue a more meaningful relationship with you, something beyond what we shared this summer, you would consider it?"

"Yes, although it will be challenging with me living in North Carolina and you living here, I'll be open to working something out if you are."

"And what about your parents? Your friends? Those who might think you've made a bad choice in hooking up with me and that you can do better?"

She leaned over and placed her finger against his lips. "I'm my own woman, Adam. If those people you named, including my parents, truly love me and want what's best for me and what will make my happy then they will know I couldn't do better. My parents are both highly educated, supposedly 'compatible,' yet all they'd done over the years is make each other unhappy. I don't want that for me. I want to live a fulfilled life with the man I love regardless of who he is and what he does. Love is the most important thing."

Adam nodded. "Yes, love is the most important thing and I would want us to continue a relationship, but that relationship has to be built on honesty, and I need to be completely honest with you about something."

He crossed the room to the dresser, opened the drawer and pulled a business card from his wallet. When he retraced his steps to her he wondered if Shannon would understand why he hadn't been truthful with her up front? Would she forgive him for his deceit?

There was only one way to find out. He handed her the business card and watched her brow bunch in confusion as she read it aloud. "Adam Corbain, Esquire. Corbain Family Law Firm. Memphis, Tennessee."

Her frown deepened; her shoulders tense when she glanced up at him. "I don't understand what this means." Silence lengthened between them. She stared at him in disbelief when it became crystal clear what the card meant. "You aren't a mechanic?"

"No."

"But—but you said you were."

He shook his head, watching the angry lines form on her lips. "No, you assumed that I was."

She stood and squared her shoulders. "You didn't set me straight and you could have. You deliberately played me for a fool. You knew what I thought."

"At the time it didn't matter to me what you thought," he said truthfully. "You only wanted one thing from me and I only wanted one thing from you. It was only later that it began to matter."

"And all those times I mentioned what you did for a living was only a joke to you, wasn't it? I can imagine you laughing behind my back."

"Some of your comments did garner a few chuckles, I admit," he couldn't help but say. "But I never made fun of you, Shannon. I was too busy trying to show you that a man's worth was not measured by what he did for a living."

"Would you have eventually told me?" she asked, her voice terse and clipped.

"No. There was no reason to do that. I needed to know that you love me for the man you thought I was and not the man who was acceptable to you and your parents. Had I not known for sure, I would not have told you. I would have allowed you to use me until you used me up, although I would have been hurting inside."

He reached out and took her hands in his. "Had I told you what I actually did for a living, I would not have known for sure if you loved me for who I am and not what I am. Does that make sense to you?"

"Yes, it makes sense now," she slowly admitted. From the first she had thought him fixing cars all day was an occupation that was unacceptable to her, but over time, it no longer mattered—and that's what he'd wanted. The big question was where they went from there.

"So what you said holds true," Adam said. "It really doesn't matter what I do for a living. Mechanic or attorney, I'm still the same man. The man you said a few moments ago that you loved. Do you truly love me, Shannon?"

She knew there was only one answer to that question. "Yes, I love you, Adam."

"And I love you, too, Shannon."

And then he pulled her into his arms and he was devouring her mouth with the passionate hunger she was used to from him. The kind that would ignite a flame within her so bright, it would set off a deep longing and intense need. Only he could do that.

"Will you spend the rest of the summer helping me restore my car?" he asked as he eased her back on the bed.

"Is that all we'll do?" she asked silkily. Electricity was shooting through her entire body from his touch.

"No. I intend to spend a lot of time showing you just how sexy I think you are. And I would love to take you to D.C. with me to meet my sister and her husband. Sydney is also an attorney and her husband's family owns a restaurant there, Leo's. You may have heard of it."

Shannon nodded. Yes, she'd heard of it. It was a well-known club, very upscale and trendy. In fact, she usually would frequent the establishment whenever she visited the nation's capital.

"And I want you to meet my parents as well, so I think a trip to Memphis is in order before the summer is out," Adam said.

When she was flat on her back, he loomed over her and she smiled at him. "I guess I need to make sure you meet my parents, too. If you're brave enough to do so."

He grinned. "I'm brave enough."

"When you meet them remember that *you're* the one who said that."

He leaned down and kissed the corners of her lips. "I can handle your parents."

Shannon believed him.

"Now to take off all these clothes." He did so, slowly, kissing her every so often through the fabric of her clothing, and when he had her completely naked, he leaned down and kissed her stomach. "How do you feel about having kids one day?"

At the moment the only thing she could feel was the warmth from the tip of his tongue as he glided across her belly, making her want him even more.

"Shannon?"

"I think," she said struggling for words, "that as long as they are your kids, kids we made together, I would love to have a bunch."

He lifted his head as a smile touched his lips. "A bunch?"

A shudder coursed through her with the way he was looking at her. "Yes, a bunch."

"That's good to know, because I want a bunch as well."

It wasn't until Adam had resumed kissing all over her tummy did she realize that a bunch was a lot. But she wouldn't mind as long as they were just like their daddy.

43

"*So that's your* Monique," Lance Montgomery said to his brother while glancing across the room at the woman talking to his wife and sister. "She's very pretty."

Lyle smiled. "I happen to think so as well. I'm glad everyone finally got a chance to meet her."

Lance nodded, remembering when Lyle, who'd had a little too much to drink one night, admitted to falling in love with the woman and losing her when she'd married someone else. "Asia likes her, and I know Carrie likes her, too," he said. "That's good because Carrie can be a hard nut to crack sometimes."

"Are the two of you discussing my wife?" Connor Hargrove said, coming up to join the men.

"Just remember she was our sister before she became your wife," Lance reminded him, grinning.

Connor laughed. "Trust me, there's no way I can forget."

"Forget what?" Logan, the oldest of the Montgomery brothers, came up to ask.

"Forget that Carrie's your sister," Connor responded.

Logan nodded. He then glanced over at Lyle. "You seem happy."

Lyle's smile widened. "I am, but I'd be happier when she decides I'm good husband material."

Logan smiled. "If Lance can make good husband material, then anyone can."

Everyone, including Lance, nodded. *That* was definitely true.

Lyle was able to pull Monique off to corner for a brief private moment. "My family likes you," he said, placing a kiss on her lips. "But then I knew that they would."

She smiled, feeling those sparks she got whenever he touched her. "And I like them. They're all nice."

"And what about me? Aren't I nice?" he asked, pulling her into his arms. Monique whispered the words she knew in her heart were true: "Oh, yes, you're the nicest of them all and everything a woman would want."

"So," he said, leaning over and kissing the corner of her lips. "What can a nice guy like me do to get a gorgeous babe like yourself to stay over tonight?"

She glanced up at him, smiling. "Well, I'm no easy case, so I suggest you start with a little sweet talk."

He grinned. "Sweet talk? Can I just convince you to have pity on a guy?"

"Not without any sweet talk."

"Okay then, listen up." He then leaned down and whispered a couple of sentences in her ear. She nodded, blushing, and then blushed some more. When he straightened up and smiled down at her, she could barely get out the words when she said, "I said sweet talk, Lyle, not hot talk. What you just promised to do almost scorched my ears off."

"Just doing what you asked," he said innocently.

She chuckled. "Like I said, that was hot, not sweet."

He pulled her back closer to him. "I guess I've been hanging around Lance so long, I don't know the difference."

Monique nodded. "And what about Logan. He's good-looking and kind. Is there anyone special in his life?"

Lyle glanced across the room at his older brother who was talking to Lance and Asia. "I think that now that Carrie, Lance, and I have found love, big brother will be doing the same if he hasn't done so already. I think he's smitten with Asia's sister, Claire, but she's currently living somewhere out of the country."

Monique smiled. "Location never stopped anyone in love, and I have a feeling that your brother is a man who, once he knows what he wants, won't hesitate going after it."

Lyle returned her smile as he continued to study his oldest brother. "I think you might be right."

An hour or so later, Lyle and Monique walked up the stairs to his bedroom. His family had left to stay at a hotel for the night, and they were all alone. As soon as she entered the room, Monique turned in his arms and kissed him.

"I never thought that I'd find love again, Lyle."

His eyes searched her face, looking hopeful, looking like a man in love. "But you have?"

"Yes."

"And after a reasonable amount of courtship time, will you consider marrying me?"

Monique didn't hesitate with her answer. "Yes! Oh, yes!" and then they were in each other's arms, sealing their agreement with a kiss.

44

Faith hung up the phone with a smile on her face after receiving calls from both Monique and Shannon saying they were planning to spend the night away and not to expect them before noon tomorrow, if even then.

She was happy for her friends, glad they had done just what Cely suggested in her letters: live each day to the fullest and do whatever they wanted to enjoy life and not live up to others' expectations and standards.

Now what about you?

Faith quickly turned around. She could have sworn she'd heard Cely's voice again. Although she knew that wasn't possible and that her imagination was getting carried away, at least the question had her thinking.

Now what about me?

She'd been doing a lot of serious thinking about that very thing since Shane had left for Orlando, and she felt good that he had called to let her know he was thinking about her. She knew that if Cely was there, she would be giving her encouragement and pushing her not to give up . . . like Cely herself had eventually done in the end.

No! She wouldn't think of the negatives. She would think only of the positives, and as soon as Shane got back, she would make it her business to let him know what was on her mind. She *was* interested in developing a meaningful relationship, if he still was.

She lifted a brow when she heard the sound of the doorbell. It was almost eleven o'clock. She wondered if it was Anna letting them know she had returned to town. After crossing the room to the door, she glanced out the peephole only to have her heart nearly stop beating. It was Shane.

She quickly opened the door. "Shane?" she asked, nearly breathless. "What are you doing here? I thought you wouldn't be back from Orlando until late Sunday."

She watched him push back off the stone column post and take a slow step toward her. "I decided to come back early. In fact, I haven't gone home yet. Sorry about dropping by so late but I came straight here. Can we talk?"

She nodded and moved aside to let him in, closing the door behind him. "Nice place," he said, quickly glancing around before bringing his gaze back to her.

"Thanks. My parents own it, and they were kind enough to let us use it this summer. Can I get you something to drink?"

"No." And then, as if there was something that he needed her to know, he said, "I missed you too much to stay away." His voice was so undeniably sensuous that it immediately lit a flame inside of her.

His words touched something deep within her, something that hadn't been touched in a long time, and she suddenly felt compelled to let him know how she felt as well. This was the opportunity she had hoped for. "I missed you, too, and I've thought of you a lot."

"That's good to know," he said, as a sexy smile curved his lips. He took a couple of steps closer to her. "I thought of you as well."

"You did?"

"Yes. That's why I'm here. Talking to you on the phone wasn't good enough. I needed to see you. And to touch you," he said, reaching out and taking her hand in his. He tugged gently and brought her closer to him. "And to kiss you again."

He chose that moment to capture her mouth with his and as if kissing her was the most important thing to him, he greedily slanted his mouth over hers, taking the physical connection deeper, making the exchange of tongues and lips that much more intense, and Faith thought there couldn't be anything more erotic.

He proved her wrong when he deepened the kiss, meshing their mouths in a way that made a warm sensation flow through her belly. The tips of her breasts hardened against her blouse. What he was doing to her mouth and the way he was doing it spiraled her to new heights and suddenly her insides seemed to burst into flames. Like before, he kissed her with such mastery, such skill and profound precision.

And with so much desire.

She felt it, and it was far more exhilarating than anything she'd ever felt before. And when he finally broke off the kiss and pulled back, every cell in her body was begging for completion.

"Make love to me," she murmured, not questioning the boldness or the rationale of her request. At that moment she wanted him. She needed him, and everything that was woman within her desired him at a degree that almost took her breath away.

"Are you sure?" he asked, his voice shimmering over her like warm honey.

"I'm positive. Monique and Shannon are gone for the night, and they won't return until sometime tomorrow. I want you to stay here with me. All night, Shane."

He gazed at her in a way that made her feel sexy, significant, and compelling, and with that look an urgency she never felt before took its toll, making her feel powerful and daring.

"Do you want to talk?" he asked, his voice barely above a whisper.

"Later," she said, taking control. She pushed him down on the sofa behind him and straddled her body over his. Something was set free inside her, and a woman she didn't know was taking over: a woman who knew what she wanted and was taking it.

She went to the buttons on his shirt while thinking there were too many of them. She eased each one open before pushing the garment away past muscled shoulders.

"Pants got to go, too," she said, easing off him to give him room to remove them, which left him in a pair of sexy black boxers. Feeling a little over the edge and somewhat out of control, she leaned over and took her tongue and traced a path down his abs, getting a good taste of his stomach. She smiled when she felt him tremble beneath her mouth.

"What are you trying to do?" he asked in a deep growl. She could hear the passion in his voice as well as the urgent need.

"What makes you think I'm trying to do anything?" she asked innocently, feeling comfortable in her new and exciting role as an aggressive woman.

Shane's chuckle was low, seductive. "I think it's obvious."

She smiled. "Oh, you haven't seen the obvious yet, Mr. Masters."

And then she eased her hands inside his boxer shorts to give him one hell of an intimate stroke. His response was automatic, and she felt his erection grow harder right in her hands. He felt warm, solid, all man. Whenever she and Virgil had made love, she'd acted prim and proper as he had wanted, but there was nothing prim and proper with the way she was behaving now with Shane. She had no qualms about abandoning her decorous ways and becoming naughty as hell. She didn't have to operate on anyone's expectations and standards tonight but her own.

"I don't think you want to continue doing that much longer," Shane warned in another thick growl, reminding her of what she was doing to him, the way she was stroking him.

"Umm, why not?"

"You keep it up and you'll find out."

She chuckled softly and released him to stand up. She wasn't one to strip in front of a man, but for some reason she wanted to bare all now. There was something about Shane that gave her the confidence to do whatever she wanted.

He watched as she removed her skirt, shimmying it down her legs and stepping out of it easily to reveal her black lacy thong. That left her blouse and bra, and she quickly and effortlessly discarded those as well.

She swallowed when she saw the way he was staring at her, and for one fleeting moment she found herself feeling restrained. She covered her center with the palm of her hand.

"Don't," Shane said, easing into a sitting position on the sofa.

When he'd arrived, he hadn't expected any of this. It seemed that Faith had become a tigress since he'd been gone, and he couldn't help but wonder at such an extreme transformation. What had made her change her mind about them pursuing a relationship?

Has she really changed her mind or are her actions being dictated by the moment? He took in a deep breath, then exhaled it when a thought he didn't like crossed his mind. He was too old for a one-night stand or even a summer fling. He needed more substance in his life. He wanted a serious relationship, a commitment, a forever kind of interlude.

He reached out and grasped her wrist and tumbled her into his lap then sucked in a quick breath when his thighs came into contact with her naked skin. "We need to talk, Faith. I need to know what's going on in that head of yours. Before I left town we were miles apart and now you want me to spend the night. Why?"

His question hung in the air surrounding them, and Faith knew she owed him an explanation. She lowered her lashes for a moment, wondering what she could say to make him understand.

She then lifted her gaze and met his. "I told you about my divorce," she said softly.

He nodded. "Yes."

"What I didn't tell you was about my friend Cely. She died earlier this year after committing suicide."

A regretful expression appeared on his face. "I'm sorry to hear that, Faith."

She inhaled deeply. "I was, too, especially since I had no idea she was going through anything. Cely, Monique, Shannon, and I have been best friends since our early teens and would spend our summers here on the island with our parents. Our friendship was special, and it still hurts to know she was going through something and we didn't have a clue. She didn't give us a chance to be there for her."

For a brief moment Faith didn't say anything else and then she continued by telling him, "She did leave letters for us, though. Not once did she explain why she did what she did. Instead she empowered us to do what she didn't do."

"Which was?"

"To live each day to the fullest and do whatever we wanted to enjoy life and not live up to others' expectations and standards." A smile touched Faith's lips. "I actually thought learning to play tennis would help me to do that. Instead, I recently discovered enjoying my life means doing something deeper, more meaningful."

She shifted in his lap to face him, determined to concentrate on him and not his naked chest. "But then learning to play tennis had its rewards, since it brought you into my life—and you, Shane Masters, turned out to be one incredibly hot encounter in more ways than one. At first you frightened me because I wasn't sure that I could handle you. Now I know that I can. I did a lot of thinking while you were gone and I've discovered you're a man worth knowing at all levels, a man I feel I can trust and the type of man that I need in my life right now. I want you."

As bizarre as it seemed, Shane loved her and needed her in his life to make it complete. He intended to take the rest of the time they would spend together over the coming weeks of summer to convince her of it.

"I want you, too," he whispered huskily. "Now the main question is do I take you here or do you prefer the more traditional locale of a bedroom?"

A big smile spread across Faith's face. She and Virgil always went for traditional, and the one time she'd convinced him to make love outside by the pool he had complained the entire time. With Shane she didn't want anything traditional. She wanted spontaneous and hot. They were alone and she wasn't expecting Monique and Shannon back tonight, so as far as she was concerned, here was just as good a place as any. For once she would love to get a carpet burn on her behind.

She met his intense gaze. "Take me here. Now."

Shane stared at her. God help him, but he intended to do just that. He had thought about this, dreamed about this, fantasized about it, and his erection was aching; he needed this like he needed to breathe.

He stood, placing her on her feet to remove the last of his clothing, and when he stood in front of her as naked as she was, he reached out and pulled her into his arms. He needed to stay in control, but the moment his lips captured hers, the ability to remain composed went out the window.

Knowing the sofa had limited space, he eased her down on the carpeted floor with him with their mouths still joined, tasting of sweetness he had come to know and love.

"Shane," she whispered softly, when he pulled his mouth away to place kisses around her lips and neck. Her hands wandered southward again, and took hold of him. His pulse escalated when she stroked the full length of him. "I want this."

"Faith," he said, breathing the name past a tightened throat. Something inside him felt she needed to be in full control this first time, and he wanted to give her that power.

But first . . .

He kissed her again while his hands went everywhere, touching her breasts, kneading her flesh, her stomach, and the area between her legs—especially there, deciding that two could play her way. And when he knew she was just as hot and ready as he was, he reached out to pull the wallet from his pants pocket. Taking out a condom, he put it on while she watched him.

"Thanks for keeping us safe," she whispered, reaching out and taking hold of him in her hands once more.

"Always," was his response. With those words he quickly changed their positions to bring her on top of him. "Ride me, Faith. Ride me until the cows come home."

He saw the surprised look in her eyes before her lips tilted into a smile. "That's a whole lot of riding," she whispered, looking down at him.

"I'm counting on it, sweetheart."

Her lips widened into an *I can do it* smile, and she straddled his body with hers. He could tell she'd never done anything like this before, and he inwardly cursed all her wasted years with the man she had married.

Shane gazed into her face and saw so much desire there, it nearly took his breath away. "Come here, sweetheart."

And then she brought her mouth down to his the same moment she lowered her body down to him, and as if his straight-as-a-rod erection were a magnet pulling her in, the heat of her slowly consumed his thick hard flesh, locking on to it tight, while he lifted his body to ease into her.

"Oh, my God," he said, pulling his mouth back, closing his eyes, and inhaling her scent. At the same time he lifted his hips higher off the floor to thrust into her to the hilt. She squeezed her thighs around him for a better fit, and he had a feeling, experienced or not, she was about to give him the ride of his life.

"Till the cows come home?" she asked.

"Unless I die of pleasure first," he said, wondering how he would survive when just the feel of her clutching him had him just about a goner. The thought that he was inside her body this way had him about ready to explode. The eyes staring down at him were so filled with passion and heat that it triggered a jolt of need deep within him.

And then she began moving her body, riding him in a way she could never have done in his dreams. She put everything into it, her hips, thighs, the groans she made, the way she tossed her head back, the rhythm she created. She continued to squeeze her thighs to lock him in, holding him hostage—not that he was going anywhere. She tightened her inner muscles to pull everything out of him, pushing him toward one hell of an orgasm.

He wanted to yell. He wanted to scream. In the end when he felt her body convulse around him, signaling her orgasm, he let out a high-pitched roar, one that nearly shook the windows. But she didn't stop riding him. She continued to move frantically over him, with him and all in him. Shudder after delicious shudder rammed through him while he groaned out her name the same way she was groaning out his.

And moments later when she literally collapsed on his muscled chest, he held her gently into his arms. Tremors that were still passing through his body made it difficult to breathe, much less speak.

But when she finally was able to lift her head and look at him, what he saw in her eyes made him love her that much more.

"Did I bring all the cows home?" she asked so sexy, it nearly stole his next breath.

He smiled. "For now," he said, forcing the words past his lips. "But I'm sure they'll wander off again sooner or later." He planned for her to ride him again at another time—she was definitely good at it.

She smiled. "Good, because I've discovered that I like riding you."

They fell asleep right there on the floor, and when they woke up some time later, they made love again, but that time in a bed. "I think I like the floor better," Faith whispered, cuddled in Shane's arms.

A smile touched his lips. "Me, too."

He then leaned in to kiss her, enjoying her mouth. In fact, he enjoyed everything about her and was a weakling when it came to keeping his hands off her. He just couldn't do it.

"This might sound rather crazy," he said, shifting their positions so he could look into her eyes, "especially since we haven't known each other an awfully long time, but I've fallen in love with you."

His revelation made her feel so good inside, she could barely stand it. She reached up and cupped his face in her hands. "That doesn't sound crazy at all because I've fallen in love with you, too."

And she had.

Faith knew at that moment that Shane Masters was everything she'd ever wanted. All those years she had waited for Virgil to bring her happiness, and in the end he had only brought her despair. She hadn't been what he wanted, and he hadn't been what she needed.

But Shane was everything to her. And this time when he leaned down and kissed her, he filled her with the taste of promises for brighter and better tomorrows.

45

The four women walked together along the beach. It was the first time in weeks they'd had a chance to be alone and talk. Everyone was happy when Anna returned from her Fourth of July trip an engaged woman, and the huge diamond ring she wore on her hand was awesome. And when she told them about how the ring had been the one her father had chosen for her mother before his death, it brought tears to the women's eyes.

Faith, Shannon, and Monique had good news to share with Anna as well. They had come to Hilton Head to have a good time but hadn't thought it would include meeting men who would change their lives forever. But they had.

The four women agreed to remain in touch and to continue to spend some time together every summer on the island. Their immediate plans were to all meet up again in D.C in January to attend Anna's wedding.

It was only when they returned to the house that they made a startling discovery. They were sitting around drinking wine as they shared countless photos with Anna of them spending other summers on the island.

"This woman," Anna said, pointing to a group picture. "Who is she?" she asked quietly, remembering that face.

Faith glanced at the photo. "That's our friend, Cely. She died earlier this year. She committed suicide."

Anna nodded. "I know. I was the one on duty in the ER when

they brought her in. She was still alive, but barely, and I tried to save her."

All eyes went to Anna. "You did?" Monique managed to ask in a shaky voice.

Anna nodded. "Yes. I fought like hell, but she refused to fight back. I'd never seen a person more determined to die."

No one said anything for the longest time, but it was apparent that each was thinking that in a way Cely had touched even Anna's life. Shannon wiped a tear from her eye before saying, "It's still a mystery to all of us why she did what she did. Cely loved life too much to give it up. I miss her so damn much."

"We all do," Faith said, chiming in. She then turned back to Anna. "You would have liked her. She was truly special."

"Yes, you would have," Monique agreed. "But even in death, she's with us. I've felt her presence the entire time I've been here."

"So have I," Shannon said.

"Me, too," Faith murmured softly. "She's the reason we came here this summer, and because of that, she's the reason we found the men we love."

"Then I think this calls for a special toast," Anna said, holding up her glass. "To Cely."

The other women nodded. "Yes, to Cely," Faith said, smiling. "For helping us to realize what a woman truly wants."

The women toasted a friend who was no longer in their midst but who would always remain in their hearts.

Epilogue

Three women who had discovered what they'd wanted just six months earlier stood in the huge church as bridesmaids—three of ten. They smiled as they watched the bride walk down the aisle on the arms of her grandfather, Robert Fuller.

"She is simply beautiful," Faith whispered to Shannon, who nodded in agreement. She then glanced across the way to the groom, who was also staring at his soon-to-be wife with total awe and love etched in his features. This was a beautiful day for a wedding, and the entrance of the bride had made it doubly so.

Moments later Anna stood beside Zachary as they faced the minister, repeating vows and pledging their lives together. There wasn't a dry eye left in the church when Zachary and Anna recited their own personal vows they had written to each other.

"I now pronounce you man and wife. You may kiss your bride, Zachary." Once the minister said the words, Zach didn't waste any time doing just that.

A hour or so later at the reception, Faith, Shannon, and Monique looked around for the men in their lives. Monique and Lyle's wedding was planned for the spring. Shannon and Adam had decided on a June wedding. Faith and Shane were looking forward to a late summer wedding on Hilton Head.

Adam, Shane, and Lyle smiled as they walked toward the women they loved, glad they had been the men these three special women wanted.

1. Do you feel Faith, Monique, and Shannon were right to feel guilty because they didn't know that Cely felt like giving up? Should they have known, since they were all close friends for many years?

2. Was Faith justified in keeping Shane at arm's length because of what she went through with her first marriage?

3. Considering Shannon's mind-set regarding the type of man she wanted, did Adam handle the situation effectively? Should he have been more or less tolerant? Why?

A Reading Group Guide

4. Why do you think it was easy for Monique to fall in love with a man like Lyle after losing "the perfect husband"?

5. Do you think Zack handled the situation with Anna properly, making sure a political career was something she wanted before deciding to run for public office?

6. What did you like most about the book?

7. Which hero was definitely what a woman would want, more so than the others? Why?

8. Do you think Faith and Monique had realistic expectations about what they wanted? Why or why not?

9. Do you think Shannon was wrong in allowing her parents to influence her feelings regarding the type of man she wanted in her future? Would you let your parents influence you?

10. Which of the four women do you think had the most emotional baggage? How did each deal with it?

St. Martin's
Griffin

Be sure to pick up these other tales from **USA Today** bestselling author

Brenda Jackson

A FAMILY REUNION

A Novel Ties That Bind

the PLAYA'S HANDBOOK
BRENDA JACKSON

NO MORE PLAYAS
BRENDA JACKSON

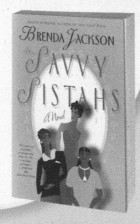

SAVVY SISTAHS

"A writer before her time."

—Carl Weber, *New York Times* bestselling author of *So You Call Yourself a Man*

St. Martin's Griffin   www.brendajackson.net   Available wherever books are sold